D1602299

NEVER
HAVE I EVER
WITH A
DUKE

USA TODAY
BESTSELLING AUTHOR

DARCY
BURKE

For the bestest buddies in the universe,
Dee, Elisabeth, and Julie.

Thank you for making me laugh (nearly) every day and always, always having my back. Love you!

Also, let's never play Never Nave I Ever with our daughters again. (But D&D is great!)

NEVER HAVE I EVER WITH A DUKE

Graham Kinsley is shocked when he inherits a debt-ridden dukedom, and now he has just one month to repay a loan. He needs an heiress—or find a way to recoup the former duke's losses. When he meets the alluring Arabella, he's entranced. Unfortunately, she's as bankrupt as he is, but if they work together they may be able to recover their fortunes. Though if they keep stealing kisses, they may lose their hearts instead.

Arabella Stoke can't afford an attraction to the penniless duke who has vowed to help rescue her family from financial devastation. She needs to find a wealthy husband before her father succumbs to the stress of losing everything. However, as Graham brings them closer to finding the swindler who stole their money, the war between what they want and what they need may ruin them both.

∿

Have you read what came before The Spitfire Society? Discover *The Untouchables*, twelve love stories featuring the most untouchable peers of the realm and the wallflowers, bluestockings, spinsters, and widows who bring them to their knees.

Love romance? Have a free book (or two or three) on me!

Sign up at http://www.darcyburke.com/readerclub for members-only exclusives, including advance notice of pre-orders and insider scoop, as well as contests, give-aways, freebies, and 99 cent deals!

Want to share your love of my books with like-minded readers? Want to hang with me and get inside scoop? Then don't miss my exclusive Facebook groups!

Darcy's Duchesses for historical readers
Burke's Book Lovers for contemporary readers

Never Have I Ever With a Duke
Copyright © 2019 Darcy Burke
All rights reserved.

ISBN: 1944576614
ISBN-13: 9781944576615

This is a work of fiction. Names, characters, places, and incidents are the product of the author's imagination or are used fictitiously. Any resemblance to actual events, locales, or persons, living or dead, is purely coincidental.

Book design: © Darcy Burke.
Book Cover Design © Hang Le.
Cover image © Period Images.
Darcy Burke Font Design © Carrie Divine/Seductive Designs
Editing: Linda Ingmanson.

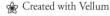 Created with Vellum

CHAPTER 1

"*N*ot so fast, Biscuit!" Arabella Stoke kept a firm hand on the small ball of fluff that was her mother's dog as she navigated into the park. It was early and she was well covered, from the oversized cap on her head to the crisp apron adorning her front to the serviceable boots that were a size too large. She had no fear that anyone would recognize her. They hadn't so far, and she'd been walking Biscuit at least a few times a week since January.

Since her father had become almost entirely bedridden.

Taking a deep breath, Arabella looked up at the blue sky. It was chilly, but clear and beautiful. In the park, snowdrops and daffodils sprouted from the drab earth as spring wrestled the ground from the clutches of winter.

Biscuit pulled at the leash again, her nose sniffing endlessly in search of something. Arabella couldn't fault her excitement. The dog was just so happy to be outside. She didn't get as many walks as she used to, not since Papa had become ill, or, more accurately, since their number of servants had shrunk to a bare minimum.

With just five retainers, including their young groom who was also employed at a smithy on Oxford Street, there was more than enough work to be done. Walking the dog had become less of a priority, and the more time Mama spent at Papa's bedside, the less Biscuit was able to stretch her legs. Not that her legs needed extensive stretching, for they were rather stubby.

Mama worried that Biscuit wasn't getting enough exercise, and she insisted someone walk her every morning. Since the servants didn't always have time, Arabella dressed herself as one of them and, unbeknownst to her mother, took Biscuit out.

Walking alone to the park had felt scandalous but exhilarating too. Now, Arabella looked forward to the outing, and Millie, the scullery maid, who was usually tasked with the job, appreciated not having to add to her work.

A small animal, perhaps a rabbit or a squirrel, dashed by in a blur. Biscuit began barking and took off so fast that Arabella wasn't able to keep hold of the leash. The dog bounded away after whatever had run past.

"Biscuit!" Arabella chased after the terrier, but soon lost sight of her as she scurried through a thick group of bushes. Muttering a very unladylike curse, Arabella called for the dog again. The barking stopped, and a bead of apprehension worked its way up Arabella's spine. A cold sweat broke over her neck. If anything happened to that dog—after everything else they'd endured—Arabella feared it would crush what remained of her mother's spirit.

Hastening her stride, Arabella moved along the path, stopping to search in shrubs and behind trees. Her worry progressed straight to terror as she feared the worst, and she soon found herself off the footpath and in a wooded area she'd never been to before.

She stopped and stood still, listening, her heart pounding a frantic rhythm. A whooshing sound from the other side of a stand of trees drove her around them. She barreled into a small clearing and nearly fell over as something dislodged her cap from her head.

A small squeak leapt from her throat as she managed to focus on a large figure. She blinked. A man. In shirtsleeves. Clutching a sword.

"Bloody hell!" He rushed forward, his features creased with horror and concern. "Are you all right?"

Arabella reached up and patted her bare head, then looked down to where the borrowed cap lay on the ground beside her. "I think so." Her voice sounded small and quiet and not entirely her own.

"Where on earth did you come from?" He bent and picked up her cap.

Closing her eyes for a moment to restore her equilibrium, she opened them again to see he was in much better focus. He was tall and lithe, with ink-dark hair and eyes. Though his face was drawn, he was objectively attractive, with angled cheekbones and a firm jaw. Objectively attractive? Yes, anyone would find him handsome until they looked at his lips. Those they might describe as sinfully gorgeous. The lower one was the thicker of the two, but the upper had a curious dip at the top, giving it the overall shape of a heart. A seductive, kissable heart.

Kissable?

Her gaze lowered to the triangle of flesh exposed by the opening of his shirt. She hadn't seen so much of a man in six long years, and when she thought of that... Well, it was no wonder she thought of kissing.

"Miss?" he prompted, holding out her cap.

Arabella took it from him, her bare hand grazing his. A frisson of anticipation danced up her arm. She snatched the cap and took a step back. "Thank you." She was thanking him? He'd almost killed her with his sword. "You nearly decapitated me."

One of his eyes squinted as he cocked his head to the side. "I wasn't even close to decapitating you." He straightened. "Besides, this blade is made for thrusting, not slicing, which is why your cap is intact."

She eyed the weapon he held in his right hand, which he pointed toward the ground. "It's made for dueling, isn't it?"

"It's made for fencing, which is what I was practicing. I'll ask again, where on earth did you come from? This is a rather remote area of the park."

It was indeed. She set the cap over her hair and glanced around, not recognizing a thing. In fact, she wondered if she'd be able to find her way back. Or find Biscuit.

Biscuit!

"I'm looking for Biscuit. My dog."

"You have a dog?"

She was dressed as a servant, and they didn't typically own dogs, did they? "My mistress's dog. She saw a small animal and tore after it. The dog, I mean, not my mistress."

A trace of a smile flirted with his kissable mouth. "I see. Then we must find… What did you say its name was? The dog, not your mistress. Biscuit?"

She nodded. "She's a terrier. About this big." Arabella held her hands apart to approximate Biscuit's size.

"Looks like *she's* the small animal," he remarked. "Where did you last see her?"

"We came in through Cumberland Gate. She ran off near there."

"You're sure she came this way? You're almost in Kensington Gardens."

Arabella's shoulders slumped. "No, I'm not sure. She was barking and then stopped. I'm worried something awful has happened."

He came toward her and patted her shoulder. "There, there. Think positive thoughts. I'm sure Biscuit is fine. You seem rather attached to your mistress's dog, but then I daresay you probably spend more time with her."

Was that a cut against the upper class? No, it couldn't be, because he was clearly upper class. Who else would be practicing fencing in Hyde Park? Wait, why wasn't he fencing at his house or at Angelo's? She ignored the tremor of awareness that radiated from where he touched her shoulder. "Why are you practicing here?"

He hesitated, and she wondered if she'd asked a question he didn't want to answer. *Goodness,* she was supposed to be a servant. She shouldn't be asking him questions at all! "My apologies." She dipped a curtsey. "I didn't mean to offend. I must go find Biscuit."

"Let me help you. Give me a moment." He went to a rock upon which she now saw his discarded clothing. Picking up the scabbard, he sheathed his sword and leaned the weapon against the rock. Next, he pulled on a waistcoat, followed by his coat. He draped his cravat around his neck, letting the white silk hang down against his lapels. There was something disarmingly attractive about his dishabille. She had to tell herself to look away or he would catch her staring.

When he appeared before her, his sword was strapped to his waist and a smart hat sat atop his dark head. "Let us find your mistress's dog." He called out, "Biscuit!" over her head. Though he was nearly a foot taller than her five feet three inches, she still flinched from the sound.

He seemed to notice, for he immediately apologized. "I didn't mean to startle you. Shall we walk toward where she ran off?"

"Yes, please." She led the way from the clearing and picked her way back to the footpath, glad she wasn't actually lost at all. Just turned around by an undressed gentleman she wished she'd seen in the act of fencing. She imagined his muscles rippled spectacularly as he thrust his sword.

Other meanings for "thrust his sword" ricocheted in her mind, and she mentally chided herself for her impure thoughts. They'd led her into temptation once, and she couldn't allow them to do so again. Especially not with a man like this. A man whose name she didn't know and wouldn't ask for.

They called out for Biscuit in turns as they walked along the path—first her, then him.

"Do you always bring the dog here for a walk?"

"Not always," she said. "And never again, probably. Assuming I find her." She couldn't quite keep the anguish from creeping into her voice.

He paused, turning toward her, and gently clasped her shoulders. "We'll find her. Don't worry."

"If I don't, my"—she'd almost said mother—"mistress will be so upset."

"I hope not at you," he said. "This isn't your fault."

"No, she won't be angry at me." She would just be inconsolable, and she was already overwrought about their troubles.

"Good."

The distant sound of a bark made them both freeze. Their gazes found each other's and locked, their eyes widening in unison.

He turned his head toward the high-pitched yap. "Is that—"

"Biscuit!" she finished.

They dashed toward Cumberland Gate, calling the dog's name in perfect time together. The terrier appeared on the path, her short legs carrying her much faster than anyone would think possible, the brown leather leash trailing behind her.

Arabella swept the dog into her arms with a relieved cry. "There you are, you silly nincompoop!"

A masculine laugh rippled across her neck as the gentleman moved closer to her. "Nincompoop? Biscuit, I think you're in trouble." He bent his head and scratched the dog's head. Then his gaze found hers again. "You won't be too hard on her, will you? I'm afraid I have a soft spot for dogs, even nincompoops."

Arabella dropped a kiss on Biscuit's silky head. "She will be showered with treats when we get home, so I wouldn't worry too much about her."

He stared at Arabella—or more specifically, at her mouth—for a moment before blinking. He cleared his throat and averted his focus toward the gate. "I'm glad to know she is safe. Please accept my apologies for knocking your cap off. I am rather single-minded in my focus when I am practicing. I didn't hear you approach." He looked at her again, and she noted a faint pink in his cheeks. That he would feel remorse and perhaps even a twinge of embarrassment made her curious.

Who was he?

Oh dear God. While she didn't know who he was, he was clearly *Someone.* Presumably, she would meet him during the course of the Season, and then what would he say? *"Why is a servant at a ball?"*

Arabella tipped her head down as if she could somehow banish her face from his memory. "I must go." She turned from him, and in her haste, nearly tripped.

He gripped her by the elbow, keeping her upright. "Careful, there."

She sent him a quick, appreciative glance. "Thank you. Er, bye."

Withdrawing herself from his grasp, she held Biscuit tight as she hurried from the park. Biscuit squirmed and yapped.

"Quiet," Arabella admonished her. "Haven't you caused enough trouble for today? If I set you down, will you promise to behave?"

Biscuit barked in response.

"Good girl." Arabella set her down, keeping a tight grip on the leash. She led her over to Oxford Street and walked quickly toward Holles Street, where they lived around the corner from Cavendish Square.

It was a narrow, unassuming house they could barely afford. When Arabella visited her neighbor, Miss Phoebe

Lennox, who lived in a large, elegant house on the square around the corner, she was aware of how far her family had fallen. Last year, they'd leased a larger house and had employed ten servants. Plus, they'd had a coach and four. The year before, an even larger house with fourteen servants. It seemed obvious now to Arabella that they'd lived beyond their means for some time. The loss of their small country estate, the house she'd been born in, last year had been quite a blow. The blow, probably, that had led to her father's sharp decline.

How she wished she could be like Phoebe, who'd inherited a fortune last year. Phoebe had declared herself a spinster and set herself up in Cavendish Square. Together with her friend, Miss Jane Pemberton, they'd formed a small group of unmarried women and ironically referred to themselves as the Spitfire Society. Spinster, they'd said, didn't appropriately encompass who they were, not as well as spitfire did.

If Arabella could inherit a fortune, she could save her family, restore her father's health, and maybe even seize the independence Phoebe enjoyed. But that was a dream, and an impossible one at that. If there was anything to be inherited, she'd have done so by now, and her family wouldn't be in the dire straits in which they currently found themselves.

Arabella walked down the steps to the servants' entrance, and let herself inside. The cook called from the kitchen, "Miss Arabella, is that you, I hope?"

"Yes, Mrs. Woodcock." She unfastened the leash from Biscuit and let the dog take off toward the kitchen. Then she removed her cap and coat, hanging them on a hook near the door.

She walked into the kitchen just as the cook set a bowl of food down for Biscuit. Mrs. Woodcock's brow furrowed. "You were gone a long time."

"Biscuit ran off." Arabella glanced fondly toward the dog as she wolfed down her breakfast.

"Again? She did that to Millie last week." Millie was Mrs. Woodcock's daughter. The cook eyed Arabella's costume. "You'd best get changed for breakfast. Millie will bring it up shortly."

Though Millie was a scullery maid, she often assisted their only other maid, Janney, who performed the tasks of a housemaid and ladies' maid. Really, every retainer in the household performed all kinds of work. They had to. Just as Arabella helped in the kitchen and did all the sewing.

"Thank you, Mrs. Woodcock." Arabella took the back stairs up to the second story, where her chamber was located. Her parents' room was on the same floor, and she would take breakfast in their sitting room with her mother—and father, if he felt up to it.

Arabella quickly changed from her servant's costume to a simple day dress. The style was three years old, so she'd relegated it to a work dress, and she planned to revise an evening gown after breakfast so she'd have something fresh to wear at the Thursby ball later in the week.

When she arrived in her parents' sitting room, she found her mother pacing before the windows that overlooked the street below. This was never a good sign. Pacing usually meant Papa had taken a turn.

"What's wrong?" Arabella asked without preamble. Her mother always preferred to get right to the heart of things.

Mariah Stoke stopped moving, her face pale and pinched. White strands had begun to weave themselves through her blonde hair, and there were new lines around her dark green eyes. "He vomited this morning, and there was blood. I want to call the physician, but he made me promise not to."

Because there was no money. Or little money. They were barely managing the household on the pittance they had remaining.

"What else can we sell?" Arabella asked, though she

feared the answer. They'd sold their coach and four, any décor of value, which included a few paintings, a sculpture, and silver, and most of her mother's small jewelry collection.

"My grandmother's pearls. Your father won't like it, but it must be done." Her gaze turned sad. "I'm so sorry, dear. I really hoped you'd be able to have those at least."

A year ago, Arabella might have felt sad, but the time for caring about material things had long since passed. She'd sell anything to save her father. They were a close family, just the three of them since her three older siblings had all died before the age of twelve. They clung to each other in the most primal, vital way, as if their survival depended on one another.

Arabella crossed the room and took her mother's hand. She gave her an encouraging smile. "It's all right. I look better in diamonds anyway."

This had the desired effect, for her mother laughed, and the lines in her face eased. The warmth was short-lived, however, as darkness overtook her mother's features far too soon. "I'll take care of the necklace later today, after I send for the physician."

"What will you tell Papa?" Arabella asked. "That our benefactor is paying for it?" It was a bald fabrication. There was no benefactor, no family, wealthy or otherwise, no kindhearted friend who would loan them funds.

Mother exhaled. "What else can we say?"

That he believed they had a benefactor illustrated he wasn't thinking clearly. How could he think when he slept so much of the time? Or stared out the window despondently? He felt so guilty for driving them into this situation with a bad investment scheme—and his expensive tastes.

"Arabella, the need for you to wed has never been more urgent. You simply must find a husband. Quickly."

Not just any husband—a wealthy one. When their financial woes had first started to surface a year and a half ago, Papa had announced it was time for her to wed his best friend's son, the Earl of St. Ives. The former earl—Papa's best friend—had agreed shortly before he'd died. However, despite the current earl promising to honor his father's wishes, the marriage had not come to pass. The earl had fallen in love with and wed someone else.

While Arabella had felt relieved that she'd escaped an arranged union, she'd also been keenly aware of her father's disappointment. Though at the time, she hadn't realized the extent of his desperation. They were nearly bankrupt, and it was only a matter of time before they ended up in debtor's prison. Or so Papa said. He refused to allow her or her mother to see their accounts, saying it wasn't appropriate for them to have to worry about it. Except, how could they not?

Arabella tamped down her irritation. She hated this situation, but she couldn't change it. She could, however, fix it by marrying a wealthy gentleman. Too bad none had offered. "There's bound to be someone at the Thursby ball," she said to her mother with a bright smile.

An image of the gentleman she'd met at the park burst into her mind. Would he be at the ball? She hoped so. With luck, he was wealthy and would declare himself in love with her. He wouldn't care that she'd masqueraded as a servant and would insist they wed at once via special license. All their problems would be solved.

She'd prefer to choose a husband by weighing factors other than financial security, but based on their short encounter that morning, he was helpful, considerate, and nearly lethal with a sword. Also bone-meltingly handsome.

Actually, she preferred to choose no one at all. After expecting to wed one man and now being expected to wed whomever she could, the idea of becoming a member of the Spitfire Society was far more attractive.

"There *has* to be someone," her mother said, clasping her hands together until her knuckles turned white. "If you don't receive an offer soon, we may need to consider forcing one."

Arabella froze. "You aren't suggesting…?" She couldn't bring herself to say it.

Mother nodded firmly and dropped her hands to her sides. "A compromise. It's not ideal, obviously, but we are in a desperate situation."

Yes, they were, but would they really sink so low? "I don't know if I can do that," Arabella said softly.

"Neither do I." Her mother burst promptly and completely into a flood of tears.

Arabella rushed to put her arms around her, stroking her hands over Mother's back in soothing circles. "We'll find a way. I promise."

After a few moments, Mother reined in her emotions, pulling back from Arabella's embrace with a pat on her back. "You c-can't t-tell any-anyone," Mother said for the hundredth time. "No one m-must know. If they find out, you'll *never* receive an offer."

"Yes, I know." Why else did she work so hard to re-design her dated wardrobe and study the latest fashion and hairstyles? She did her best to look as though they weren't destitute and thought she did a fair job. But someone was going to puzzle it out eventually, particularly when they noticed she and her mother traveled to balls in a gig with a tiger—their young groom—on the back.

Mother sniffed. "We're running out of time. Your father could very well die, and then where will we be? If I don't end up in debtor's prison, we'll have to impose on my cousins in Hertfordshire, and they are hardly in a position to provide assistance. What kind of future is that for you? Obscurity on a farm in the middle of nowhere, probably spending your life alone." She shook her head. "This is not how things were supposed to go. You should have wed that gentleman your first season. What was his name?"

"Miles Corbett." Papa had refused Miles's suit, insisting she would wed the heir to the Earl of St. Ives when the earl was ready.

Miles had asked her to elope to Gretna Green, but she hadn't possessed the courage to leave her family. No, that wasn't quite right. She hadn't possessed the will to disappoint them. She didn't regret her decision. Most of the time.

"Whatever happened to him?" Mother asked.

"He left England to find his fortune." Because Papa had made it clear he wasn't worthy of Arabella. She sometimes wondered what had happened to him, for he would always be her first love.

"Ah well, he wouldn't have the funds to save us from our misfortune." Was it misfortune if Papa had been able to avoid it?

Arabella stiffened her spine. Such thoughts were unhelpful. This was their reality. This was what they had to face. "I'll wed soon, Mother. I promise."

There was simply no other option.

CHAPTER 2

*H**ell and damnation.*
Blast it all.
Son of a bitch.

A dozen other curses pounded Graham Kinsley's brain as he strode from the bank toward the hack he'd just hailed. After instructing the driver of his destination, Graham climbed into the vehicle and scowled.

The mortgage hadn't been paid in three years, and the bank was done being patient. They planned to foreclose on Brixton Park unless Graham could deliver the overdue payments. It was an astronomical sum, and since Halstead Manor, his entailed estate, wasn't profitable and the former duke had left him a mountain of debt, there was simply no way to stop the foreclosure.

Bloody, bloody hell.

Graham scrubbed a hand over his face and tossed his hat onto the seat beside him. There had to be a way. He refused to lose Brixton Park. The third Duke of Halstead had built the stunning country house just outside London, and the seventh duke wasn't going to lose it on account of the sixth's duke stupidity.

The realization that he, Graham Kinsley, son of a secretary and a secretary himself until six months ago, was now the Duke of Halstead washed over him again as improbable and unbelievable as when he'd first heard the news that he was heir presumptive.

The bank manager's advice echoed in Graham's brain: *"Sell Brixton Park before we take it from you."*

Sell the one thing Graham's father had cared about the most aside from his late wife and beloved son? Graham couldn't do it. Though neither he nor his father had ever lived there, it represented their legacy, the life that had been stolen from them. Their attachment to the estate was very personal and very real. There had to be another way.

Two ways, actually. The first was to recover the money the former duke had invested in a terrible scheme. He'd literally lost a fortune—a fortune he didn't have because he'd already been in debt up to his eyeballs. Graham had pored over the records a hundred times and still had no clue whom he'd invested the money with, and the duke's secretary claimed he didn't know either.

Without recovering the investment, that left only one other option: marry an heiress.

Graham had just inherited a dukedom. His entire life had been upended. Finding a wife was the furthest thing from his mind. Rather, he wanted it to be. He knew he had to marry someday—duty and all that—but right now, he simply needed to find his feet.

The hack pulled to a stop in front of Graham's former employer's—and best friend's—residence. Graham paid the driver and walked up to the house belonging to the Earl of St. Ives. The butler, Trask, opened the door and greeted him.

"His lordship is in his study, if you'd care to join him. And her ladyship is in the drawing room entertaining Lady Northam and Lady Ware."

"Thank you, Trask." Graham handed his hat and gloves to the butler, then took the stairs to the first floor.

The door to the drawing room was just to the left of

the stairs, so he stopped in to say hello to the ladies before continuing to David's study.

"Well, if it isn't the new Duke of Halstead!" The Marchioness of Northam, who was a dear friend of the Countess of St. Ives—Fanny—exclaimed with a welcoming smile. "Fanny was just telling us that you spent the night. Are you leasing a house for the Season, or is Brixton Park close enough to make it unnecessary?"

He dropped into a chair. "Definitely unnecessary. Brixton Park is just five miles away."

"I do hope you'll plan to host an entertainment," the marchioness said. "The last duke didn't extend invitations." Likely because he'd been selling off the interior of the house piece by piece to pay his creditors.

"She wants to investigate the rocks on the estate," Lady Ware explained from beside the marchioness on a settee.

Graham recalled that Lady Northam was a geologist. "I'm sure there will be occasion for you to explore." Though not this Season. It was going to take time—and money—to restore the estate to what it deserved to be, to what it once was, to what his ancestor had built.

"When do you plan to make your debut as the duke?" Lady Northam asked.

"I've been trying to convince him to attend the Thursby ball," Fanny said, glancing his way before looking toward her friends. "Six months is an appropriate length of mourning, especially for a family member he didn't know."

"You didn't know the former duke at all?" Lady Ware asked.

Graham shook his head. "Never met him. We were distantly related. No one was more shocked than I when I became the heir presumptive last summer." That had been when his father had died suddenly, just weeks after *he'd* become heir presumptive. The duke had followed him within two months.

Nearly two months in which the duke could have—and should have—invited Graham to visit the estates he would inherit, to review the accounts, to prepare him for the crippling debt he was about to be saddled with. But he hadn't. He'd ignored Graham as much then as he and his predecessors had ignored Graham's line of the family for four generations. All because of a lie.

Fanny's countenance dimmed. "About the Thursby ball—" She shook her head. "Never mind. I'll let David explain." She summoned her usual sunny smile. "You will be the most sought-after bachelor of the Season." She cast a look toward Lady Ware. "Along with Anthony, of course." Anthony was Lady Ware's brother, the Viscount Colton.

"Anthony might be sought after, but he's not doing any seeking." Lady Ware's brow puckered. "He's still struggling after our parents' death." She brightened, clearly not wanting to dwell on that unhappy memory—they'd been murdered by a highwayman last year—and focused on Graham. "What about you? Will you be seeking a wife straightaway?"

Lady Northam chuckled. "He won't have to look very hard. Misses will flock to him, I'm sure." She narrowed her eyes slightly. "You aren't a terrible rake like the Marquess of Ripley, are you?"

Graham wasn't entirely aware of everyone's titles and reputations, but Ripley he'd heard of. In fact, he'd seen him at Brooks's last night—with the Viscount Colton. He decided not to mention that. "I am not a rake. At least I don't think I am."

"Nevertheless, you will be studied and discussed—be forewarned," Lady Northam said.

"Thank you?" He laughed. "So if I'm to be dissected, I should like to know whom I should steer clear of. *If* I were to be interested in the Marriage Mart, which I am not. I'd rather not find myself leg shackled just yet." Unfortunately, want and need were not the same thing, and he needed an heiress. Perhaps they could help without realizing what he was after.

"Definitely stay away from anyone who is in their first Season," Lady Ware said. "They are the hungriest. You'll be safer with more mature ladies."

Lady Northam nodded in agreement. "Like Jane and Phoebe, though I daresay they won't be at many events."

Lady Ware reached for a cake on the table in front of the settee. "Not since forming the Spitfire Society."

"What on earth is that?" Graham asked.

"Their own private club of sorts—for spinsters," Fanny explained. "Phoebe—Miss Lennox—inherited a vast sum of money last year and set herself up in Cavendish Square as a spinster. Jane declared her own spinsterhood and joined her."

"It's marvelous." Lady Northam's tone was deep with respect and admiration. "If I hadn't met Beck, I would have joined them."

Graham heard what they said, but his mind was rather fixated on one part: that Phoebe Lennox had inherited a vast sum. She sounded perfect—mature, uninterested in marriage, and rich. Well, he needed her to be at least vaguely interested in marriage, but perhaps they could come to a mutually beneficial arrangement. Her money for his…what? She didn't sound like the type to be swayed by a title, not even duchess.

Oh, hell, he had an uphill climb.

But Graham had never backed away from a challenge… However, they'd also said Miss Lennox didn't attend social events. No matter, he'd simply pay a call.

David, Earl of St. Ives, entered the drawing room with a smile. "I thought I heard you, *Your Grace.*"

Of course David didn't need to use such formal address, but it was a game, and Graham had started it. They'd been friends for as long as either could remember and had always called each other by their first names. Until David had inherited the earldom, which had been expected, of course. Graham had insisted on calling him "my lord" most of the time, despite David telling him not to. Now David took great delight in addressing Graham, who'd never expected to be a duke, as "Your Grace."

Graham had taken to embracing it. He smirked up at David. "Yes, that's right, I do outrank you."

"Quite," David said, stifling a smile. "Though I do chair a committee in the Lords, while you do not." David had just recently been put in charge of roads.

Graham flattened his palms against the arms of the chair. "Thank God. If I had to manage something like that right now in addition to everything else—" He stopped speaking before he uttered something he didn't plan to, then jumped to his feet. "We're boring the ladies."

"Not at all," Fanny said.

"Let them go so we can talk about the Duke's prospects after they leave." Lady Northam winked at Graham, who laughed in response.

"Please tell me how I fare," he said before departing the drawing room with David.

They went into his study across the hall. "How was your appointment?" David asked.

Graham had considered telling David about his financial woes on more than one occasion, but the words never made it from his brain to his tongue. Graham had been the one with the highest marks in mathematics at Oxford, the one who'd stepped into managing David's affairs, as if he'd been doing it for years. Granted, he'd been learning at his father's side, but the transition had been seamless.

Now, Graham was in possession of a broken-down, entailed estate and a gleaming house and parkland that he was on the brink of forfeiting. It was beyond humiliating, despite the fact that none of it was his fault.

"Yes, it went well." As well as could be expected upon learning your legacy was about to slip through your fingers. "I appreciate you letting me come to stay. I'll be on my way to Brixton Park in a short while."

David sat in a chair near the hearth. "You are more than welcome to stay—now, anytime."

Graham knew that, but it didn't change a thing. David hadn't even been wed to Fanny a year, and they were as in love as two people could be. They certainly didn't need him hanging about. "I would never intrude for long." Graham took the other chair angled near the fireplace.

"You aren't intruding."

"Tell that to Fanny." He winked, and David rolled his eyes.

"Fanny would be the first to insist you stay."

Well then, he wouldn't be able to find more things to sell at Brixton Park. It was blessed hard to try to liquidate one's assets while at the same time trying to keep one's financial situation quiet. He didn't want all and sundry knowing the dukedom was on the verge of bankruptcy. If he was going to find an heiress, he'd be better off not advertising that he needed one.

"I have plenty to keep me busy at Brixton Park," Graham said.

"I imagine you do. I do appreciate the time you spent with my new secretary."

Graham had worked with the young man, bringing him up to snuff, over the holiday season. "He'll work out fine."

"What of your retainers?" David asked. "Have you been able to assess both Brixton Park and Halstead Manor?"

"Not fully." That was a lie. He knew enough to deduce that Halstead Manor was a neglected, run-down pile of stone, with tenants who desperately needed a landlord who cared. Brixton Park, for all its glory, was in need of some repairs and was currently operating at a fraction of its normal retainers. Many had left or retired when the former duke died. And of course, Graham couldn't afford to hire any more. It was all so bloody overwhelming.

He had to focus on what he needed first: money. Which meant an heiress.

David scrutinized him for a moment. "Did I really hear you discussing marriage with the ladies?"

"Only in a general sense. They terrified me with predictions of young misses clamoring after me."

David's gray eyes glinted with humor. "You *are* a duke."

"Improbably, yes. I suppose I must consider marriage."

"You needn't rush into anything. Unless you want to?"

"I don't particularly." But again, want and need were not the same things. "Fanny and the others mentioned more mature women who aren't desperate to wed. They sound more appealing than those who hear my title and swoon."

David laughed. "Has that actually happened?"

"Not yet, but then I haven't been to a Society event. Upon Fanny's recommendation, I've accepted the invitation to the Thursby ball." Graham pinned him with a probing stare. "I expect you to guide me. Do *not* abandon me to the wolves."

David's head dipped. "It's not as bad as all that. However, I do have to abandon you. I'm taking Fanny home to Huntwell to await the birth. I'm afraid we just decided earlier today to leave the morning of the Thursby ball." He grimaced as he awaited Graham's reaction.

Graham groaned, casting his head back against the chair. "You're a terrible friend."

"I know. Fanny feels particularly bad since she talked you into attending the ball." David gave him an encouraging nod. "You'll be fine—you like dancing and you were always the most popular gentleman at every assembly in our district."

Graham lifted a shoulder but knew David was right. He *did* like dancing, and he liked the company of women. Perhaps it was the absence of his mother—she'd died in childbirth when David was two—that had driven him to seek female companionship.

"How's your wardrobe?" David asked.

Small. "If you're asking whether I have a ball-ready costume, the answer is yes. I'm not a heathen. Though, some will assume it, won't they?"

"I doubt that. You have many well-placed friends, both from school and from last Season when you managed the wagering for Ware's races."

That was true. Graham had met more people from Society than he could remember. "Ware can help me if I need it."

David grimaced again. "I'm afraid not. Ware—and Northam—are also leaving town. I've asked Anthony to provide you support."

"Wonderful." Graham sent him a teasing glare, then smiled. "As you said, I'll be fine." Graham had to focus on his problems anyway, and it would be difficult to keep them from David if he were here in town.

Graham shifted in his chair, feeling slightly uncomfortable that he wasn't discussing his situation with his best friend. He suspected David would offer him money, but Graham wouldn't accept anything but a loan. And right now, he couldn't afford one.

"I'm delighted for you and Fanny, and I better be the first person you write to after the child is born," Graham said with a faux stern tone.

"Of course you will. Now let me bore you with the names Fanny wants to use." His eyes twinkled with anticipation. How could Graham be bored when his dearest friend was so infectiously enthusiastic?

A short time later, Graham rode from London toward

Brixton Park. The more he thought about it, the more he decided an heiress would solve his problems. Not just any heiress, but the one Lady Northam had mentioned: Miss Phoebe Lennox. A self-declared spinster with an enormous fortune and no desire for the Marriage Mart.

She sounded absolutely perfect.

CHAPTER 3

"*L*et us have tea and cakes in the garden room," Jane Pemberton suggested.

Arabella looked longingly at the bookshelves being constructed in the room Phoebe was converting to a library. "You do realize I may visit your library one day and never leave?" Arabella said to Phoebe.

"You would be more than welcome. You *are* more than welcome—any time." Phoebe gave her a warm smile.

"When you've had enough of the Marriage Mart, which you likely will soon, I do hope you'll officially join the Spitfire Society," Jane said as they departed the library and went to the back of the house to the aforementioned garden room.

Phoebe's first project after purchasing the house had been transforming this breakfast room into a "garden room." She'd installed tall windows and a glass-paned door that led to the garden. The walls sported green wainscoting and a floral wallpaper so that it felt like you were sitting out in the garden instead of just looking at it. Potted plants finished the effect, and it was easy to see why it was Phoebe's favorite room in the house.

Phoebe was two years older than Arabella's twenty-three, but when she'd inherited a fortune last year, she'd suddenly seemed even older. Or perhaps that was because of the confidence and serenity she now exuded. She'd escaped a marriage to a philandering gentleman when she'd left him at the altar last year—and then she'd escaped London. She'd gone to stay with her great-aunt, who'd died a few months later, leaving Phoebe everything she had.

"I am not yet tired of the Marriage Mart," Arabella lied. "I have great hope this will be the year I find success." It had to be.

Jane gave her a skeptical look as they sat around a circular table situated in the corner near the windows. "Are you certain that's what you want? You could abandon the Marriage Mart as Phoebe and I have."

"One might argue we didn't abandon the Mart so much as the Mart relegated us to the shelf," Phoebe said before her lips curled into a mischievous smile. "Not that I mind." She sobered as she looked toward Arabella. "I do understand preferring marriage to this. Becoming a social outcast isn't for everyone."

"My mother would suffer a fit if I left the Marriage Mart," Arabella said. And not just because of how it would negatively impact their financial situation. She found Phoebe's spinsterhood a disappointment, and she would undoubtedly be horrified if Arabella followed her example. "She would argue that I wouldn't be happy, that I'd be lonely without a husband. She and my father are quite in love, so she expects I will experience the same fortune."

Phoebe studied her closely. "You don't sound as if you agree."

The butler delivered a tray with tea and cakes along with butter biscuits, which were Arabella's favorite. After pouring the tea, he asked if they required anything further.

"Not at the moment. Thank you, Culpepper." Phoebe

smiled up at the middle-aged butler, who inclined his head, then departed.

Arabella reached for a butter biscuit and immediately took a bite. Flaky deliciousness spilled over her tongue, and she nearly closed her eyes in rapture. After she swallowed, she asked, "If I lived here, I would ask for these every single day. Every. Single. Day."

Jane laughed. "Why do you think I visit so often?"

"It's true," Phoebe said. "She doesn't come for my company at all. I'll get you the recipe so your cook can make them."

In that moment, Arabella was wholly and unabashedly jealous. It wasn't just the biscuits. It was Phoebe's complete autonomy.

"You neatly skirted Phoebe's comment," Jane said. "Are you in search of a husband because you're afraid of being lonely? You'll always have us." She reached over and patted Arabella's hand.

"Yes," Phoebe agreed. "You are a member of the Spitfire Society whether you want to be or not."

Emotion pinched Arabella's throat for a moment. "Thank you. I treasure our friendship so much. To answer your question, while independence is incredibly attractive to me, I think I might like to fall in love." It was a lie—she didn't think she would fall in love again, and she didn't expect love to feature in any match she might be fortunate enough to make. However, she couldn't tell them she wanted to marry for money without explaining why. "Again." She said this last with a hint of a smile. She'd never discussed Miles Corbett with anyone.

"Again?" Phoebe and Jane spoke in unison, just as one was about to take a bite of a cake and the other a sip of tea. Their eyes pinned Arabella with brazen curiosity.

"I fell in love with someone six years ago. Alas, my parents did not approve of his suit."

Phoebe frowned. "How awful. What happened to him?"

"He left England to find his fortune. He thought if he was wealthy, he could convince them to reconsider, even if he didn't have a title."

"Did you never hear from him again?" Jane asked, setting her teacup down.

Arabella shook her head. "I hoped he might return, and I managed to keep suitors at bay while I waited. However, I gave up on that a few years ago."

Phoebe gave her a soft smile of encouragement. "How extraordinary to have been in love, though. May I ask how it felt?"

Arabella found it hard to conjure the desperate longing she'd felt back then. "I remember thinking he was the kindest, most handsome, most wonderful man I'd ever met. He was attentive and thoughtful. He made me feel like the center of the universe—his universe, anyway." While she didn't still feel a pull toward him, she realized she missed that sensation, that feeling of being in love.

Jane sighed. "That sounds marvelous."

"He sounds like a singular gentleman," Phoebe said. "I'm sorry he didn't return to you."

Arabella had been sorry too, but that time had passed. "It was ages ago, and we were very young." And foolish. She'd behaved in ways she oughtn't.

Even so, she would never regret it. Especially if she never wed.

But she had to! The people she loved most depended on it. She longed to tell Phoebe and Jane the truth so that they could help her find the husband she needed. Which was absurd. They couldn't help her. They'd no sooner go to a ball or a rout than they'd go to Almack's.

"Not to change the subject, but I wondered if you might do me a favor," Phoebe said, reaching for a butter biscuit.

Arabella nodded. "Of course, anything."

Phoebe swallowed her biscuit before continuing.

"While the Spitfire Society may not be for you, it will likely be helpful to other young women. I plan to host biweekly social gatherings here in the afternoon during the Season."

"But only for unmarried women," Jane said.

"How lovely. I wish I could come."

"You are more than welcome, but I daresay these events will become known as unofficial meetings of the Spitfire Society." Phoebe pressed her lips together in a resigned expression, then lifted her teacup. "Not that *I* mind. But I want you to be fully aware of your potential association with our *outrageous* club." Her eyes glowed with mirth, and once again, Arabella felt a pang of jealousy. How wonderful it must be not to care what people thought or said.

"Did someone say that?" Arabella asked.

Jane made a face. "The Duchess of Holborn, but she's a horrible snob. Lady Satterfield, on the other hand, was absolutely lovely at her ball."

Arabella recalled that, for she'd been there too. Lady Satterfield was immensely popular and didn't possess a cruel or supercilious bone in her body as far as Arabella could tell.

Phoebe set her cup down. "If you encounter anyone you think might enjoy attending my events, please let me know so I may extend an invitation."

"I'll do that. You're incredibly thoughtful and kind."

Culpepper returned. "Miss Lennox, you have a caller. I tried to tell him you were occupied, but he insisted on delivering his flowers in person."

It was Jane who answered. "*He?*"

"The Duke of Halstead," Culpepper replied.

Phoebe looked at Jane. "Is he the one who just inherited?"

Jane nodded. "I met him last Season at Ware's races. He was the Earl of St. Ives's secretary."

Arabella had heard about Halstead, but not that he'd

been a secretary. "Now he's a duke? How did that happen?"

Phoebe's eyes sparked with curiosity, and her mouth tipped into a mischievous smile. "Should we ask him? Normally, I would send him away, but this sounds like a good story."

"Oh yes, invite him in," Jane said, already rising from the table and moving to the seating area in the center of the room.

Phoebe looked to her butler as she rose. "Send him in, Culpepper."

With a nod, Culpepper turned and departed. When he returned a moment later, Arabella had taken a place on the settee, while Phoebe and Jane were in chairs that flanked it.

"His Grace, the Duke of Halstead," Culpepper announced.

Arabella's eyes widened. He was the swordsman.

He looked different now that he had all his clothes on, and she wasn't entirely sure it was better. His dark hair was neatly styled, his cravat blindingly white and stiffly starched, his ebony boots gleaming.

His gaze fell on her, and the mutual recognition was instantaneous. Would he say they'd met before? It would be scandalous, for she'd been without a chaperone and she'd misled him about her identity. However, neither Phoebe nor Jane would care. In fact, they'd likely find the tale delightful.

To his credit, however, he only bowed to all three of them. "Good afternoon, ladies. Thank you for accepting my call, Miss Lennox." His gaze drifted with curiosity from Jane to Phoebe and finally to Arabella. She realized he didn't know who was who.

"Allow me to introduce my friends," Phoebe said, gesturing first towards Jane. "This is Miss Pemberton. And this is Miss Stoke." She swept her hand in Arabella's direction.

"It is my pleasure to meet you all." He bowed again, then stepped to Phoebe's chair, where he handed her a gorgeous bouquet of daffodils. "These are for you."

"Thank you." Phoebe looked past him to where Culpepper still stood. "Please put these in a vase?"

The butler came forward and took the flowers, then left.

"Please sit," Phoebe invited.

He could either sit next to Arabella or in the other vacant chair. He chose the settee.

Arabella's spine tingled in spite of the six inches that separated them.

He cast her a sideways glance, and she suddenly realized he was a duke. A *duke*. She'd met a duke that morning and hadn't even realized it. What's more, she'd led him to believe she was a servant. He could be the answer to her family's prayers, and she'd probably bungled any chance she had.

"It's rather bold of you to pay a call on me," Phoebe said. "I don't believe we've met." It wasn't clear to Arabella whether Phoebe had been aware that he didn't know who she was, but perhaps she was trying to find out without embarrassing him.

"Haven't we? I was sure we'd met last year during Ware's races. I managed the wagers."

Phoebe shook her head. "I didn't attend them. I'd left town by then. Perhaps you aren't aware I abandoned my betrothed at the altar." She lowered her voice to a conspiratorial tone. "I'm somewhat of a pariah."

"Well, I think that makes you interesting." Was he flirting with Phoebe?

Phoebe's eyes sparkled as she laughed softly. "You went from being a secretary to inheriting a dukedom. That makes you *fascinating*. Please do tell us how that came about."

Halstead shifted slightly, and Arabella had the impression he wasn't enthusiastic about answering that question. "It's not a very *fascinating* story, I'm afraid. I was distant cousin to the former duke, and when his son and my father died, I became heir presumptive. I scarcely had time to adjust to that role before the duke joined his son in the hereafter."

"And there are no other family members left?" Phoebe asked.

"There are a great number of aunts and cousins who aren't in the line of succession." He grimaced. "More than I can count, frankly."

"You say you were a distant cousin of the duke," Jane said. "Had you not met any of those people?"

"No. My branch of the family had become estranged from theirs over the years." He slid a glance toward Arabella.

"How did you become a secretary?" Jane asked.

Arabella felt a strange need to provide assistance to the duke. For what, she wasn't sure, but he seemed uncomfortable. Arabella smiled brightly and injected her voice with humor. "Is that an equally mundane story, Your Grace?"

"Quite. My father was secretary to the Earl of St. Ives, along with his father before him, and his father before him."

"I imagine it's an adjustment," Phoebe noted. "I know what it's like to have your fortunes completely changed in the blink of an eye."

The clock chimed the hour, and Arabella realized she had to get home. Mother wasn't enthusiastic about her visits to Phoebe's house, and Arabella had at least promised to keep them somewhat brief.

"I'm afraid I must go." Arabella wished she didn't sound disappointed, but she didn't want to leave. He was a duke! And likely wealthy. Except it seemed he might be interested in Phoebe. Why *had* he called on her?

Halstead rose quickly and offered his hand. She took it, wishing he wasn't wearing a glove, because she wasn't.

"It was a pleasure to meet you, Miss Stoke." His gaze bore into hers as he said her name, and she knew he wanted to ask why she'd lied.

She lifted her shoulder the barest degree. "I look forward to seeing you soon. Perhaps you'll be at the Thursby ball?"

"In fact, I will. I look forward to seeing you there." He let go of her hand, and she felt another flash of disappointment. But it was fleeting, for she would see him again in just two days.

That gave her two days to determine his financial status, which *had* to be more than acceptable, and two days to devise a plan. She winced inwardly—that sounded so calculating. And yet, this was what things had come to. She had to make a match.

Arabella said goodbye to her friends and left through the door leading to the garden. As she walked home through the gate Phoebe had installed between their gardens, she thought of the duke and how fortunate it was that he'd crossed her path. While she scarcely knew him, she found him attractive, and he *had* helped her catch Biscuit. Perhaps finding a husband wasn't going to be as terrible as she'd feared. Perhaps fortune had smiled upon her.

It was about damn time.

~

When Graham had walked into what the butler had called the "garden room," he'd seen Miss Stoke and thought she was Miss Lennox and that she'd lied about her identity the other morning. Well, she *had* lied about her identity. And why was that? He was dying to know, and perhaps he'd ask her to dance at the ball just so he could find out.

However, she wasn't the woman he was looking for, which was actually a trifle disappointing. There was something about her that had lingered in his thoughts. Something he couldn't quite put his finger on.

Something he *must* put from his mind because she was not Miss Lennox—the heiress he needed to woo. She sat before him, with intelligent green eyes and a lovely countenance that he could see himself gazing into for the next fifty years.

Could he? Or was he trying to talk himself into the benefits of marriage? It was the latter, honestly, but did it matter? He was out of options, so he'd do whatever he must to rouse enthusiasm. And so far, Miss Lennox was charming, if overly inquisitive. He'd appreciated Miss Stoke's assistance with deflecting the interrogation, and for that reason was sorry to see her go. *Just that reason?* his mind asked.

Yes, just that reason.

Miss Lennox's brow creased as she edged forward in her chair. "I hope you don't think me coarse, but I must ask why you've called. I don't get many gentlemen callers. Actually, I receive none."

"I'd expected you might hint at asking me." He hadn't, however, anticipated her candor. "You must forgive me. I'm new at this and probably not doing it the right way. I'll be equally frank. The Marriage Mart terrifies me. As a duke, I must now consider whom I might make my duchess, and I much preferred meeting someone like you than some young lady fresh out of the schoolroom." He squinted at her briefly. "Is that terrible?"

She exchanged a look with Miss Pemberton, and then they promptly broke into laughter.

Graham smiled along with them, but wasn't sure why it was so amusing.

Miss Lennox caught her breath. "My apologies, Your Grace. We aren't laughing at you but at the situation. I am not remotely interested in marriage—not even to a duke. However, if I were, you would be precisely the kind of man I'd consider. I value little more than honesty, and a man who's willing to risk his masculinity and come right out and say what he wants is incredibly refreshing." She looked over at her friend. "Isn't it, Jane?"

"It's downright bizarre." Miss Pemberton studied him a moment. "How many sisters do you have?"

"None."

"I would have wagered half of Phoebe's fortune you had at least five."

"Good thing you can't," Miss Lennox said to Miss Pemberton in mock horror before laughing again. "I see what you mean. Gentlemen with numerous sisters tend to be the most palatable."

"I'm afraid I'm a touch lost. I'm still stuck on 'risking my masculinity.' How on earth did I do that?"

"By saying the Marriage Mart terrifies you," Miss Lennox answered. "I suspect it terrifies most men, but they'd never admit it. At least not to a woman."

"I am not most men," Graham said. "I will gladly disclose when something frightens me, especially the prospect of putting myself on display for the purpose of courtship." He tried not to shudder and failed.

They started laughing again. "Oh my goodness!" Miss Pemberton drew a deep breath. "You must realize how amusing it is to hear a *man* say those things. We're the ones who have to select just the right wardrobe and perfect all the best skills. We have to be beautiful, witty, charming, flirtatious without being fast, and most of all, *biddable*." She made a face and settled back in her chair.

Miss Lennox nodded vigorously. "This is why I have forsaken marriage. It can't possibly be worth the monstrous effort." She gave him a pitying look. "I am sorry you must engage in the circus, but I understand that a duke has a duty." She turned her head toward Miss Pemberton as her mouth bloomed into a beatific smile. "How lovely it is to be a spinster no one cares about."

Miss Pemberton smiled in return, and Graham couldn't help but feel left out. He also couldn't help but feel completely stymied. Miss Lennox had made it abundantly clear she wasn't interested in marriage. And yet she *had* said that if she were, Graham would be just the sort...

She drew him back from his thoughts. "And here I suspected you called on me to discuss how I've adjusted to inheriting a fortune."

He pounced on that notion. "I did think it was something we would have in common." He offered his most charming smile. "You came into your inheritance quite suddenly, I take it?"

"Yes. My great-aunt changed her will after I went to live with her. She told me as she lay dying that in her final months, I had made her happier than she'd been in years." Miss Lennox looked away briefly, blinking rapidly.

"I'm sorry for your loss."

She delicately cleared her throat. "Thank you. Now, I wonder if I might help you."

He arched a brow, curious. "In what way?"

"While I am not interested in marriage, I may know other women—more mature women such as you would prefer to meet—who might be. Bluestockings and...spitfires." She stifled a laugh so that it ended as a giggle.

Miss Pemberton grinned, then briefly rested her fingertip against her cheek. "I am not—yet—the pariah that Phoebe is. I'm sure I can come up with at least a few ladies who might be interested in meeting a duke."

He needed more than a meeting. He needed courtship and marriage and not necessarily the courtship. But they had to be rich spitfires. Or at least one of them did. "I would appreciate that, thank you." In the meantime, this arrangement would ensure he saw Miss Lennox again, and he could perhaps find a way to change her mind about marriage.

Miss Pemberton began listing names, and Miss Lennox contributed until there were seven. He wanted to ask if any were heiresses, but to do so would expose himself. He would need to conduct covert research. "I don't suppose you could write those names down?" he asked.

"Of course." Miss Lennox stood and went to a small writing desk, where she sat and quickly dashed off the list.

Graham realized this was the second time that week women had suggested other women to him. What on earth had happened to him? This was not the life he was used to. He flirted with women. He charmed them. He bedded them. The end. *Hell,* maybe he *was* a rake. He had no idea.

Miss Lennox rose from the desk, and Graham quickly got to his feet. She handed him the folded parchment. "Do let me know if I can be of further service. You seem a pleasant sort."

Miss Pemberton stood, exclaiming, "Oh! What about Arabella? Why didn't we put her on the list?"

"Well, now I feel incredibly foolish," Miss Lennox said, shaking her head. "Yes, add Miss Stoke. She's lovely —and you already know her."

"I do." And if he were honest, he wanted to know her better, if only to get to the bottom of why she'd lied to him. No, if he were honest, he wanted to know if she was an heiress. An heiress who pretended to be a retainer so she could walk her mistress's dog. Only she didn't have a mistress. Did Biscuit belong to her?

So many questions. He looked forward to getting answers.

Perhaps this heiress hunting wouldn't be as bad as he'd expected. Conversely, it could turn into a total disaster, particularly if his desperate situation became known.

As he left Miss Lennox's house, he was certain of two things: He was only incrementally closer to his goal, and he was an absolute, unmitigated imposter.

CHAPTER 4

"*Y*ou look as though you'd rather be anywhere else," Arabella whispered to her mother as they entered the Thursby ballroom after greeting their host and hostess.

"Not anywhere else, just at home with your father." She took a deep breath and relaxed her brow, though she didn't quite smile. "I do hope he eats while we're gone."

Today had been difficult. Some days he ate, some he nibbled, and some, like today, he couldn't force himself to take any sustenance. Mrs. Woodcock had made his favorite pudding for dinner, and they were hopeful he would eat it.

"Let us not think of that," her mother said, straightening her spine. "We must focus on the matter at hand, which will have the ultimate goal of improving your father's health: finding you a husband."

Arabella had drafted a mental list of eligible bachelors with the Duke of Halstead at the top. When she'd learned the handsome swordsman she'd met in the park was a duke, she'd been nearly giddy with excitement. Or at least relief. She'd found him engaging, which was more than she could say for most gentlemen she met.

However, he had called on Phoebe, and Arabella hadn't yet been able to discover why. She'd been too busy managing the household while her mother focused on her father, and there hadn't been time to pay another visit to Phoebe.

Mother looked over Arabella with a critical eye. "I wish we'd been able to afford a new ball gown," she murmured. "But you did well with this."

Arabella had taken one of the two new gowns they'd purchased last Season and had changed the ribbons at the sleeves as well as the embellishments at the hem and on the bodice. The dark rose dress was the same, but the new gold ribbons and sparkly gold beaded flowers gave it fresh life.

"The bandeau is especially charming," her mother noted.

That was entirely new, made of a gold silk taken from one of her mother's old gowns and adorned with roses and pearls. Arabella lifted her hand to the back of her head and gave her nape a slight stroke. "Janney is getting better with my hair." The ladies' maid portion of her job was not her forte, but she was learning, just as Arabella was.

Mother kept her voice low as the ballroom began to fill. "She is indeed. I look forward to when she doesn't have to work so hard. To when we all don't have to."

Conversation had gathered around them, but there was a sudden lull. Heads turned toward the main entry, and everyone stared at the Duke of Halstead as he made his entrance. He registered the attention with a smile and was immediately waylaid by a group of guests. People began talking again, and Arabella heard the same word over and over: "Halstead."

She hadn't told her mother she'd met him. It wasn't just that she oughtn't to have met him at Phoebe's house, but also that she didn't want to raise her mother's hopes. Although if Halstead followed through on what he'd said the other day and asked Arabella to dance...

The arrival of the Countess of Satterfield interrupted

Arabella's thoughts. In her late fifties, Lady Satterfield was a well-liked Society matron. Her stepson was the Duke of Kendal, and she had a reputation for helping young ladies navigate Society, including her daughter-in-law. The duchess had reentered Society as Lady Satterfield's companion years after a scandal and had soon found herself wed to the duke. It was a heartwarming love story that young ladies like Arabella sought to duplicate for themselves.

After exchanging greetings, Lady Satterfield glanced toward the crowd surrounding Halstead. "Looks like we have a new reigning Untouchable."

Arabella had heard of that name—a few years ago, a group of young ladies had taken to calling the most sought-after but reluctant-to-marry bachelors Untouchables. They often had nicknames such as the Duke of Desire or the Duke of Ruin. "Does Halstead have a nickname?" she asked the countess.

Lady Satterfield laughed. "I don't think so. I suppose he'd be the Surprise Duke."

"Or maybe the Sudden Duke," Arabella's mother suggested with a smile. It was nice to see her enjoying herself —and it didn't seem to be an act.

"Oh, I like that," Lady Satterfield said. "Have you met him?"

"We haven't," Arabella's mother answered, and now Arabella definitely had to behave as if she hadn't either. Hopefully, he would play along. If he even spoke to them this evening.

"I'll be sure to introduce you. He's a lovely fellow, very genuine. Inheriting a dukedom when one didn't expect it could bring out the worst in someone. However, that doesn't seem to be the case with the Duke."

"I don't suppose he's looking for a duchess yet?" The hope in Arabella's mother's voice was unmistakable—at least to Arabella. She added a lighthearted laugh, as if she were joking.

Lady Satterfield looked toward Arabella. "The Marriage Mart is a priority for you this year?"

"Yes."

Lady Satterfield's gray eyes widened briefly. "My goodness, I didn't mean to make it sound as if you hadn't prioritized it—when and even whether to marry is no one's business, but of course, most of Society makes it their business. You know I am not one for gossip, just making conversation."

Arabella gave the countess a warm smile. "You've the most generous heart of anyone in Society as far as I know. I don't feel the least slighted by your query. The truth is I've had trouble standing out amidst the other young ladies. I'm afraid I'm not as…" She searched for the right word.

"Aggressive?" Lady Satterfield offered helpfully.

That was the perfect word. "Exactly. I suppose I was naïve to think the right gentleman would happen to cross my path. This Season I mean to be a bit more…focused." She winked at the countess, who laughed softly.

"Well done, my dear. If I can be of any service, I do hope you'll tell me. You should meet Halstead. As I said, he's quite charming, and maybe he's just the gentleman you've been waiting for." She turned her head, clearly seeking the duke out.

Arabella watched as the countess's gaze seemed to meet Halstead's. A few moments later, he was heading in their direction.

"How did you do that?" Arabella's mother asked in wonder.

Lady Satterfield elevated a slender shoulder. "For some reason, the younger set responds to me."

The duke arrived with much attention showered in his direction. However, he ignored it all as he bowed to the countess. "Good evening, Lady Satterfield. It's a delight to see you."

The countess dipped a curtsey. "And you, Duke. May

I present Mrs. Stoke and her daughter, Miss Arabella Stoke?"

Arabella and her mother curtsied, Arabella holding her breath as she did so, waiting to see if the duke would pretend they hadn't already met. He bowed in return, first to Arabella's mother, then to Arabella, seeming to go along with the ruse. "It's my pleasure to make your acquaintance."

With an exhalation, Arabella relaxed. "Good evening, Your Grace. It's an honor to *meet* you." She put a slight emphasis on the word meet, just to confirm that they must pretend this was their first meeting.

"Lady Satterfield was just extolling your virtues," Arabella's mother said.

"Was she?" he asked, his left brow arching briefly as he glanced toward the countess.

Arabella tried not to stare at him, but it was impossible for her to look at him and not see his open shirt from the first time she'd actually met him—before she'd known he was a duke. Tonight, he was completely covered, however, and even more resplendent than he'd been at Phoebe's. His dark coat was impeccably tailored, and she wondered what would happen if he picked up his sword. When he parried, would the seam split, or would the garment move with his athletic form?

"I am happy to do so," Lady Satterfield said. "I am always eager to help others, especially young people, find their way in this confusing maze. How are you enjoying the Season so far, Duke?"

"A confusing maze is an apt description. I am managing, however. I am fortunate to count the Earl of St. Ives a close friend."

"Well, when he escorts Lady St. Ives to the country for her lying-in, you must not hesitate to call on me and Lord Satterfield if you desire assistance, or even if you do not. You could also call on Kendal. He knows far more about being a duke than I do."

"In fact, the earl and countess left this morning. I appreciate your support and will gladly accept any counsel you might offer." He turned his attention to Arabella. "May I have your company for the first set?"

Arabella nearly exhaled with relief a second time. "I would be honored." She slid a glance toward her mother, who looked as though she might burst with joy.

Halstead offered his arm to Arabella, and he led her to the dance floor just as the musicians were preparing to play.

"Thank you for pretending we hadn't met," Arabella said.

"Which time?" He sent her a wry glance. "I'm beginning to wonder if you're a serial liar."

She tensed and worked to keep her muscles from tightening. In one sense, she was a liar, given her efforts to hide her family's destitution. And so the lies, or at least half-truths, would continue… "My apologies. Biscuit is my mother's dog, and I like to take her for walks by myself sometimes. I know it's not seemly—that's why I dress as a servant."

"So you can be anonymous. I can understand—and appreciate—that."

The music started, a minuet, and they took their places for the dance. She touched her hand to his. "Thank you, Your Grace. It was never my intent to deceive you."

"Not me personally, no, but you intended to shield your identity for propriety's sake, and I can find no quarrel with that." His common sense and ordinariness were refreshing. Most people she met in Society would have been horrified, but then she never would have revealed any of this to most people.

She'd been quite lucky that she'd run into Halstead instead of someone who would have told everyone she'd been walking the dog alone. She had to be more careful. Or stop walking the dog. Since she didn't expect their situation to change anytime soon, she'd just have to do the former.

"Yes, for propriety. That's why it was also necessary that we not disclose we met at Phoebe's house," she said. "That wasn't a proper introduction either."

He grimaced. "I hadn't thought of that, to be honest. I'm afraid my social skills are not above reproach."

"I'd be glad to help, if you like. If you have specific questions."

"Thank you, that's awfully kind.

He moved effortlessly through the steps of the dance as they conversed. "And yet, I would expect most young ladies couldn't wait to tell their mother they'd met a duke." His gaze found hers. "I am not surprised to learn you are not most young ladies."

As heat barreled through her, suffusing her with a flush of awareness, she focused on her steps lest she crash into him. "You're an excellent dancer, Your Grace."

"I rarely missed an assembly back in Huntingdonshire."

She imagined him dazzling all the women in the district with his easygoing nature and handsome features, along with his dancing skill. "All those assemblies, and you are unwed?"

He shrugged. "Marriage wasn't my priority."

She nearly laughed as she recalled Lady Satterfield's comment. "Mine either."

"And now?" he asked, his eyes briefly locking with hers.

"I hope to marry this Season."

"I see. I probably should too," he said casually, giving her the impression the "probably" was the most important word in his statement.

Did that mean he was definitely looking for a duchess, or was he simply open to the idea? She didn't want to prod him. "It shouldn't be too difficult for you. I think every young lady in the room has her eye on you."

When his gaze found hers this time, his focus lingered. "Does that include you?"

As he looked at her while their hands touched, a connection was forged between them. She nearly tripped. She definitely botched her steps. "Sorry," she muttered.

He easily guided them back to where they ought to be. "Don't be."

Once she had her bearings again, she answered his question. "I could be saucy and say that of course I have my eye on you—perhaps too much since I nearly caused us both to sprawl across the dance floor." She allowed her lips to curl flirtatiously. "But I'll be more direct. Yes, I have my eye on you. What young lady wouldn't want to catch the attention of a duke?"

"I am just a title to you, then?" He sounded slightly disappointed.

"Not at all. Having met you on several occasions, I have determined I *like* you. I can't say that about many gentlemen, duke or not." She was flirting—she had to—but she meant it. While he was a means to a desperately needed end, she *did* like him.

He gave her a sly smile. "How lovely to hear, Miss Stoke, for I like you too."

Was that some sort of indication as to his intentions? Her heart picked up speed, and she worked to keep her excitement in check. It wouldn't do to appear overeager. It was one thing to be frank and another to be desperate.

But then she *was* desperate.

Hopefully, she wouldn't have to reveal that. Doing so would surely ruin her chances with him and anyone else.

The set came to an end, and they were soon leaving the dance floor, her hand curled around his arm.

"Would you care to promenade around the ballroom once before I return you to your mother?" he asked.

"Indeed, thank you." Her mother was going to be positively ecstatic, but Arabella didn't want to get her hopes up. Though, her own hopes were escalating.

"Since you offered assistance, I wonder if you might help me identify someone, a gentleman named Piers Tibbord."

Arabella almost said no, but the name tickled her mind. "The name sounds familiar, but I'm afraid I can't summon his image, nor do I recall how I might know him." She glanced up at him apologetically. "That's not terribly helpful, is it?"

He laughed softly. "No, but that's all right. I have an excellent recollection of names. However, sometimes I can't place them to a face. So I see someone who looks familiar, and if their name doesn't come to me, I have to sort through my brain to find it. Sometimes I can, and sometimes I pretend." He winked at her, and it was hard not to let her hope run rampant.

Before they returned to her mother, she wanted to ask him a specific question. "If I take Biscuit for an early morning walk again soon, is there a chance I'll see you practicing with your sword?"

"Unfortunately, no. I don't have a house in town. It seems silly when I have an estate—Brixton Park—a mere five miles away."

Disappointment spiraled through her, but she only nodded. They were depressingly close to her mother. "Thank you for the dance," she said, wondering if he would ask to call on her. Her stomach knotted in anticipation.

"Thank you," he responded, steering her to her mother. Lady Satterfield was no longer with her.

Mother smiled at them, her features practically brimming with excitement. "There you are. You looked lovely together."

Arabella stared at her, silently begging her to stop before she said something like, *"You should get married!"*

Taking her hand from Halstead's arm, Arabella moved away from him. With great reluctance. He smelled very nice, like sandalwood and spice. Being next to him felt…good.

Now, however, she was next to her mother as he bid them good evening. And then he was gone. Without any indication that they would spend even another moment alone together.

But then, he *had* answered her question about seeing him in the park with the word, "unfortunately," as if he'd rather run into her again. Had he meant it like that? It was possible, she decided, and possible was good enough for now.

Mother turned to face her. "Quickly, before it's time for you to dance with someone else, tell me everything."

"He's trying to find his way as a new duke," Arabella said pragmatically, trying to keep her emotions from getting the best of her. Inside, she was a tangle of anticipation and apprehension. She thought back over the dance. "He said he liked me."

Warmth bubbled inside her, giving weight to the anticipation over the apprehension. He *had* said that. Perhaps he didn't think he could ask to call on her yet. He was, as he'd said, not very adept at the social game.

Mother beamed at her. "Well, that is spectacular. Is he going to call?"

"He didn't say so, but he's still trying to get his bearings."

"True. We shall endeavor to put you in his path as much as possible." She paused briefly, clearly thinking. "Do you know where he lives?"

"His estate outside town—Brixton Park."

"Of course." She pursed her lips. "That will be difficult to wander in front of. We'll find other ways. Surely he will be a regular fixture at events like these. I only hope our invitations keep up. People are very sympathetic about your father's illness. So many ladies have stopped by tonight to wish us well." She lowered her voice even further. "No one seems to be aware of our true situation." Her tone was heavy with relief.

Arabella was glad to hear it. She wondered what Halstead would think if he knew they were destitute. Perhaps he wouldn't care. And if he did, perhaps he'd fall madly in love with her and ignore such trivialities.

Their very future hung in the balance. It was *not* a triviality.

She recalled the name he'd mentioned and addressed her mother. "Do you know the name Piers Tibbord?"

The color completely drained from her mother's face. "Why are you asking about him?" she whispered through gritted teeth.

"The duke mentioned the name, and I couldn't recall how I knew it."

"He's the dastardly scoundrel who swindled your poor father!" She kept her voice to a low growl, but her distress was palpable.

Arabella felt foolish for not remembering. "I'm so sorry I brought it up. Please forgive me, Mama." She touched her mother's arm, and her complexion slowly returned to normal.

"Why did the duke mention him?" her mother asked. "If he is in league with that villain—"

"He didn't seem to know him," Arabella said quickly, hoping to soothe her mother's anger before she worked herself into high dudgeon. "He's merely trying to keep track of names and faces."

She recalled what he'd said about knowing names and not faces to match with them. Maybe he did know him... Still, she couldn't think he would be associated with such a despicable sort.

"I hope that is all it is, because if Halstead is aligned with Tibbord, there is no amount of money that could support a union with him. It would kill your father." Mother's lips pressed into a firm line, and the creases of concern that almost constantly inhabited her forehead returned in force.

Arabella stroked her arm. "Come, Mama, we must be optimistic. Things will work out." They had to.

She glanced around the ballroom and nearly wept with relief at the sight of Sir Ethelbert Plessey coming toward them. She'd met him at Lady Satterfield's ball, and while he wasn't astoundingly wealthy, he was situated well enough to save her family. Probably. Assuming he didn't run screaming in the other direction when he learned of their insolvency.

It was best she not think of that.

~

By the time Graham escaped the Thursby ball, he'd danced five sets, taken three promenades, and dodged countless barrages of flirtation, as well as two distinctly sexual propositions from married ladies. He was exhausted.

But he couldn't go home yet. First, he needed to visit Brooks's to see if he could find someone who knew Piers Tibbord. Graham had found the name scrawled in the margin of one of the former duke's ledgers.

Hopefully, he'd encounter Colton. If David hadn't returned to Huntwell that morning, Graham would have gone to him directly.

Graham scrubbed a hand over his face as his coach traveled the streets of Mayfair toward St. James, where he was now, inexplicably, at least to him, a member of several gentlemen's clubs. This new world was still that: new.

He fervently wished someone had introduced him to the dukedom. Not to being a duke—that he could work out with assistance—but specifically to being the Duke of Halstead. But that never would have happened. Since his great-great-uncle had banished Graham's great-great-grandfather from the family, Graham's forefathers had worked as secretaries to the Earls of St. Ives just as they'd continued their abiding hatred of the Dukes of Halstead —and the sentiment had been mutual. As such, Graham had had no interaction with the duke, not even after he was named heir presumptive. Since the duke hadn't sold the property or willed it to one of the other relatives, it was as if the duke had wanted Graham to inherit a nightmare and be at as much of a disadvantage as possible.

"Well done, you," Graham muttered. "If that was your intent, you succeeded marvelously." He narrowed his eyes as he stared into the near darkness. "However, I do not surrender so easily."

Graham wasn't going to give up fighting for Brixton Park. It existed because of his ancestor's hard work, and Graham meant to claim the legacy that had been denied his line for four generations, all because of a lie.

He had no idea if Piers Tibbord was connected to the massive investment the duke had made last year, but so far, Graham hadn't been able to find any record beyond the ledger entry that only said, "investment scheme" with the staggering amount of money listed beside it. An amount of money that was impossible to support if the scheme went bad, which it apparently had.

Graham wasn't even certain where the former duke had gotten the money. The accounting was a mess—both for Brixton Park and for Halstead Manor, which didn't even make enough money to sustain itself. If not for his Parliamentary duties, Graham would go there to try to turn things around. For now, he'd manage it from London, then spend the summer and fall in Essex and ensure Halstead Manor became profitable. If he could.

No, he refused to think like that. Come hell or high water, Graham would right the former duke's wrongs. First and foremost, he'd find where the money had gone and determine what had happened. It couldn't be unrecoverable. The duke wouldn't have made such a horrid financial decision, would he?

Unfortunately, there was no one to ask. The duke was dead, of course, and most of his retainers had retired or moved on, including his secretary, who'd relocated to Bath. Or so Graham had been told. His letters to the man had gone unanswered, and Graham had to consider paying a visit.

As if he had time for that. He had no time at all. The mortgage must be paid, or he'd lose Brixton Park.

Which brought him back to his mission—recovering the money from that investment, if he could, or marrying an heiress. He summoned an image of Miss Stoke, not that it had taken much effort. She'd been the best part of the ball. Charming, engaging, and refreshingly honest, she was a singular young lady on the Marriage Mart.

Though her father was untitled, dare Graham hope he was incredibly wealthy? Could Graham be lucky enough to find a lovely young woman who was everything he needed?

Some would say he'd been lucky enough to inherit a dukedom. However, no one knew the truth, and sometimes Graham wished he could go back to being David's secretary.

Was that really true? Yes and no. Graham missed the simplicity of worrying about someone else's fortune—it was an altogether different sort of commitment when the money didn't belong to you and your livelihood didn't hang in the balance. In many ways, it was far easier, for there was no emotional attachment. Which was what Brixton Park was. If Graham were not emotionally attached, he would do as the banker advised and sell it now. But Graham couldn't disappoint his father. He might not be here to see it, but Graham would reclaim what had been stolen from his family.

By his family. What a twisted tangle.

The coach drew to a stop in front of Brooks's, and the coachman opened the door for Graham to step out. "Thank you, Lowell."

The coachman inclined his head and asked if he should wait or return in a while.

"I've no idea," Graham said, thinking. "Why don't you wait?"

"Very good, Your Grace."

Graham went into the club for just the second time. It was a trifle overwhelming with the grand staircase and the sound of heightened conversation from the subscription room. As he headed for the stairs, he encountered Viscount Anthony Colton.

Tall with dark, wavy hair and sad blue eyes—sad because they seemed to have lost their spark since his parents had died last year—he grinned upon seeing Graham. "Why, it's the new Duke of Halstead. Good evening, Duke."

At his side was the Marquess of Ripley again. He was not quite as tall as Colton, but his hair was darker, and his dark blue eyes held all the vivacity that Colton's did not. In fact, tonight, as with the other night when Graham had made his acquaintance, Ripley appeared as if he were scheming something. Something decadent and likely scandalous. Or maybe that was because Graham was aware of the marquess's outrageous reputation.

Graham moved toward them. "Good evening, Ripley, Colton. How fortuitous that I've run into you. I was in search of companionship."

Ripley's lips curled into a devilish smile. "You've fallen across the right path. We are just on our way to find feminine companionship by way of a gaming hell. Join us."

Hell, he hadn't meant female companionship. He should have said camaraderie. Ah well, he could certainly go along to the gaming hell and then beg off. "My coach is just outside."

"Fortuitous indeed," Anthony said, walking up to Graham and clapping him on the shoulder. "You saved us having to find a hack."

The trio went outside, where Graham led them to his vehicle.

"You've a nice coach, if slightly outmoded," Ripley remarked. "If you're looking for a newer model, I can recommend someone."

Graham only said, "Thank you." He'd be lucky if he could survive the Season without having to sell the bloody thing.

Ripley directed the coachman to Covent Garden before climbing inside and taking the forward-facing seat. Colton sat opposite him. Graham entered last, sitting beside the marquess.

"So what's the likelihood you'll wed by Easter?" Colton asked as he leaned back against the squab.

The coach moved forward, and Graham blinked. What the hell had they heard? No one knew of his desperate urgency in finding a wife. "Why do you ask?"

Ripley settled into the corner, angling himself slightly toward Graham. "You're not aware of the wager?"

"What wager?"

"In the betting book at White's," Anthony answered. "There's a bet as to whether you'll be wed by Easter."

Graham's muscles loosened with relief. "And what are people saying?"

Ripley lifted a shoulder. "Most say you'll be wed, but it's early yet. The wager was just placed this afternoon."

The betting book was well known to Graham even if he hadn't ever participated in placing wagers. He supposed he'd fully arrived in Society now. "At least the bet isn't about *whom* I will wed."

Colton chuckled. "Oh, that may come."

Ripley regarded Graham for a moment. "It's too early to say because no one knows you well enough to guess. What sort of woman is your type? A great beauty? An unimpeachable reputation? A bluestocking? An heiress? A wallflower?"

This could be a great opportunity. Graham's pulse sped as he smiled mischievously. "All of them."

Colton laughed, and though it took Ripley a moment, he joined in.

When their humor subsided, Graham looked from one to the other. "Who would that be?"

"What do you mean?" Colton asked, his brow creasing.

"I mean, who possesses all those traits?" He kept his tone wry, but he was deadly serious—he wanted to know who was an heiress, and this was a spectacular way to do so without asking, *"Who are the richest ladies on the Marriage Mart?"*

"So you do plan to wed?" Ripley asked with interest.

Anthony looked to Ripley. "We should go back and place our wagers."

"Not necessarily." It was still important that Graham not appear as if he was in a hurry, lest people think he was desperate and then ferret out why.

Ripley smirked at Colton. "He's being coy." He turned his attention to Graham. "I can't think of anyone who would fit all those descriptions."

"Miss Phoebe Lennox," Colton said. "Actually, no, her reputation is less than distinguished since she abandoned her betrothed at the altar last Season."

"Oh, she sounds like *my* type," Ripley said with a glint in his eye.

Colton snorted. "Hardly. She's not a widow. Or a courtesan." He glanced toward Graham. "Ripley wouldn't bother with a young, virtuous lady like Miss Lennox."

Ripley frowned. "But you said her reputation was in tatters."

"I did not say that. I said it was less than distinguished. My sister knows her. She's quite nice, or so Sarah says. Leave her alone, Rip."

The marquess raised his hands in mock surrender. "I

wouldn't dream of tarrying with someone like her. We're just having fun. Now, let me think of who else I know…"

"How about Mrs. Billingford?" Colton suggested.

Ripley's lips spread into a wide, sinful smile. "Halstead didn't say he wanted a tigress in bed."

Graham couldn't resist saying, "Halstead didn't say he *didn't* want that."

Laughter erupted in the coach, and it was a long moment before Ripley said, "We are definitely going to the right place, then."

"Mrs. Billingford's house?" Graham asked innocently.

This was met with more laughter. "Can you imagine?" Colton asked. "If all three of us showed up?"

Ripley smoothed his hair back over his temple. "She'd be quite happy to accommodate us, I'm sure."

Bloody hell. Graham was speechless.

"Well, we can discuss that if we want, but I'd rather partake of Mrs. Alban's stock." Ripley fixed his gaze on Graham. "She owns the brothel above the gaming hell. Actually, she owns the gaming hell too. We'll gamble for a while and then head upstairs. Or I suppose you can head up straightaway, if you prefer."

He preferred to return to Brixton Park. He wasn't in the mood for Mrs. Alban's "stock"—what an awful description—and he sure as hell wasn't going to gamble. He didn't have a shilling to lose.

"I should probably return home after I drop you at the hell," he said. "I've a bit of a drive to get to Brixton Park."

"You are welcome to stay with me," Ripley offered. "Provided you don't mind a smudge on your good name."

Yes, he minded that a great deal. His good name was just about all he had at present.

Colton chuckled. "Rip isn't kidding. I know my reputation has taken a beating since we became friends, not that I care. I stayed at his house *once*, and you'd think I killed someone in a duel."

The coach moved into Covent Garden, and Graham realized he hadn't addressed his most important question. "I don't suppose either of you know Piers Tibbord?"

Ripley shrugged, but Colton answered. "He's a swindler. Or so I've heard. Never met him, and as far as I know, no one has. He conducts all his affairs through an intermediary." Colton's gaze narrowed at Graham. "I hope you aren't tangled up with him."

Bloody hell. Graham couldn't tell them the truth of where he'd found the name. "No. I heard the name and thought he sounded familiar. Clearly, I was mistaken." His mind whirled as he tried to think of his next move. He couldn't very well ask where he might find Tibbord, not after what Colton had just revealed.

The coach came to a stop.

"You sure you won't join us?" Colton asked. Tibbord had apparently been forgotten. Good.

"I'm sure, but I appreciate the invitation." Graham yawned for good measure. "I'm still finding my London legs."

The door opened, and Colton climbed down first.

Ripley clapped the top of Graham's shoulder. "Do let me know if you ever need a place to stay—my door is open to you." He clambered around Graham and out of the coach.

Graham bid them both good night and was soon on his way toward Brixton Park.

The events of the evening and the information he'd gleaned played through his mind. How was he going to find Piers Tibbord if no one had actually met him? Perhaps he should ask Lord Satterfield or the Duke of Kendal. Lady Satterfield had seemed genuine in her offer of assistance.

However, then he'd have to come up with a reason that wasn't the truth. If he said the former duke had possibly done business with him, the reality of Graham's situation could get out. Or not—if he was careful. This was going to take careful consideration.

Finding Tibbord was going to be difficult and perhaps even impossible. He had to think of other ways to track down the duke's investment. Recovering the investment money—*hell,* even determining what the investment had been—seemed an insurmountable task.

Even if he found Tibbord, how would he go about getting the duke's investment back? He wouldn't think about that right now. He had to locate the swindler first —or at least get a little closer to that goal.

Which brought him back to an heiress. Phoebe Lennox was still his best option.

And yet Arabella Stoke kept creeping into his mind, along with the hope that her father was fabulously wealthy. She'd be the answer to all his problems, and he could think of plenty of benefits of making her his duchess that had nothing to do with her bank account.

He'd turned down an invitation to a brothel, and yet here he was fantasizing about Miss Stoke. About the soft lilt of her lips when she smiled at him. The elegant curve of her neck as she danced with him. The delicious scent of sweet pea that washed over him as he escorted her around the ballroom. Closing his eyes, he leaned his head back and mentally pulled the pins from her light brown hair. Strands of gold mixed with the brown, bringing to mind the rich color of ripe, dark wheat. Her green eyes were tinged with brown at the very center, giving them an earthy, seductive vibrancy.

Damn, he was at half-staff and growing harder by the minute just thinking of her. He forced himself to think about his lack of funds instead. It was an effective, if depressing, tool.

His efforts were going to take time. Too bad he had about as much of that as he did money.

CHAPTER 5

*M*ama walked into the small sitting room at the back of their narrow town house. "Your father had a good lunch. He's actually sitting up in bed and will have a bath later."

Arabella smiled at the warmth and happiness in her mother's voice. "Wonderful news. I'll go up and see him in a while."

"He'd like that." Arabella's mother sat in her favorite chair near the fireplace and picked up the newspaper she'd set down earlier. "Perhaps you can read to him from that novel." She was referring to *The Castle of Otranto*, which was Arabella's father's favorite.

"Of course." Arabella returned her attention to the ball gown she was embroidering. She'd designed clusters of flowers and was stitching them onto the sleeves to update the two-year-old garment.

Their butler, Baxter, entered and presented a card to Arabella's mother. "His Grace, the Duke of Halstead."

Arabella's fingers froze, and her spine went stiff. She snapped her gaze to her mother, who looked down at the card, her eyes widening. Then she promptly surveyed the room. "Are we presentable?" She turned her attention to Arabella. "Hide that gown so he can't see what you're doing."

Why, because ladies didn't embroider their gowns? Arabella stood, and the butler came forward.

He took the garment. "I'll give it to Janney."

"Thank you, Baxter."

"Then please send the duke in." Mama stood and hid the newspaper under the cushion of her chair. She blinked as the usual lines of worry creased her brow. "Unless we should go up to the drawing room?"

To do so, they'd be visible going up the stairs from the entry, and what would be the point of that? "I think it's fine if we receive him here," Arabella said. "This is a lovely room."

"Yes, but it's perhaps too…comfortable." Mama frowned. "Never mind, none of our rooms are as splendid as they should be." She sounded as if she might cry, and Arabella hated that.

"I'll bring a plate of fresh butter biscuits," Baxter offered. "That will ensure he remembers this visit for all time." The cook had tried Phoebe's cook's recipe the other day, and even Arabella's father had eaten some.

Mama relaxed slightly, her mouth finding the ghost of a smile. "That's true. Thank you, Baxter."

He inclined his silver head as he ambled from the sitting room with Arabella's gown.

Mama looked over at Arabella. "Why do you suppose he's here?"

"To pay a call?" Arabella didn't mean to sound flippant, but really, why else would he be there?

"Yes, yes, of course," Mama said with a hint of smiling exasperation, which buoyed Arabella's spirits where she was concerned. "I mean, what should we make of his call?"

Footsteps sounded outside the door. "I'm sure we'll find out," Arabella murmured.

Mama dashed over to her side and urgently whispered, "Remember, you must find out why he asked you about Tibbord!" She hastily pasted a welcoming smile on her face just as the duke entered.

Halstead bowed. "Good afternoon, ladies."

They curtsied and greeted him in return.

"It's an honor to welcome you into our home," Arabella's mother said. "Please sit." She gestured toward the settee, then sent a look at Arabella that clearly said she should sit beside him.

Arabella perched on the settee, and he lowered himself next to her. It was a small piece of furniture that left only a few inches between them. The familiar sense of awareness that his proximity aroused washed over her.

"It's a pleasure to see you both again," Halstead said. "I had such a lovely time dancing with Miss Stoke the other night that I thought I should come and thank her in person." He turned his head to Arabella. "Thank you."

Arabella cast a glance toward her mother, who looked as if she might weep with joy. She refocused on the duke. "You are in for a treat because the cook just made butter biscuits, and they are perhaps the best butter biscuits you will ever have."

He waggled his brows at her. "I am aquiver in anticipation."

It was barely a flirtation, but the simple act of his being here meant he was at least interested in getting to know her better. Arabella would do everything in her power to pass muster.

Baxter entered with the plate of biscuits along with a pot of tea and three cups. He removed the items from the tray onto a small, low table at the center of their seating arrangement. "Shall I pour?" he asked Arabella's mother.

"That won't be necessary. Thank you, Baxter."

After the butler had departed, Arabella's mother urged the duke to try a biscuit. As he removed his gloves and reached toward the table, he asked, "Where do you spend your summers? You've a country home, I imagine?"

Arabella was afraid to look at her mother and see distress flash in her eyes. They'd sold their country house—where Arabella had spent her childhood—last year. Not that it had made them any money, for it had been mortgaged to the hilt.

"We do not," Mama said in a surprisingly smooth tone. "We prefer London."

That was a simple, and believable, enough answer.

Mother continued, "You've two country homes, do you not? Your seat in Essex and the magnificent Brixton Park? You probably have a Mayfair town house as well."

"You are correct." He finished his first butter biscuit and looked to Arabella. "That *is* the best butter biscuit I've ever had. I don't think my cook at Brixton Park makes those, but I shall ask." He transferred his gaze to her mother. "I don't see a need for a house in town, not when Brixton Park is so close."

"What a reasonable and wise choice," her mother said with warm approval. Arabella could practically see the inside of her mother's mind as she deduced he must be responsible with his money if he chose not to waste any on a house in London when many other gentlemen in his position would. "I should love to see Brixton Park. I've heard it's quite grand."

The duke angled himself toward Arabella. "Do you ride?"

Damn, another question that could provoke her mother's panic. "Yes, but I admit I lost interest in recent years as I began to focus on the Season," Arabella said.

"Her horse was put out to pasture a few years ago, and we've never gotten around to replacing her, have we, dear?" Mother threw in a light laugh along with the fabrication.

They'd surreptitiously sold off their horseflesh over the past few years, as Papa had begun to gamble too much and became interested in flashy investments guaranteed to increase their wealth. He'd hoped to recover from a spate of bad losses at the gaming tables but had only succeeded in driving them deeper into debt. While the duke was perhaps good with money, her father was exceptionally *bad*.

Arabella saw no need to answer the question and instead queried the duke. "Do you ride, Your Grace?" It seemed he must, particularly since he lived outside town.

"I do."

"And do you have a passion for fast vehicles like so many young gentlemen?" Mother asked. "Perhaps you have a high-perch phaeton."

"I do not have either of those things," he said. "I was not raised with privilege, so I don't necessarily have all the trappings you might expect of a duke." His tone was even, but there was something charged beneath the surface of his response, perhaps a current of frustration.

Her mother *was* interrogating him somewhat, though she was doing a good job of hiding it in casual conversation. In fact, one could argue he was doing the same thing, asking about their country home and whether Arabella rode. She began to feel a vague sense of discomfort, which was silly. Just because they were trying to determine his financial status didn't mean he was trying to determine theirs.

Except he might be. Particularly if he were interested in marriage. Wasn't that something families discussed as part of a marriage contract? Only her father wasn't in a position to discuss such matters, and even if he was, what could he say except *"We're insolvent, but please, marry my daughter anyway?"*

"I'd forgotten you recently inherited, and my goodness, you were a secretary before that, were you not?" Mama asked with genuine interest and not a shred of disdain for the duke possessing the background of a commoner. But then *they* were commoners, and it was by sheer luck that Papa's close friendship with the former Earl of St. Ives had elevated them in Society.

"I was," Halstead said. "I enjoyed being a secretary

very much, and since I worked for the Earl of St. Ives and consider him a close friend, I was raised in tandem with the nobility. I went to Oxford with St. Ives and learned all the same things he did." In some ways, Halstead's relationship with the earl mirrored Arabella's father's with the earl's father. Both had benefitted from friendship with the Earls of St. Ives.

Mama seemed impressed, her eyes lighting. "You may not be aware, but Arabella's father was quite close with the former earl. They went to school together and remained dear friends until the earl's passing."

"I am aware," the duke said gently.

Arabella gauged her mother's reaction. Thankfully, she only responded with a serene nod before continuing.

"I imagine it's quite an adjustment going from secretary to duke," Mama said. "What do you like best about being a duke? Is it the ability to purchase anything you'd like?"

Well, that was rather *too* obvious, wasn't it? Arabella studied the duke for his reaction and again had the vague sense that Mother's questioning was putting him off.

"I'm not sure I've thought about that." Halstead reached for another biscuit. "So far, I think I like these biscuits best." He smiled before popping it into his mouth.

It was a nonsensical answer, as if their biscuits had anything to do with being a duke, but she supposed one could argue that if he hadn't become the duke, he would have had no occasion to be there in this sitting room with Mrs. Woodcock's delectable confections.

Arabella grabbed one for herself.

"About Brixton Park," Mama said, making Arabella tense. He'd already ignored Mama when she'd said she'd love to see his estate. "Dare we hope you'll host an event there? It would be a wonderful place to host a picnic, being so close to town. I've heard the parkland and gardens are extraordinary."

Arabella noted that the muscles in his jaw flexed. She glanced down at his hands, which appeared rigid. Instead of lying flat against his thighs or at least at ease, they were slightly curled. His entire body seemed to thrum with energy. She feared her mother was pushing him to the brink of his endurance, and he'd leave, never to return. Then where would they be?

He gave her mother a placid smile that seemed at odds with the small observations Arabella was making. "I don't think I'll have the time to organize such an event, not with all I must learn."

"You need a duchess," Mama declared brightly, her gaze moving to Arabella in the least subtle silent communication ever.

"Why don't we take a walk in the garden?" Arabella suggested abruptly, already rising from the settee. "It's small, but the day is too pleasant to ignore. You can watch us through the window, all right, Mama?"

The duke quickly got to his feet and offered his arm before her mother responded.

As if she would say no…

"Go ahead! Take your time," Mama encouraged, directing an urgent stare at Arabella that was likely meant to convey a variety of things: Ask him about Tibbord! Find out how much he's worth! Obtain an offer of marriage!

While she liked the duke, Arabella couldn't help but feel awkward. Because whatever transaction might arise between them, it would be because of need, not want, and she hated that.

As soon as they were outside, she started to relax. "It's a very small garden." She pointed toward the back of Phoebe's house. "You can see Miss Lennox's house there."

He looked in the direction of her hand. "Ah, yes. I may pay a call when I'm finished here."

It was as good as saying, *"You are not the only young lady I am considering."* Which made sense. Why would he focus on her when there were far better options? Daughters of dukes or at least earls. Beautiful young debutantes like Miss Dahlia Wemple. Wealthy heiresses like Phoebe.

Or perhaps he was saying, *"This call has gone horribly. Your mother is ridiculous. It's been nice knowing you."*

Arabella sought to undo some of the damage her mother may have done. "I'm sorry about my mother's questions. She gets overexcited sometimes, particularly when dukes call."

He arched a dark brow at her. "Does that happen often?"

"Never, in fact."

He visibly relaxed, his frame losing its tension as they circuited the garden. "Ah, well, I didn't mean to cause a stir."

"It's quite all right. I hope she didn't offend."

A smile pulled at his lips. "Of course not." He glanced around. "It seems we are nearly finished with our walk around the garden."

She laughed softly. "I told you it was small. We can go round again." At the very least, she had to ask him about Tibbord. She didn't think an offer of marriage was forthcoming. "I wanted to ask you about Mr. Tibbord."

The tension returned to his body. He stiffened briefly, and she wondered if he had to work at hiding it. Was there something about Tibbord? Or was she reading into his reaction because she knew what Tibbord was?

"What did you want to ask?" His voice sounded a bit thin, and she began to doubt his behavior was a figment of her mind.

She stopped and turned toward him, keeping her hand on his arm. It was a gamble, but she decided to plunge forward so she could study his reaction for the truth… "Tibbord is a swindler. I am curious as to how you know him."

And there it was. A slight widening of his gaze and nostrils followed by a tightening in his jaw. "How do *you* know that? I can't imagine you'd be associated with someone like that." He regarded her intently, his gaze piercing hers.

It seemed, *maybe*, that he knew Tibbord was a thief. If he knew what she knew, had he—? She cut off the thought and blurted, "Did he cheat you too?"

Too late, she realized what she'd done. Before she could find a way to retract what she'd said, he moved closer. "He cheated you? How?"

"I don't know precisely," she answered softly, her chest churning in anguish. "Please, you can't tell anyone. My mother will be devastated, and my father…" She couldn't bring herself to finish.

His gaze softened, and he put his hand over hers on his arm. "I won't. The questions your mother was asking… You're looking to marry a wealthy gentleman, aren't you?"

She didn't trust herself to speak. No, she couldn't speak. Mortification and despair surged inside her. She nodded.

He pressed his mouth into a grim line. "I'm sorry to tell you that I can't be that gentleman. You're correct that Tibbord swindled me—not me, the former duke—and I haven't a farthing to my name that isn't owed to someone else."

And just like that, Arabella's fantasy died. Her future had never seemed more bleak.

~

*G*raham watched the play of emotions across Miss Stoke's face. From horror when she'd mistakenly revealed they'd been cheated to sadness to humiliation and lastly to utter devastation. He wanted to do more than touch her hand, but now more than ever, he couldn't.

He'd felt a similar array of sensations, culminating in

abject disappointment that she wasn't the heiress he needed. However, perhaps they could help each other in a different way...

Miss Stoke blinked at him. "You're bankrupt?"

He bristled at her phrasing—*he* wasn't bankrupt. He had a small but tidy savings, which he'd had to access to support his new station for appearances' sake and to keep from having to sell Brixton Park immediately. It wasn't going to last much longer, however. It was expensive being a duke, particularly one who was trying to attract an heiress. "The dukedom is, yes. However, I'm trying to rectify that."

"By marrying an heiress." Realization swept over her features. "That's why you called on Phoebe."

Dammit. Since it wasn't a question, he didn't address the comment. "I'd appreciate if you would keep my situation secret, just as I will yours."

She nodded quickly. "Of course. I completely understand."

He continued with the idea that was dancing in his head. "As I said, I'm trying to rectify the matter and not just by marriage. I'd prefer to avoid that, if I can."

"You don't want to wed?" She asked this with genuine curiosity, and he saw no reason not to answer her plainly.

"Not right now, and not for money." The desire he felt for Miss Stoke wove its way through him. He'd rather marry for much different reasons. He wouldn't speak plainly about *that*.

"We are in agreement on that," she said.

He hated the resignation in her voice. It was tinged with sadness, and he wished he could tell her she didn't have to marry for money. He could perhaps do the next best thing. "I'm hopeful that I can find this Tibbord thief and recover my fortune. And yours. He can't get away with fleecing people."

She inhaled sharply. "You think you can do that?"

He clenched his jaw. "I'm determined to do it. If we

work together—combine our knowledge—perhaps we can find him."

"I'm afraid I don't know who he is. I didn't even remember his name when you mentioned it the other night. I asked my mother about it, and she nearly had a fit. I don't think she knows much either. My father made the investment with Tibbord and has refused to tell us anything about it." Anguish crept into her gaze, and Graham wanted to banish it forever.

"When did this investment occur?" he asked.

Small pleats lined her brow. "I'm not sure exactly. Maybe a year ago?"

"I believe the duke made his late last spring or summer. There is frustratingly little information. Just the record of the investment and the amount recorded in a ledger. I found Tibbord's name scrawled in the margin of an entirely different ledger."

"But you seemed to know he was a swindler," she said. "Am I wrong?"

Again, he saw no reason to lie to her, especially if they could help each other. "No. I asked a couple of friends about him, just as I did you at the Thursby ball, and one of them informed me he was a known thief. He also told me no one knows him directly, that he always acts through another party, though he didn't say who." Graham would follow up with Colton on that. "Was that the case with your father?"

She shook her head, grimacing. "I don't know."

"Can we ask him?"

Her grip tightened briefly on his arm. "He's very ill. I fear asking him about Tibbord may only worsen his condition. I'm sorry."

Well, that was bloody disappointing. "There has to be a way to track the scoundrel down."

"Couldn't the duke's secretary help?"

Graham frowned. "Unfortunately, he moved to Bath when the duke died and hasn't answered my correspondence. I may need to pay him a visit." Again, he didn't particularly have the time, but he was running out of options. How else would they find Tibbord? He kept returning to her father. "I'm sorry your father is so ill." Graham stroked his thumb along the top of her hand.

"As our financial situation worsened, he became more and more unwell. He scarcely leaves his bedchamber anymore." Her eyes filled with worry. "I fear he isn't long for this world."

Graham's gut twisted. What would happen to her and her mother if her father died? Presumably, they had no money in trust or any means of support. "Miss Stoke, I would very much like to help you, if you'll let me. However, we desperately need to know everything your father can tell us about Tibbord and their transaction if we have any hope of recovering your money."

"Do you really think that's possible?" she asked, a bare thread of hope detectable in her voice. "Investments go bad all the time—this is not the first time my father has lost money."

"While that's true, there's something wrong here. I can feel it. I've handled investments and financial transactions for the Earl of St. Ives in my position as secretary, as did my father before me. The amount of money the duke invested with Tibbord was far too great. Either the duke was an utter fool, or Tibbord cheated him somehow."

"Unfortunately, my father *is* a fool," she said quietly. "Though it pains me to say so."

Graham was all too aware of her touch and her nearness. And his desire to take her in his arms and hold her, soothe her, kiss her...

Kiss her?

Yes, he wanted to kiss her and probably even more than that. However, he couldn't. In fact, he shouldn't even be standing with her like this. What must her mother think?

"We've been out here for quite some time. I'd wager

your mother is already planning your wedding trousseau."

"Paid for by money neither of us has." She smiled up at him sadly. "I am very sorry you're poor."

He wasn't entirely sure if she meant it purely for the purpose of financial rescue. There was a hint that, like him, she'd hoped for something more. "No sorrier than I." He removed his hand from hers. "We should go in so I may take my leave."

"Yes." She sounded as reluctant as he felt. "I will learn all I can from my father. How shall I let you know when I have something to share?"

"Perhaps we should set our next meeting time and place."

"I could walk Biscuit in the park again," she suggested. "Or I could meet you at Phoebe's."

Miss Lennox's would probably be better, for propriety's sake. However, Graham didn't want Miss Lennox thinking he was interested in Miss Stoke. Even though Miss Lennox had said she didn't wish to marry, Graham nurtured a small hope that he could change her mind. "The park, I think. Early, as we did before, and in the same place. Will Wednesday morning give you enough time to speak with your father?"

She glanced up toward a window on the house, perhaps her father's chamber. "I'm not sure. It depends on how he's feeling, and I honestly have no idea how I'm going to do this without upsetting him."

While it pained him to see her fret over this and he had no wish to cause her father distress, he couldn't see an alternative. "I wouldn't have asked if there was any other way."

"I understand. And I agree—this is too important." She paused, flicking a look toward the house again. "Perhaps I'll tell my father that an investigator contacted us."

"Won't you have to include your mother in such a ruse?"

"I can't, not without revealing what we're doing, and she can't know that you are aware of the truth. If my father asks her about the investigator, she'll think he's rambling nonsense. He does that, unfortunately." There was no mistaking the doubt stealing over her features. "It's possible he may not be able to help. His mind is not always there."

"I'm so sorry, Miss Stoke." And he truly was. "Losing my father last year was incredibly difficult. I miss him every day."

Her gaze softened, and she lifted her free hand but dropped it to her side before touching him. "I am sorry for your loss. It sounds as though you loved him very much."

"I did." He wanted to cheer her—and himself. "But listen to us being the sorriest people in London. We don't have time for that." He offered her a bolstering smile. "I'm going to do everything I can to hunt down Tibbord and recover our money."

Light and hope warmed her features as she smiled in return. "That would be wonderful. We should go in. I'm not at all sure what I'm going to tell my mother. She's bound to think an offer has occurred or is forthcoming given how long we've been out here. Instead, I must tell her we don't suit."

"Don't do that," he said quickly, looking toward the house. "Not yet. I may need to call on you again or dance with you. Or promenade—we need to be able to share information."

"You make a good argument." The flirtatiousness he'd come to anticipate crept into her eyes and voice. "If we *must*."

Graham chuckled softly as he led her back to the house.

After a brief conversation with Mrs. Stoke, during which she gave him a hastily copied recipe for the butter biscuits, Graham took his leave. As he took the reins of his horse from their young stable lad, he marveled at how the Stokes had managed to shield their financial situation. So had he, but they'd been at it much longer. He wondered if anyone had begun to notice. He had to help Miss Stoke—it was vital.

Maybe, if he was able to return them both to financial security, he could actually court her. He paused before mounting his horse. Did he want to court her?

No. He wanted to grow accustomed to his new position. He didn't have time for a wife, no matter how lovely and tempting Miss Stoke might be. The timing was wrong, unfortunately, and he'd do well to remember that. The relationship between him and Miss Stoke must remain purely professional.

Graham climbed atop his horse and set off toward Brixton Park. The back and forth would likely become tedious, and he supposed he could stay at David's town house now that he and Fanny had returned to Huntwell. It could at least serve as a base so that Graham didn't have to return to Brixton Park before going out each evening when he had engagements. Something to consider.

For now, he needed to return to Brixton Park and then come back to town tonight so he could speak with Anthony. On second thought, if he could run Anthony down right now, he could avoid another trip tonight since he didn't have any commitments.

A weariness swept over him. He'd never asked for any of this. And yet when he thought of his father, Graham knew he had to fight. When the duke's son had died, Graham's father had been thrilled to be named heir presumptive. At last, their branch of the family would reclaim its birthright.

Graham heard his father's voice: "It isn't about the dukedom. It's about our right, as Kinsleys to be a part of the family. More importantly, we can finally claim our place at Brixton Park, which *my* great-grandfather built."

Yes, Graham had to fight. For his father, the person

who'd meant most to him in the world. Now that Graham was alone, that was all he had left.

You don't have to be alone.

The voice at the back of his mind buzzed at him like an annoying gnat.

No, he didn't have to be alone, and if he couldn't recover the money from Tibbord, he couldn't afford to be. He needed to find the bloody man. And then Graham would make him pay for stealing from an old man and ruining a young woman's future.

CHAPTER 6

*A*fter lunch the following day, Arabella's mother took Biscuit for a walk around Cavendish Square. She'd only be gone a short time, so Arabella had to move quickly.

Making her way to her father's room, she armed herself with a plate of butter biscuits, which had quickly become his favorite treat. It was the one thing he could be relied upon to eat.

"Papa, I'm here with biscuits," she said, walking into his dim chamber. The curtains were only half drawn from the windows.

He was sitting up in bed, having recently returned after managing a half bowl of duck soup for lunch. The newspaper sat beside him, folded.

"What was that, dear?" His voice had thinned in recent months. Arabella prayed it would return to its deeper strength when his health finally improved. *If* it improved.

No, she refused to think like that.

"I don't really want to see Biscuit just now."

He meant the dog, whom he'd found bothersome since becoming ill. Biscuit could get overexcited when she came into his chamber, probably because she missed seeing him, and Papa preferred she stayed out. It was troubling because Arabella felt certain Biscuit could improve his disposition. It was impossible not to smile when she laid her head on your lap and let her tongue hang out while you scratched the underside of her chin.

"Not Biscuit, Papa. A plate *of butter* biscuits." Arabella closed the door and went to set the plate on the table next to the bed. A chair was angled nearby—it was where Mother spent so much of her time and where Arabella read to him.

Papa chuckled, and, though thready, it was a wonderful sound. "Those I will gladly welcome."

Arabella sat in the chair. "Mother is out walking Biscuit, though I daresay you would benefit from a visit with her. Dogs have mysterious restorative qualities."

He reached for a biscuit and gave a noncommittal grunt in response.

Arabella regretted discussing the dog. She didn't wish to get off on the wrong foot. Today was his most lucid of the past few, which was excellent timing for what she needed to do. She must take full advantage.

She inwardly winced. She didn't wish to take advantage of *him*, but couldn't dismiss the sensation that she was doing precisely that.

No, you're doing this for *him. For all of you.*

"Papa—"

"Tell me about your Season, dear." He started speaking on top of her, so she let him continue. "Your mother says the Duke of Halstead called yesterday. I am sorry I missed it." His gaze turned sad as he ate the biscuit. Thankfully, the emotion seemed fleeting as he enjoyed the confection.

"The Season is going well, Papa. The duke is very charming, but he is not the only gentleman paying me interest." She didn't want him to get his hopes up, especially when she had no future with the duke.

Papa's brows arched briefly. "Is that right? Who else has called?"

It suddenly felt as if no one was interested. "No one."

"Ah well, no matter, not with a duke on board! How wonderful if you could land him." His eyes narrowed, and his lip curled. "I'd like to see what St. Ives would say about that, the blackguard."

This was a familiar line of conversation. No, not conversation, because Arabella didn't encourage it. Diatribe was a better description. "He's not a blackguard." He'd simply fallen in love with someone else, and Arabella couldn't fault him for that.

Papa scoffed. "He's worse than that to have thrown you over. His father is likely tossing in his grave. The boy lied to his father on his deathbed." He shook his head. "Unforgiveable."

Arabella saw no point in trying to defend the earl to her father. Furthermore, she had no desire to agitate him right now, not when the reason she'd come to see him would do that well enough on its own. Instead, she joined in his disdain. "Good riddance to him anyway," she said. "I can't say I really cared for him."

"Of course not, dear. You've far better taste." He gave her a half smile and reached for another biscuit.

Biscuit! Her mother would return soon. Arabella didn't have a moment to lose.

"Papa, I met with an investigator about…Mr. Tibbord." She hesitated briefly before saying the man's name, her body tensing as she awaited Papa's reaction.

He'd just taken a bite of biscuit and now sat up straight to sputter and cough. Arabella jumped to her feet and patted his back.

"Are you all right?" She felt horrible for rushing forward without paying attention to the fact that he'd just eaten a biscuit.

He quieted and leaned back. "An investigator?"

She nodded and sat back down. "Tibbord is a thief—we are not the only people he has fleeced." She thought of Halstead, not that *he'd* been fleeced, but he was a victim of the man's misconduct just the same.

"Of course not," Papa said. "Who hired the investigator?"

"I'm not sure." She hated lying to him, but it was necessary. This was for their benefit. Their livelihood depended on it. "But we can help if you tell me about what happened."

He shook his head. "I must speak to the investigator, not you."

She'd anticipated he might insist on meeting the investigator. "Papa, it's not possible. You are too ill. Mama would never allow it." That much was true.

He frowned. "But I am the head of this family."

"Yes, but you are also too ill to get dressed." She edged forward in her chair, clasping her hands together tightly as she looked at him pleadingly. "You must let go of some of the burden. I can handle this. Please."

He was quiet for a long moment. "It isn't right."

Arabella held her breath. She was running out of time before her mother returned.

Papa exhaled. "If it will punish Tibbord for what he's done, I'll help."

Inside, she relaxed with relief. Outside, she smiled. "Thank you, Papa. The investigator would like to know how Tibbord managed to steal from you." His eye twitched, and she felt wretched for dredging this up.

He looked toward the window. "He gained my trust. I invested a small amount at first, and it earned a tidy return, so I invested more. Tibbord required it, you see, to stay in the game. If I didn't invest more, he would find another investor and I'd lose my spot. When I lost a goodly sum at the tables," he winced, "I invested more."

Tibbord had preyed upon a man who possessed little

financial acumen. Then, when Papa had fallen into financial distress, Tibbord had gone in for the kill. "How did you come to know Mr. Tibbord?" she asked gently.

"I heard about him at a gaming hell, er, establishment." He looked away and folded his hands in his lap.

Arabella didn't think there was anything she could say to ease his embarrassment. Furthermore, it wasn't up to her to alleviate his conscience. While she'd forgiven him for jeopardizing their well-being with his gambling, it wasn't easily forgotten. "I know you went to gaming establishments, Papa. Most gentlemen do. How did you meet Mr. Tibbord?" she prompted, all too aware that her mother would return soon.

"I didn't meet him." Again he looked away, and a faint flush of pink crept up his neck. "I conducted all business through his assistant." The confirmation that there had been an intermediary wasn't surprising, but it was frustrating. She'd been hoping her father had perhaps met the man.

"Then how did you even hear of Tibbord?"

"Everyone at the hell knew of him. He was known for his clever handling of investments. He was aware of all the latest shipping interests and building schemes. Gentlemen were eager to invest with him. When Osborne—that's his man—spoke to you, everyone seethed with jealousy."

That couldn't still be the case, not if Tibbord's reputation was now that of a thief. "Has that changed? I imagine it must have if someone is investigating him."

"I was not the only person who lost a great deal of money with him. Those of us who did were evasive about the specifics, of course."

Of course. "Who else lost money to him?" she asked.

Papa pressed his lips together firmly. "That I won't say. It's not my place to reveal others' secrets."

The sound of Biscuit's bark carried into the bedroom.

Papa scrunched up his face. "Would you mind keeping the dog out?"

"Mama won't bring her in." Arabella wasn't quite finished with her questions, but she was out of time. Rising, she asked, "In which hell did you make Osborne's acquaintance?"

"The Thundering Stag," he said. "In Covent Garden."

The dog yapped again, and it sounded as though they might be in the sitting room just outside the bedchamber. Arabella gave her father a pointed stare. "Remember, don't tell Mama about this. She would worry, and she already has enough weighing on her mind."

"She is far too encumbered." His voice was sad and full of regret.

Arabella's heart melted. She moved to the bedside and took his hand. "Things will get better. Perhaps this investigator will be able to recover the money you lost."

He gave her an encouraging smile that didn't reach his eyes. "Yes, that would be lovely, dear." He obviously didn't think it was possible. "You must keep me apprised of what's going on. Promise me." He sat forward, and his features were more animated than she'd seen them in weeks.

She squeezed his hand. "Yes, Papa. I will."

Biscuit barked again, and Arabella quickly stepped out into the sitting room, where her mother was just handing the dog off to Millie.

Mama patted Biscuit's head before turning to Arabella. "You were in with your father?"

"I brought him some biscuits."

"You shouldn't overtire him. He needs his rest."

Arabella didn't agree. What he needed was exercise. However, it wasn't worthwhile to argue with her mother.

Mama went into the bedchamber, and Arabella followed. Papa was out of the bed and heading toward his dressing chamber.

"Yardley, what are you doing?" Mama asked with alarm.

"Getting dressed. I'd like to go out to the garden."

As he disappeared into the dressing room, Mama spun about and blinked at Arabella. "What happened?"

Apparently, she'd given him something to get out of bed for. Arabella stifled a smile. She'd been so worried about how the Tibbord conversation might adversely affect him, she'd never imagined it might do the opposite. "Nothing. We ate biscuits. He really loves them."

Mama shot a look toward the plate on the bedside table. Only two biscuits remained, showing he'd eaten several more since Arabella had left the room. She smothered another smile.

"Mariah, will you lend your assistance?" Papa called.

"Of course." Mama hurried toward the dressing chamber with alacrity, and Arabella retreated to the sitting room.

That had gone much better than she'd hoped. Not only had she gathered vital information, Papa seemed to be energized by the prospect of the investigator. Too bad it wasn't true.

A shard of discomfort sliced through Arabella. What if nothing came of Halstead's inquiries? What if nothing changed, and Arabella was forced to marry for money? Worse, what if Arabella wasn't able to do so?

Ice coated her spine. She wouldn't think like that. There was too much at stake. She would be back on the Marriage Mart tonight. *And* she would pursue Tibbord. She would save them all at any cost.

With Halstead's help. She was eager to tell him what she'd learned. Tomorrow couldn't come soon enough.

∾

*S*itting in the House of Lords was perhaps the strangest aspect of Graham's new life. He was still learning so much, but the sheer importance and responsibility of being a duke was slowly—and firmly—settling in. He'd been so focused on his personal financial issues that he hadn't paid proper attention to his other duties. Yet another reason he needed to solve that problem once and for all.

As he left a committee meeting at Westminster, an unfamiliar voice called his name. Stopping, Graham turned about and recognized the man who was looking for him. "Lord Satterfield, it's a pleasure to see you," Graham said.

The earl was perhaps sixty or so, but in possession of a youthful countenance, despite his nearly bald pate. His brown eyes met Graham's. "How are things? Lady Satterfield asked me to check in on you." He smiled warmly. "I hope you don't mind."

"Not at all, that's very kind of her. Things are going well, thank you." Inside, Graham laughed riotously at the blatant lie. He seized upon the opportunity to discover something about Tibbord. "I wonder if you might help me with something." He beckoned for Satterfield to join him off to the side in the vestibule.

"I'd be delighted to provide assistance however I may," Satterfield said, his gaze open and eager.

Graham started with another lie. "I'm helping a friend track down a rather scurrilous fellow, a gentleman named Tibbord. Have you heard of him?"

Satterfield's features darkened. "I'm sorry to say that I have, if you mean the Tibbord who's known for making faulty investments. He fleeced a friend of mine last year. Fortunately, it wasn't too bad, but I understand others have not been so lucky."

"Indeed? What have you heard?" Graham's breath lodged in his throat as he waited to hear if Satterfield knew anything that could cast Graham into a poor financial light.

"Just rumors, really. I know for a fact he invested money for my friend—or said he did. Who knows what he really did with the funds. My friend earned a return for a short time. When he invested more, things started to turn. He then heard whispers of this happening to other investors. Then Tibbord vanished."

"When was that?" Graham asked, hoping he didn't sound too impatient.

"Late last fall, perhaps?" Satterfield gave his head a shake. "I'm not entirely sure. I know he preyed on gentlemen who were down on their luck at the tables. You could ask around at a few gaming hells. I believe he spent much of his time in Covent Garden. At least that's where my friend always encountered him."

Graham was thrilled to learn even this much, but wondered if there was more to be gleaned. "Did your friend ever meet Tibbord? It's my understanding he typically worked through an intermediary."

"That's my understanding as well. I will never comprehend why someone would agree to invest under such circumstances, but then I have never found myself in desperate need of a financial windfall."

Just as Graham was now. Would he take what remained of his savings and sink it into such an investment if he thought he could save Brixton Park? He didn't think so, but he had the benefit of knowing what had happened to Tibbord's victims. Absent that information, he might have been desperate enough. It was a sobering and discomfiting thought.

Satterfield peered at him with curiosity. "You're looking for Tibbord on behalf of a friend?"

"Yes." Graham offered a weak smile. "I'm afraid it's difficult for me to completely relinquish my former life as a secretary."

"Ah, that makes sense. You're a good friend." Satterfield nodded approvingly. "Will you visit some hells in Covent Garden?"

It seemed he must. While it appeared he was closer to finding Tibbord, searching for the man in the hells of Covent Garden seemed a daunting task, especially if he hadn't been seen in months.

"I may," Graham said. "I do appreciate your help, Satterfield."

"It's my pleasure. Will you be at the club later? Kendal has a private suite, and we often meet there, if you'd care to join us."

"Thank you. I'm not sure of my evening plans, but will drop by if I can." On his way to Covent Garden, perhaps.

After taking his leave of Lord Satterfield, Graham rode back to Brixton Park, his mind turning over all he'd learned. If Tibbord had preyed on men losing at the tables, where had the former duke been gambling? Though Graham hadn't known his relative, he couldn't imagine the man frequenting gaming hells over White's or Brooks's.

Graham took his horse to the stable with the intent of speaking with the head groom who'd been in the former duke's employ. Dyster was a fairly young man, maybe a year or two short of Graham's twenty-eight. With a bright thatch of blond hair and a crooked smile, he was exceedingly good-natured as well as being stellar at his job. Which was a very good thing since the stable workers consisted of him, Lowell, the coachman, and one much younger lad.

Dyster took the reins of Graham's mount, the one animal he'd never be able to bring himself to sell. Uther had been a gift from his father six years ago, and Graham loved the beast as much as he'd loved his dog who'd died five years ago.

"Good afternoon, Your Grace," Dyster said.

Graham dismounted and patted Uther's neck. "Good afternoon, Dyster. Take good care of him for me."

"Always."

"May I speak with you a moment?" Graham asked.

"Of course." The groom inclined his head toward the boy, who came forward to take the horse. Dyster turned his attention to Graham. "I'm at your service."

"What can you tell me of the former duke's habits with regard to going into town?"

Dyster's brow gathered into neat, furrowed lines. "I'd say he went into town about twice each week, primarily for business in Parliament, though he did visit his club periodically, I think."

He thought? Graham pressed for more information. "Did you drive him?"

"I did not. He preferred Rockley drive him, but Rockley moved on after His Grace passed."

"Rockley was the head groom?" At Dyster's nod, Graham continued. "Do you happen to know if His Grace ever visited Covent Garden? Specifically, did he ever frequent gaming hells?"

Dyster's eyes widened briefly. "I can't imagine His Grace doing anything like that. However, he did like to place bets. He was always wagering at his club. I overheard him talking about it sometimes with Rockley." Dyster grimaced. "I beg your pardon. I shouldn't have listened."

"I'm quite glad you did," Graham said with an encouraging smile. It wasn't much, but he at least knew the duke had liked to gamble. Graham would definitely need to visit some hells in Covent Garden, but maybe not tonight. He wasn't sure he wanted to return to town, particularly when he would be meeting Miss Stoke there early tomorrow.

Graham thanked Dyster, then went to the house, his mind fixating on his morning appointment with Miss

Stoke. Had she learned anything of value from her father? Graham dearly hoped so.

Beyond that, he looked forward to seeing her. She had a keen mind, and he appreciated her drive to help her family. He would do everything he could to aid her in avoiding an unwanted marriage. Indeed, there was no one better to provide assistance in that endeavor than him, someone who was equally motivated to avert a union.

The butler, Hedge, greeted Graham as he arrived at the house. Hedge had been a footman Graham had promoted when the prior butler, like so many other retainers at Brixton Park, had left upon the death of the previous duke. The man was young to be a butler, or so Graham supposed, but he still had five years or so on Graham.

"Good afternoon, Hedge."

"Good afternoon, Your Grace. I trust you had a pleasant day in town."

"I did, thank you. Tell me, did the former duke spend much time in London?"

"Not much, as far as I could tell," Hedge said, seeming to ponder the question. "He did go to Westminster regularly."

"What about entertainment? Did he attend many social occasions? Visit his club?"

"I believe he went out in the evening at least once a week. I'm afraid I can't say for certain, nor can I say where he went."

Graham handed him his gloves and hat. "Quite all right. I was merely curious."

Hedge nodded once in affirmation. "I placed a stack of correspondence on your desk."

"Excellent." Graham went upstairs to the office the former duke had used. Situated next to the sitting room that led into the ducal bedchamber, it completed the three-room apartment where the duke had apparently spent much of his time. Graham had learned that the office had been moved upstairs to make it easier for the duke who suffered from arthritis and detested the stairs.

For now, Graham had no plans to relocate the office to downstairs. He was far too focused on other things. Besides, why should he go to such trouble when he might not even live here in a few months?

Stop that!

The voice of his father echoed in his brain. Graham couldn't think negatively. Things would turn out as they should—they had to.

He went to the desk and sifted through the letters. The first was from the bank. His entire body tensed as he read the missive. They were giving him until the end of the month to pay a substantial sum, or they would force him to leave. Which they had every right to do since they held the deed. That they hadn't yet taken possession of the property was a testament to their faith in the prior duke. Graham was fairly certain they didn't have the same trust in him.

Scrubbing a hand over his face, he set the letter aside and loosened his cravat. Perhaps he *should* go back into town tonight. He couldn't afford to waste any time.

Yes, he'd go back and spend some time in Covent Garden, then he'd spend the night at David's town house. That would allow him to be near the park for his morning appointment with Miss Stoke.

His body thrummed at the prospect of seeing her again. He mentally chided himself. Whatever had sparked between them had to be forgotten like any plans he'd had before he'd inherited this bankrupt dukedom.

Graham plucked up the next letter. It was from Miss Lennox. His pulse picked up speed, but not in the same way it had for Miss Stoke.

Stop that!

That admonition came from him, not his father.

He scanned the note and was pleased to see that Miss Lennox wanted to introduce him to a potential spitfire.

He smiled at her use of the word. He liked it. Except when he thought of it, he thought of Miss Stoke. Of a woman who ignored propriety by walking her mother's dog and fooled the entire ton when it came to matters of her family's financial state.

Stop it. Really.

The spitfire Miss Lennox wanted him to meet was a widow with a young son—an earl—who needed paternal guidance. An earl... Chances were she was wealthy.

He continued reading. Yes, she was "charming, beautiful, and wealthy, if slightly eccentric."

She sounded perfect. But then Miss Lennox had sounded perfect too, and she wasn't. Or she wasn't yet. Graham still wondered if he might be able to change her mind about marriage. He ought to spend more time with her. Yes, that would be another facet of his plan as he hunted down Tibbord.

Miss Lennox concluded the letter by inviting him to meet Lady Clifton on Friday. Of course he would. This would give him the opportunity to pursue two women who would suit his needs.

As Graham sat down to write a response, he pushed away the shame his predatory behavior wrought. He wasn't doing anything unusual, he reasoned. This was how all people participated in the Marriage Mart. It was, at least, how *most* of them did.

How he wished it wasn't necessary. But it was that or give up now and let the bank take Brixton Park. He could feel his father's anguish crushing his bones. Graham refused to give up.

He dashed off a note to Miss Lennox, then composed, more slowly, a response to the bank, saying he would have no problem meeting their deadline. He would do whatever was necessary: frequent gaming hells, romance wealthy, marriageable women, sacrifice his own hopes and desires.

Desire.

That word summoned a vision of Miss Stoke, and Graham had to yell at himself a third time to leave off such futile thoughts. He couldn't pursue her. He couldn't even *think* of pursuing her. And yet, he would see her tomorrow and would continue seeing her until this disaster was reconciled.

He only hoped it ended the way they both wanted—the way they both *needed*.

CHAPTER 7

*A*rabella made her way to the area of the park where she'd met Halstead for the first time. Armed with treats for Biscuit, to lure her back should she bolt away again, Arabella walked quickly and with great anticipation. She couldn't wait to share what she'd learned with him.

Or maybe she was just eager to see him fencing. Both, she decided, and she refused to feel any shame about it.

Any plan she might have had to sneak up and watch him for a moment was destroyed by Biscuit's sudden yapping as soon as she saw him. Halstead, who had been fencing, lowered his sword and grinned widely upon seeing them.

"A most ferocious beast!" he declared, looking down at Biscuit, who was quite pleased to see him.

"Actually, that's her happy bark," Arabella said. "She clearly likes you."

Halstead sheathed his sword and leaned it against a tree, then squatted down to pet Biscuit, who was more than happy for the chin scratches, then promptly plopped on the ground for belly rubs. "How nice that she remembers me, but then dogs have an uncanny ability to remember things, especially people. There was an old man at Huntwell who took care of my dog one day when he was a puppy—he'd run off after being spooked, not long after I got him. After that, Zeus insisted we visit the man regularly and when he died, Zeus was very sad. In fact, when the man took ill, Zeus seemed to know, as he made sure we visited him that very day."

"Zeus sounds like a wonderful dog. I take it he is no longer with you?"

Halstead finished petting Biscuit and rose to his full height. "He's been gone some time now. I got him as a boy. We had many wonderful adventures together—along with David." He glanced away briefly. "St. Ives, I mean."

She thought of that awkward moment when he'd called on her and St. Ives had come up in the conversation. Looking at Halstead now, seeing the sudden discomfort in his expression, she assumed he was thinking of it too.

Perhaps they should confront the topic directly. "You said you were raised with St. Ives?" she asked softly.

"As close as brothers, really." He grimaced. "I'm terribly sorry for any hurt he caused you."

"I was not hurt. I barely know him. Furthermore, I would have hated to marry him if he was in love with someone else. What a horribly tragic situation that would have been." She was fortunate to have avoided it.

"I'm glad to hear it. He felt absolutely awful about the whole thing."

"I will tell my father that, though he will likely never forgive him. He and the previous earl were the best of friends, and my father considers the current earl's failure to marry me a betrayal." She seized the opportunity to shift the conversation. "Speaking of my father, I have news."

He grinned, his eyes glittering with excitement. "I was hoping you'd say that." When he looked at her like that, her belly fluttered and her heart flipped.

Biscuit tugged at the leash, eager to explore. "Let me just tie her leash to a tree," Arabella said.

"Allow me," Halstead offered.

Arabella handed him the leash, her gloved hand brushing his bare one. He guided the dog to a young tree and squatted down to fasten the leash around the trunk. From this angle, it was impossible not to appreciate his backside.

He straightened and turned. "Now, your father?"

"Yes." Arabella shook herself from staring at him, hoping he hadn't noticed. "He was quite helpful. He said he heard of Tibbord in a gaming hell in Covent Garden."

"I learned the same thing from Lord Satterfield," Halstead said. He squinted one eye at her. "I don't suppose he told you which hell?"

"The Thundering Stag."

His face lit with such jubilation that she couldn't help but smile in response. He took a half step forward as if he meant to do something, but then stopped himself. "Wonderful. I visited a few hells in Covent Garden last night—not the Thundering Stag—and didn't learn a thing. No one had heard of Tibbord—or didn't want to admit it."

"It wasn't even Tibbord," she said. "My father confirmed he used an intermediary, a man called Osborne."

"Bloody hell, your father was deuced helpful." He shot her a look of apology. "Didn't mean to say that in front of you. I got carried away by my enthusiasm."

"I understand. I was so anxious to tell you everything, I could hardly wait until this morning." Her gaze found his, and the air around them seemed to still as mutual understanding bloomed between them. There was a connection and then, just as quickly, the realization that it couldn't ever strengthen or lead anywhere.

He coughed and looked away toward Biscuit, who was busily sniffing every inch of ground she could reach. "Did you learn anything else?"

"Yes, he said the investments were smaller at first and

went very well. So well that he was eager to do more and more and had to in order to 'stay in the game.' That's when the investments started to turn bad and when my father began losing heavily."

"That aligns with what Satterfield told me—he knew of gentlemen who lost money. Satterfield also confirmed there was an intermediary." He cocked his head to the side. "I don't suppose your father described Osborne to you?"

She should have asked, but then she'd run out of time when her mother had returned from walking Biscuit. "No, but I'll find out."

"That would be most helpful for my next foray into Covent Garden."

Envy pulsed through her. She wished she could go to Covent Garden gaming hells and help with the investigation. Sometimes being a woman was truly awful. Or an unmarried woman anyway. She wondered if Phoebe or Jane would ignore propriety and go. Her envy shifted to them.

She forced her attention back to the matter at hand. "When do you plan to go?"

"Tonight. I've plans with Lord Ripley and Lord Colton."

"Ripley? I'm surprised you'd go out with him."

"I don't know him very well. In fact, I barely know Colton, but he's a friend of David's." He grimaced and apologized again.

"If you apologize to me every time you mention St. Ives, it will become most tedious. He is clearly one of your dearest friends, and I have no quarrel with that." Besides, it wasn't as if their association would last forever. It likely wouldn't even last the Season.

"You make a good point. I will endeavor to cast that absurdity away." He inclined his head and gave her a charming half smile. "As I was saying, Colton is a friend of David's, and David's wife is a close friend of Colton's sister."

"Lady Ware," Arabella said. She vaguely knew her, and of course she'd met Lady St. Ives briefly last year when both she and Arabella had sought to gain St. Ives's favor during one of Lord Ware's races.

Halstead nodded. "With David leaving town, he wanted to make sure I had someone who would guide me if I needed it."

"And he recommended Colton? He is fast gaining a rakish reputation, especially since he's been cavorting with Ripley."

He laughed. "Cavorting? I have no plans to *cavort* with them. We will visit a few hells, namely the Thundering Stag, and I will hopefully locate this Osborne fellow."

"I wish I could go with you." She hadn't meant to say it aloud, but the words had leapt from her mouth before she could stop them.

His brows rose. "Why on earth would you wish that?"

"It sounds exciting. I don't ever get to do anything exciting." Except this. Dressing as a servant to walk her mother's dog in order to meet the Duke of Halstead in the park during the early morning was the most exciting thing she'd ever done.

He studied her for a moment. "Would learning to fence be exciting?"

A thrill rushed through her. "I think it would." Particularly if he was the tutor.

"Then allow me to teach you to fence." He went and unsheathed his sword, cutting it through the air. "An introductory lesson, if you will."

It was scandalous and wonderful, and she'd never wanted to do anything more. She pushed her shoulders back. "Tell me what to do."

"Take the sword, for starters. It's not too heavy. At least it shouldn't be." He handed her the weapon.

She wrapped her hand around the hilt and hefted it, testing the weight. "No, it isn't heavy."

He flashed her a smile that held just the best twinge of arrogance. "Wait until you wield it a few minutes." Then he winked, and she feared she would melt into a puddle. She focused her attention on the sword. "What will you teach me?"

"Proper stance to begin." He moved around behind her. "Is it all right if I touch you?"

Her breath became trapped in her chest while the beat of her heart picked up speed. "Yes." The word came out higher than she usually spoke, and she prayed he didn't notice.

He lightly touched her shoulder. "Drop your shoulders and relax your muscles. If you're tense, your accuracy will suffer." She did her best to flush the tension from her body, but it was very difficult to be completely at ease when he was so close behind her.

"I see you are right-handed," he said. "Because when I proffered the sword, that's the hand you used to reach for it."

"You are very astute."

He didn't respond to her comment but continued with his direction. "You will lead with your right foot, so point that foot forward." She complied, and he went on. "Put your back foot ninety degrees compared to your front foot."

She adjusted her back foot. "How far apart should they be?"

He stepped to the side so he could see her face, and she turned her head to look at him. "Mine are usually three feet or so, but it depends on your height or the length of your legs, actually. How long are your legs?"

It was both an innocuous question and an incredibly intimate detail to share. Men weren't supposed to see a lady's legs, let alone discuss them. He seemed to realize this, for he quickly said, "Never mind. They are shorter than mine, so perhaps two and a half feet or so. Next, you will bend your knees so you can move quickly."

She positioned her feet as he'd instructed, then bent her knees. "And the sword?"

"Hold that at forty-five degrees to your body." He clasped her wrist and positioned her arm at the appropriate angle. "Like this."

His body came close to hers as he showed her what to do. The scent of sandalwood and spice enveloped her. She wanted to close her eyes and inhale deeply, to immerse herself in his touch and scent.

She didn't, however. She stared at the sword and tried to ignore the way her body reacted to his proximity and attention.

"Now, as you move forward, you'll lead with your front foot with the back foot following." He spoke softly near her ear, and now she had to contend with the sound of him as well as the rest.

"When do I move?"

"When you lunge."

"Isn't that an attack?" She knew barely anything about fencing, but that much she was aware of.

"Yes. Fencing is a series of attacks and defenses and counterattacks."

"Do you fence at Angelo's?" she asked.

"I do."

She wished she could watch him there, but didn't say so. It was enough to tell him she didn't ever get to do anything exciting and quite another to tell him that watching him excited her. *Oh dear,* this was becoming a problem. She'd been drawn to another man in this way, and things had not turned out well. He'd left the country, and she'd been heartbroken. She couldn't follow that path again.

As Halstead had predicted, she could see that holding

the sword aloft for an extended period of time would require practice, for it already felt heavier than when she'd first taken it from him. Lowering her arm, she stepped away. "That was an excellent introductory lesson," she said, holding the sword toward him.

He shook his head. "If that's your attempt at a lunge, it's terrible."

"It isn't. I thought we were done." She wanted to be done. No, she *needed* to be done. Spending time with him like this was not in her best interest.

"I wasn't done, but perhaps you are. I thought to show you how to lunge." He sounded a bit disappointed, and she hated that. Probably because she was disappointed too. Or sad. Or frustrated. Or angry at her circumstances. She decided she was all those things.

Turning away and taking a few steps, she adopted the stance he'd showed her, holding the sword at the appropriate angle. She spoke as she moved forward, extending her arm, which he hadn't said to do, but which seemed like the natural course of action. "Like this?"

She directed her lunge toward him, with plenty of feet to spare, and his eyes widened briefly before lighting with approval.

"Yes, just like that. And I didn't even show you how to thrust the sword."

Oh, she wanted him to show her that, all right, but not with that sword. Good Lord, she was a wanton and her mind was not where it should be *at all*.

She handed him the sword. "That's enough for today."

He took the weapon, pointing it down. "Does that mean I will get to give you another lesson someday?"

"Who can say? It depends on our future interactions." Which they had to keep to Tibbord. They had no other reason to associate, and she would do well to remember that. "Where shall I send the description of Osborne?" she asked.

He picked up his scabbard and sheathed the sword. "Brixton Park." He shook his head. "That's too much trouble if you're sending one of your retainers. Have them take it to Colton."

"What's his address?"

"He has rooms at the Albany."

"I'll send it there, then. I'll be dying to hear how it goes." She wanted to suggest they meet again tomorrow, even as she knew that the more time she spent with him, the more she was in danger of repeating what had happened with Miles. Or not. She had no inkling if Halstead was as attracted to her as she was to him. And it was for the best if she never learned.

He thought for a moment, his head tipping briefly to the side. "I will be visiting Miss Lennox on Friday. Perhaps we can arrange to meet then? Either at her house or 'by chance' on the street." He gave her a sly, warm smile.

She felt an absurd urge to cry for she was horribly jealous that he was visiting Phoebe. Instead, she gave him a close-lipped smile in return. "I will be sure to stop by."

"Excellent. This has been a most favorable meeting. Here, hold this." He handed her the sword, then went to untie Biscuit's leash from the trunk of the tree.

Arabella averted her gaze from his backside as the warmth of the sword handle—from his bare hand—seeped through her glove. He stood with Biscuit in tow, and they exchanged items, the sword for the leash.

"I'll see you Friday, then," she said.

He inclined his head toward her at a jaunty angle. "I look forward to it."

Why did he have to say *that*? She nodded, then spun around and walked away before she said something foolish such as *"Not as much as I do!"*

Only she *did* look forward to it. Far, far too much.

∼

*B*efore leaving town after his appointment with Miss Stoke, Graham had stopped by the Albany to let Colton know that a message would be delivered later that day. However, Colton hadn't been receiving. His manservant had said he was indisposed, which Graham ought to have expected given the earliness of the hour. Even so, he was reminded of Miss Stoke's comment about the viscount's reputation.

It was said he was grieving his parents' death, which Lady Ware had also told him. That made sense to Graham. He still suffered moments of sharp sadness regarding the loss of his father. Perhaps he could lend support from someone who'd also recently lost a parent.

Graham was anxious to meet with Colton and Ripley. They'd planned to rendezvous at the Thundering Stag—at Graham's suggestion. He'd sent notes to them after meeting with Miss Stoke. He arrived a few minutes early and stationed himself at a table not far from the door so Colton and Ripley would see him easily.

"What can I bring ye to drink?" a serving maid asked. Petite, with dark brown hair and wide, deep-set brandy-colored eyes, she was attractive. And if the way her gaze lingered on him and dipped to his lap meant anything, she found him attractive too.

Not that anything would come of it.

Why not? She was precisely the type of woman he would have tumbled back in Huntingdonshire. Furthermore, he'd felt unsettled all day. Since seeing Miss Stoke.

Provided unsettled meant aroused. Which in this case, it most certainly did.

Seeing her had been lovely enough but then he'd had to go and touch her, to teach her to fence, to try to appease her desire for excitement. How he longed to appease her in other, far more *exciting* ways.

The serving maid pulled him back to the present.

"Sir? Do ye want a drink or not? Or something else?" She winked suggestively and cocked her hip out.

"An ale, thank you. Bring three. I'm expecting friends." Before he could dissuade her expectations for later, Ripley and Colton arrived at his table.

"Evening, Halstead," Ripley said, taking a seat. His gaze roved appreciatively over the maid. "I wondered why you chose this establishment, but I can see why. Excellent selection." He gave her a provocative smile.

The maid licked her lower lip as she returned his stare. "Happy to entertain all three of ye, if ye want."

Ripley took her hand and brought it to his lips for a brief brush of a kiss upon the back. "That's not my preference, love. However, if *you* have two friends, do let me know."

She let out a throaty chuckle. "I'll see what I can do. I'll be right back with yer ales." She lifted her shoulder and gave Graham a look of apology before she took herself off.

"Blast, did I steal your fun?" Ripley asked. "That was never my intent. I'll leave her to you."

"No, that's fine—do as you like. We did not make any arrangements."

Ripley settled back in his chair. "Excellent."

"Here's your letter," Colton said, pulling the missive from Miss Stoke from his coat and handing it to Graham.

Ripley's dark brows rose as he looked at Colton. "Since when did you become his butler?"

"Since he arranged to receive this at my apartment. Came at an ungodly hour to say so too. I'd barely arrived home."

"It was a rather late night," Ripley said with a satisfied chuckle.

Graham listened to their conversation as he opened the letter, then promptly tuned them out.

Dear Duke of Halstead,

I was able to gather Osborne's description. He is in his middle thirties, exceptionally tall with a sharp chin and nose. His hair is dark with gray at the temples. He dresses somberly, always gray and black, and he carries a walking stick with a raven on the top.

I hope this helps you and look forward to your report.
Yours,
Miss Stoke

Yours. How he wished that were true. *Hell,* he was more than aroused. Perhaps he should lay claim to the serving maid after all.

"Who's it from?" Ripley asked.

"No one." Graham folded the parchment and placed the letter into his coat, where it warmed him through his waistcoat and shirt. What a ridiculous thought.

"I doubt that," Ripley said, his brows lifting once more. "You arranged to have it sent to Colton instead of Brixton Park. Why would you do that?"

Graham bristled. "Because I needed the information tonight, and I didn't want to waste time having it delivered all the way to Brixton. Does that satisfy your curiosity?"

"No. I asked who it's from, and 'no one' is not an accurate answer." Ripley's answering stare was even, and Graham had the sense he was not easily intimidated.

Well, neither was Graham. He leaned forward slightly and stared at Ripley across the table. "Then let me be more accurate. None of your business."

Colton, who sat to Graham's left, interjected. "Now, ladies, can we put our claws away?"

Ripley relaxed and laughed. "I was just trying to get a rise out of Halstead, which I did." He winked at Graham. "My apologies. As most people will tell you, I'm a right ass."

Graham flicked a glance toward Colton, who nodded. "It's true. But he's entertaining as all hell. I'm glad you arranged for us to meet tonight. You need a proper introduction to London. It occurred to me that your friend St. Ives and his friends are all married and boring. It's good they left town so you won't be dragged down by their domestication."

The maid brought their ales, depositing them on the table with a lingering stare at Ripley, her dark eyes full of promise and her body swaying with anticipation. Ripley picked up his tankard and held it toward her, his eyes twinkling. Graham feared the maid might swoon.

After she left, Graham gripped his mug and regarded Ripley with an arched brow. "I don't think the ladies care if you're an ass."

Colton snorted. "They definitely do *not*. He could throw them from a moving carriage, and they would show right back up at his doorstep. It's disgusting."

Ripley blinked in mock affront. "You exaggerate. And not prettily. I would never cast a woman from my carriage, moving or otherwise."

"Of course you wouldn't," Colton said with a laugh. "My mistake."

Ripley sipped his ale. "You're starting to give me competition—both as an ass and a lothario."

Colton shrugged. "You're the model of a hero, apparently." He took a deep pull from his tankard, then set it down with a clack. He turned his head toward Graham. "Now, why are we here at the Thundering Stag?"

Graham had crafted a story to tell them that would hopefully satisfy their curiosity without exposing his financial woes. However, he was marginally concerned about Ripley given how he'd gone after the letter and who'd written it.

"I'm looking for a gentleman called Osborne. He made an investment on behalf of the former duke and there has been no return. I mean to find him and demand the reimbursement of the investment or the interest I am owed."

Colton paused in lifting his tankard to his mouth. "You mean to find him in a hell? Seems an odd place to find a man who makes investments."

"This is where he operates," Graham said. "He preys on men who are losing at the tables."

"Then Rip has never heard of him." Colton grinned before taking a drink.

Graham rotated his attention to the marquess. "I take it you don't lose?"

Ripley lifted a shoulder. "Not usually."

"Ha, not ever. Now he's being coy." Colton rolled his eyes.

"I've recently decided not to play anymore," Ripley said, sounding disappointed.

"Because some men won't participate if he does," Colton explained.

Ripley ignored the comment and narrowed his eyes at Graham. "Does this have something to do with Tibbord?"

Graham nodded. "Yes. Osborne is Tibbord's intermediary."

"When you asked us about Tibbord before," Colton said, "I told you he was a swindler, and you acted as though you didn't know that. You said something to the effect of Tibbord just being a name you'd heard."

There was no mistaking the curiosity in Colton's tone, as well as a slice of skepticism. "Forgive me," Graham said. "I was trying to gather information, and I didn't want to disclose my suspicions at the time. I suspect Tibbord has either been making bad investments or, and this is what I truly believe, he isn't making investments at all."

"Your reticence is understandable since you barely knew us." Ripley stood abruptly. "Give me a moment."

He took a swig of ale, then wove his way to the back of the establishment.

Graham watched as the marquess spoke with the serving maid, then they disappeared through a doorway. Swinging his head toward Colton, he asked, "Did Ripley just leave to go shag that maid?"

Colton laughed. "Probably. He's done it before. Once or twice."

"Good God, how does he not have every disease?"

"French letters," Colton answered promptly. "He swears by them. Can't say I've ever bothered, but I should probably start if I mean to keep up with him."

"Is that your intent?" Graham sipped his ale.

"Not really." Colton's eyes gleamed. "My intent is to enjoy myself and live for every moment of pleasure I can find." He said this with such fervor that Graham couldn't help but feel his passion.

"Life feels very different after losing someone," Graham said softly. "Don't you think?"

"Of course it does." Colton's response was cold, and Graham feared he'd overstepped.

"I didn't mean to cause you any pain. I lost my father last year. We were very close. It's been difficult. I only meant to offer my support—and condolences."

"I do appreciate that, but I don't need either." He finished his ale and waved toward another serving maid for her to bring another.

A moment later, she brought two fresh mugs to the table and swept the others away, even though Graham hadn't quite finished his. "Why didn't she stop to flirt?" Graham asked, seeking to lighten the mood after he'd unintentionally darkened it.

"Because Ripley's not here?" Colton laughed. "She's likely just busy since one of her coworkers is otherwise engaged."

Graham sipped his ale and wondered if he could possibly keep up with Colton and Ripley. Their lives were not his, nor did he think he wanted them to be. What *did* he want his life to be?

That was a question he hadn't pondered. There hadn't been time. From the moment he'd become the duke, he'd been overwhelmed with learning his new role. Whatever life he might have wanted or expected was gone.

He'd never dreamed of more than he'd had. In fact, he'd been quite content to be a secretary and manage Huntwell. However, now that he had the chance to manage a magnificent estate like Brixton Park and an ancestral pile in need of a complete refurbishment, he was energized. Yes, that was the life he wanted—a duke who worked to better what he had for future generations.

Really? He'd never thought of future generations except for St. Ives. He managed Huntwell for David and his children and his children's children. But now he could do that for himself.

The thought gave him a thrill of anticipation. Tempered by grave concern. How could he do that if he was bankrupt?

Scowling, he took a long pull from his mug.

"You look rather upset all of a sudden," Colton remarked. "What's the matter?"

Thankfully, Graham didn't have to answer, for Ripley returned.

"That was quick," Colton said drily.

Ripley's answer was fast and smooth. "Speed is no measure of gratification. However, I was not pleasuring the fair maid. I asked her about Tibbord and Osborne, and she took me back to speak with the owner of the hell."

Graham kept his excitement in check. Barely. "What did you learn?" He hoped he sounded calm and collected instead of desperate.

"They may or may not be what you suspect—he wouldn't confirm it. He did say they'd left London for a time, but appear to have returned recently," Ripley said. "It seems it's your lucky night."

"How's that?" Graham looked around, wondering if they were here.

"They aren't here, if that's what you were hoping— sorry to disappoint you. But I can arrange for you to meet them, I think. Apparently, they were seen at a Cyprian ball the other night.

"They—both Osborne *and* Tibbord?" Graham asked. "Tibbord isn't typically seen."

"I didn't clarify," Ripley said. "I do think he said 'they,' but I could be wrong. In any case, I would be happy to host a Cyprian soirée at my house and will do my best to make sure they attend. We'll have gambling to sweeten the pot, since Tibbord preys on those who are failing at the tables."

Graham couldn't quite mask his surprise. "You would do that?"

"As your friend, I want to help you get what's owed to you." His eyes darkened, and the aura of danger overtook that of a careless rake. "The scoundrels can't get away with stealing."

"Thank you." Graham was quite glad to have the marquess on his side. He didn't think he'd want the man as an adversary. "I appreciate your friendship." Too late, Graham considered the ramifications of his attending a Cyprian party at the Marquess of Ripley's house. He could ruin, or at least taint, his reputation, and that might very well be all he had. He certainly needed it intact to find an heiress.

Graham took another drink of ale before speaking. "While I am delighted by your generous offer, I don't think it would be wise for me to attend." He grimaced. "My apologies."

Ripley waved his hand. "No need to apologize. I completely understand. Masks will be optional, and people need not disclose their identity. That way, you can come. Furthermore, you can either come before the party or enter through the back so no one sees you arrive."

That could work. And right now, it was his best option. "The owner of the hell couldn't give you any information about Tibbord or Osborne? Not where they live or where they might be found?"

Ripley shook his head. "I'm afraid not. I did ask."

"A Cyprian ball sounds like a terribly fun evening. I hope it's soon," Colton said before finishing off his second tankard.

Ripley looked toward Graham. "Is Saturday too soon?"

Anticipation thrummed through Graham as he fought to keep his voice even. "Saturday is perfect—if you think you can organize it so quickly."

"I wouldn't have offered if I couldn't. I'm usually ready to entertain at a moment's notice." His mouth stretched in a catlike smile. "Come early."

Graham nodded. "I will." He could hardly wait to tell Miss Stoke.

Wait. Should he tell Miss Stoke? A Cyprian party was hardly the sort of thing one should discuss with a young lady. And yet, he had to keep her apprised. He'd leave out the Cyprian part.

"What will you do when you run Tibbord to ground?" Colton asked.

Graham had thought about it, but so far had nothing beyond simply threatening the man. "Insist he return the duke's investment."

"It's entirely possible, likely even, that insistence will get you nowhere." Ripley's tone was wry. "Extortion would work better. If you could find something to use against him."

Bloody hell, Ripley definitely possessed a dangerous edge. He also was not wrong. "Hard to find something to use against him when I can't even find the man."

Colton shrugged. "Something to consider."

It was indeed. Feeling both energized and thoughtful, Graham nearly polished off his ale before setting his tankard down on the scarred table. "Shall we go to Brooks's?"

Ripley blinked in surprise. "Before I've tumbled the lovely maid? I think not. Give me a few moments this time." He rose and went to find the serving maid.

"Let us gamble, then," Colton said, standing quickly. He wobbled a tad and braced his fingers on the table to steady himself. "We are in a gaming hell after all."

Graham had never felt more boring. He had no interest in shagging a maid nor was he going to play any games of chance. Since he didn't wish to leave Colton alone, he rose along with him. "Yes, let's." Graham would simply go along and hope that Colton was perhaps inebriated enough to notice he didn't play.

He'd had all the curiosity he could handle for one night. Even so, it had turned out well. He hadn't found Osborne or Tibbord, but he felt certain they were within sight.

CHAPTER 8

*F*riday afternoon, Graham sauntered into Miss Lennox's garden room wearing an expectant smile. Present were three ladies—Miss Lennox, Miss Pemberton, and presumably Lady Clifton.

Three ladies, not four. He was disappointed Miss Stoke wasn't there.

All were seated, but Graham could tell Lady Clifton was taller than average—at least she appeared so compared to the other two. Her pale blonde hair was pulled into a neat style atop her head with small curls gracing her temples.

He bowed, extending his leg. "Good afternoon, ladies."

"Good afternoon, Your Grace," Miss Lennox said. "Allow me to present Lady Clifton. Lady Clifton, His Grace, the Duke of Halstead."

Lady Clifton rose and offered a curtsey. "I'm pleased to make your acquaintance, Duke."

"The pleasure is mine." And it should have been, for she was as lovely to behold as her bank account was necessary to his future. However, he was having a hard time focusing on what he needed to do today. Which was to woo her. Or Miss Lennox. *Hell,* he couldn't woo two women at once. He bet Ripley could. Perhaps he should ask the man for lessons.

No, that wasn't Graham. He felt strange enough wooing a woman for financial purposes instead of something… Something what? Nobler?

Lady Clifton sat, and Graham did the same, taking a chair near the settee where she resided next to Miss Pemberton. "You are new to the peerage, I understand," she said.

"Yes. It's been rather a whirlwind." Graham was also disappointed to see there were no butter biscuits. No biscuits and no Miss Stoke. How…deficient. "I'm delighted to have friends such as Miss Lennox to help me acclimate." He gave his hostess a warm smile.

"I think I've decided that helping people is my calling," Miss Lennox said. "Though we must credit Jane for bringing you two together. I think that may be her calling." She and Miss Pemberton exchanged a quick look before Miss Lennox shifted her gaze to Graham and Lady Clifton. "Perhaps you two should take a walk in the garden."

It wasn't very subtle. But then why bother with pretense if the intention was to see if they might suit?

"That sounds lovely," he said, thinking his voice sounded foreign. "Lady Clifton?"

"I would be honored."

As she rose, he leapt to his feet, then offered his arm. Her touch did none of the things to him that Miss Stoke's did, and *bloody hell*, he had to stop thinking of her.

Graham guided Lady Clifton outside to the garden, his gaze immediately straying to the gate that connected with the Stokes' garden. Would Miss Stoke come through it at any moment? He hoped so, and yet… It would be awkward for her to see him with Lady Clifton.

Why? They weren't courting. They had no relationship whatsoever. At least not one that ought to engender jealousy. Still, when he put himself in her position, he decided he didn't like thinking of her walking in a garden with some other gentleman. Or dancing with him. Or fencing with him.

He chuckled—as if she would fence with anyone but him.

"What amuses you?" Lady Clifton asked.

Bugger, he'd quite forgotten she was beside him. He was a cad. "I was just thinking...of a joke I heard last night. Something about birds, but I can't recall the specifics. How gauche of me." He needed to focus on Lady Clifton. Not just for his goal, but because she deserved his full attention. "I understand you have a son?"

"Yes, he's eleven." She launched into a warm description of the young Lord Clifton—his love for astronomy and treacle pudding.

At one point during their conversation as they circled the garden, something hit Graham in the shoulder. "Is there something on my coat?" he asked, fearing a bird had just relieved itself on him. He took his arm from Lady Clifton and turned so she could see his shoulder. Belatedly, he realized he probably shouldn't ask a countess to check him for bird excrement.

"I don't see anything," she said. "What happened?"

"Nothing, apparently." He offered his arm once more and they continued. A moment later, it happened again, but this time lower on his back. Whatever it was wasn't coming from above.

Narrowing his eyes, he looked surreptitiously behind him. There, peeking just above the gate, was Miss Stoke. He inclined his head ever so slightly to signify that he saw her. Hopefully, she would stop pelting him with pebbles or whatever she was using.

He continued his conversation with Lady Clifton as he steered her back toward the garden room. They went back inside, and Lady Clifton said she needed to be going.

"I trust you had a nice promenade," Miss Lennox said, her eyes alight with interest as she looked between the countess and Graham.

"We did, thank you," Lady Clifton said. "I do hope we'll have the chance to do so again." She curtsied to Graham once more, and he bowed in return.

"It would be my privilege, Lady Clifton." Impatience tore through him as he fought to keep from going back outside to Miss Stoke.

The countess took her leave, and Graham looked toward the garden, wondering how he could excuse himself to go back outside. But there was Miss Stoke coming toward the door.

"Oh, look, it's Arabella," Miss Pemberton said.

"How lovely." Miss Lennox turned her head to Graham. "How was your walk with Lady Clifton? You seemed to be getting on quite well."

Miss Pemberton laughed softly. "We're not ashamed to say we were watching."

Miss Lennox stood and went to the door to let Miss Stoke in. "Come in, Arabella. Look who's here."

Miss Stoke was a picture of fresh loveliness, her light brown hair gathered into a chignon at the back of her head while wavy strands framed her heart-shaped face. Her gaze landed on him and didn't move for probably a moment too long. He was entranced.

"Good afternoon, Your Grace." Miss Stoke curtsied, and Graham almost forgot to bow.

He presented his leg. "Good afternoon, Miss Stoke. What a delight to encounter you here."

"You just missed meeting Lady Clifton," Miss Lennox said to Miss Stoke. "She is an old friend of Jane's, though she's slightly older than you, isn't she?"

Miss Pemberton nodded. "Oh yes, by several years. We were neighbors, and our families often visited when I was a child. We became correspondents, and I do consider her a dear friend. She is widowed and looking for a father for her son, someone who can guide him into the earldom he's inherited at such a young age." She glanced toward Graham with a smile. "I understand His Grace is new to the peerage, but his experience as St. Ives's secretary allowed him to directly support an earl. Surely that will be of excellent help to the young Lord Clifton."

"I agree," Miss Lennox said. "Jane thought—and rightly so—that Lady Clifton and His Grace might suit. They took a walk in the garden, and he was just telling us how it went." Miss Lennox looked toward him expectantly. "Will the banns be read on Sunday?"

A great wave of discomfort washed over Graham. He didn't want to discuss this in front of Miss Stoke. He didn't want to discuss it at all. "That's a bit premature," he said softly.

"But you got on well, didn't you?" Miss Pemberton prodded.

"We did." He stole a glance at Miss Stoke, whose expression was completely impassive. It seemed she didn't give a whit that he might be courting Lady Clifton.

And why on earth should she? They'd made no expectations of each other. On the contrary, they both knew the other had to wed someone with money or suffer the consequences. For him, that was losing Brixton Park, but for her, it was far more serious. He felt like a cad *again*. Of course she wasn't trifling with feelings of jealousy.

Miss Pemberton smiled widely. "Marvelous. I was certain you'd suit. We'll make sure you both attend the next ball so you may ask her to dance."

Graham was fast losing interest in this conversation, if he'd ever had any to begin with. He wanted to speak with Miss Stoke, but couldn't imagine how they would accomplish that.

"It's actually quite fortuitous that His Grace is here," Miss Stoke said, pivoting toward him. "I've a need for someone to reach something. The butler is out, and no one else is tall enough." She smiled and shook her head, then gave Graham a look tinged with urgency.

Was there a problem? He hoped her father was all right.

"Allow me to help," he said. "Lead the way."

"Oh, thank you." She glanced toward Miss Lennox and Miss Pemberton. "We'll just be a moment." Then she turned and led him from the house before the other ladies uttered a word.

Graham inclined his head before following Miss Stoke into the garden. They didn't speak until they reached the gate, which he hurried to open for her. "Is something amiss?" he asked.

"No. It was an excuse to give us a few minutes so you can tell me what happened at the gaming hell." She moved into her garden.

Graham closed the gate, then shot a glance at her house. "Can anyone see us out here?"

"Of course they can—if they look. They won't, however. My mother is busy with my father, and everyone else is so overworked, they hardly have a moment to stop moving, let alone gaze out at the garden." She sounded cool and maybe even irritated. But then he would be too if his father was very ill and there was barely enough money to run a household.

Now he darted a look at Miss Lennox's house and wondered if she and Miss Pemberton could see them. Perhaps the top of his head. He squatted down.

Miss Stoke narrowed her eyes at him. "What are you doing?"

"Ensuring Miss Lennox and Miss Pemberton can't see me."

"Oh." Miss Stoke stared at him a moment, then laughed. "I'm sorry. You look rather ridiculous hunched down."

"Yes, well, I feel rather ridiculous too. Furthermore, I'm not sure how long I can squat like this, so let us be quick. I was not able to find Osborne or Tibbord, but I did learn that they left London several months ago." She frowned, and he nearly took her hand. "Don't despair, for they have returned, and I've a plan to coax them into the open."

Miss Stoke's green eyes lightened. "What is it?"

"Actually, it's Ripley's plan. He's the one who learned they were back in town. He's going to host a party Saturday evening and invite them. I will also be in attendance."

"The Marquess of Ripley is helping you?"

"He has, er, certain skills," Graham said slowly. "So far, he's been quite resourceful."

Her lips flattened into a line. "What sort of party is this? Can you make sure my mother and I receive an invitation?"

She couldn't mean to go to Ripley's house? Regardless of the type of party—and he had no intention of telling her—her reputation wouldn't support it. She *could* wear a mask as he planned to do, but no, she couldn't. She just couldn't.

"You can't attend a party hosted by the Marquess of Ripley, even if you were invited. And no, I won't ask him to do so." She started to frown, so he seized on another tactic. "Your mother would never allow it."

She exhaled. "That is, unfortunately, true." She cocked her head to the side. "What of your reputation?"

Graham shifted his weight. As he predicted, squatting in this position was not terribly comfortable. His legs were beginning to ache. "Masks are optional, and I intend to wear a mask. With luck, no one will know who I am. My only goal is to finally talk to Tibbord—or at least Osborne—face-to-face. Er, mask to mask potentially."

"How will you even know he's there if everyone is masked?"

"Ripley has a plan—his retainers will know who I am and will ensure the meeting occurs." At her skeptical stare, he added, "I trust him. He's been incredibly helpful so far."

"And what if they don't show up?"

He'd thought about that. "Then we'll try something else."

"Does that 'we'll' refer to me or Ripley?" Yes, she sounded annoyed, not that he blamed her.

"You."

Now she looked surprised. "I haven't done a thing."

"That's not true. The information you gathered from your father was most helpful. I never would have known to go to the Thundering Stag."

She seemed to relax slightly, but there was still an edge to her today. A grooved line scored the flesh above her nose, and her body seemed tense and tight.

He surrendered to his desire to touch her and clasped her hand. "We're getting closer, I know it."

She looked down at where they touched, then lifted her gaze to his. The connection between them was still there, and it seemed to him in that moment that they were both fighting a losing battle.

"You know, you could sell your name to the highest bidder," she said softly. "You may not have money, but you have an excellent title, and there are heiresses who would pay for the privilege to become your duchess."

Why the hell hadn't he thought of that? Because it turned his stomach. He was essentially doing that in looking for an heiress to wed, but at least he wasn't outright advertising his desperation. "I couldn't."

Her lips lifted in a slight smile. "I didn't think so. However, I thought it bore mentioning."

Because it would help him. He squeezed her hand. "We're going to make this work, I promise you. We are both going to make it through this without suffering total disaster. Please trust me."

"I do."

He could have stared into her eyes and held her hand

for another hour or a day if not for the ache in his calves. "Good God, my legs hurt. I must go."

"Stand and we'll go through the gate." She reached for the latch, and he reluctantly released her other hand.

"Would you like to meet for another fencing lesson in the park so that I can tell you what happened at the party?" He held the gate open for her.

She peered up at him with a saucy glint in her eye. "They're 'fencing lessons' now?"

He laughed. "Why not? You demonstrated an aptitude. It would be a shame not to continue."

She preceded him into Miss Lennox's garden. "Then yes. Sunday morning, or will you need to recover from Ripley's party?"

There was a note of envy in her voice, and he hated that she wasn't able to participate in any of the investigation. "I'm happy to meet you Sunday morning." Even if he was exhausted. He could stay at David's house again. It was the least he could do for her.

In truth, he wanted to do much, much more.

~

*E*nduring the Marriage Mart was growing harder and harder. Arabella had danced with Sir Ethelbert again last night and also with Mr. Alexander Litcott. While he didn't have a title, he was rather wealthy due to his family's success in textiles. He was also just a year older than Arabella and not particularly adept at conversation. He'd spent a good portion of their dance staring at her breasts.

Duty called once more tonight, but Arabella wished she could go to the Marquess of Ripley's party instead. If she wore a mask, she could...

"What?" Papa jolted awake, startling Arabella in the process. She dropped her needle, not that she'd been actively sewing the past few minutes while her mind had wandered.

She looked to the bed where Papa lay blinking his eyes, his head elevated on a stack of pillows. He'd fallen asleep while she'd read to him a short while ago. While he seemed better overall since she'd talked to him about Tibbord, he still lay down in the afternoon and napped. "Do you need anything?" she asked.

"Some water, please."

Arabella set her sewing onto the basket beside her chair and went to a dresser in the corner, atop of which sat a pitcher. She poured water into a glass, then returned to the bed, where Papa was struggling to sit up.

After setting the glass on the bedside table, she helped him to a better position, then handed him the water. "Better?" she asked with a smile.

He finished drinking and handed her the glass, his brow furrowed. "I had a rather troubling dream. It was about Tibbord. Did you warn the investigator about what he might do?"

Arabella had no idea what her father was talking about. "No. Why would I warn him?"

The lines in his forehead deepened, and he sat up further, his back coming off the pillows. "I told you—he will seek revenge in some way. If any of us who invested with him complained about losing money or wanted to walk away or worse, if we said we'd tell others that Tibbord was fleecing us, Osborne threatened to share the truth of our financial states."

"He extorted you to keep investing money or at least to keep quiet about his fiendishness?" Arabella's blood chilled. "You didn't tell me anything about that."

"Of course I did. The other day, when you came to tell me about the investigation. I told you if Tibbord knew about it, whoever hired the investigator would find themselves exposed." He hadn't either, but she wasn't going to continue to argue with him, not when he was like this.

"Perhaps they don't care." Arabella could think of who *would* care—Halstead. If he cornered Tibbord or Osborne tonight, he might find his insolvency revealed to the entire ton. While he could probably recover in ways she couldn't, he didn't want anyone to know.

She had to warn him.

It seemed there might be a mask in her future after all. First, she'd have to claim a headache and beg off attending the soirée with her mother. Hopefully, she'd be able to convince Mama to go without her. Slipping out would be far easier if Mama wasn't home. Although, she would likely spend the evening with Papa, so perhaps it wouldn't matter…

"They *should* care," Papa said, bringing her back to the conversation. "They won't like being the butt of a jest, nor will they appreciate the condescension they will likely encounter."

Arabella knew he was speaking for himself as much as anyone else. He was so utterly humiliated by what he'd done. It was, she'd thought, the crux of his illness. However, his lapses in memory were troubling. He clearly thought he'd told her about this the other day, when he absolutely had not.

"That is likely true," Arabella said. She wanted to appease her father's concern. "I will make sure the investigator knows to keep our name out of things."

"Thank you, dear." He settled back against the pillows. "Are you going to keep reading to me?"

She had read to him before he'd fallen asleep, then she'd picked up her sewing while he napped, knowing he might wake and expect her to continue the book. "Of course." Agitation raked at her—she was eager to plan for the evening. She needed a disguise.

〜

*S*o far, everything had come off perfectly. Mama had seemed relieved when Arabella had claimed a headache, and consequently Arabella's efforts to encourage her to attend the soirée without her had failed. No matter, for Mama had taken dinner in Papa's chamber and remained there ever since.

Next had come the costume. Arabella had spent the remainder of the afternoon and the evening repurposing an old gown. She hadn't worn it in a couple of years, so hopefully no one remembered that it had once graced the form of Miss Arabella Stoke. She needed to be completely inconspicuous.

The mask had been easy enough to create—black fabric that covered her face from her hairline to her lip. She reached back to touch the knot at the back of her head, checking to make sure it was still secure.

Getting there was the easiest part, for the marquess lived in Hanover Square, a very short walk just over Oxford Street. She'd considered asking the groom to accompany her, but had decided against it. Asking him to lie to her mother was out of the question. And unfortunately, that would have been necessary.

As she walked toward the notorious Marquess of Ripley's house, she realized it was dangerous and scandalous and probably many other words that ended in "ous." Yet she couldn't quash the excitement thrumming through her veins.

She prayed the marquess's house would be easily discernible because of the party. Entering the square, she looked about. To her left was a larger house with coaches queued in front. That had to be it.

Summoning all the courage she possessed, she strode toward the house. Light and laughter spilled from the front door as it opened to admit a gentleman in front of her. She quickened her pace and followed him inside.

If the foyer was any indication, the marquess's house

was quite grand. The marble floor gleamed beneath the dozens of candles flickering overhead. Art adorned the walls, and an immaculately turned-out footman stood sentinel at the door. He greeted her without looking directly at her.

The primary noise of the party seemed to be coming from upstairs. Arabella picked her way through the foyer, where a handful of people milled about, and went up the staircase. The sound of conversation grew louder as she ascended, and when she arrived on the first floor, she knew to turn to the right to reach the heart of things—and hopefully Halstead.

She only hoped she could find him.

Though he was wearing a mask, she thought she could identify him. She was very aware of how tall he was, the width of his shoulders, the slope of his jaw. Yes, she'd spent far too much time staring at him, thinking about him, dreaming of him.

A blush crept up her neck. She had, in fact, dreamt of him last night. An aching, torturous dream that had left her feeling completely unfulfilled despite her attempts to find satisfaction. Sometimes she wished she'd never lain with Miles. Knowing what you were missing by remaining unwed was far worse than not being aware of anything at all.

As she reached the threshold of the drawing room, she nearly walked straight into another liveried gentleman.

"I beg your pardon," the footman said. "Is there anything you require?"

She suddenly recalled what Halstead had told her—that Ripley's retainers would know who he was. "I wonder if you could direct me to the Duke of Halstead. He's expecting me." It was a bald lie, but the mask made her daring.

The footman seemed surprised, his eyes slightly widening, but he inclined his head. "This way."

That was so easy! Triumph surged in her veins as the footman led her up the stairs to the second floor. She could deliver the warning about Tibbord and be on her way without having set foot into the actual party.

"Just in here," the footman said, opening a door.

She stepped inside. To a bedchamber. What an odd place for a meeting, but perhaps it was the only place available if the party had spilled over into the other areas of the house.

"Wait here." The footman closed the door, leaving her alone in the dimly lit room.

The realization that she would soon meet with Halstead alone in a bedchamber sent a slick pulse of desire straight to her core. Wanton didn't begin to describe her. She wanted what she couldn't have. And in a few minutes, the temptation to claim it would nearly overwhelm her.

She couldn't let it. He'd be horrified anyway. She suspected he was attracted to her too, but he wouldn't act on it. He was a gentleman *and* a duke.

More's the pity.

CHAPTER 9

*R*ipley's party was a smashing success. If one was seeking to wager great sums or indulge in lurid fantasies. Graham had started in the drawing room and watched as men and women paired off and left. He quickly moved to the saloon, which had been set with a variety of gaming tables. This was where he would find Osborne or Tibbord.

However, he'd been here over two hours, and there was still no sign of them. Impatience was fast giving way to frustration.

A wide-lipped Cyprian with rouged cheeks and a generous bosom sauntered toward him. With her light brown hair and green eyes, she reminded him vaguely of Miss Stoke. But then so had the other two women who'd approached him tonight, and their hair hadn't been light brown nor had their eyes been green.

She came right up to his side and put her hand on his bicep. "Good evening. You look lonely."

Hell, this one smelled of sweet pea—and rose. Not quite the same as Miss Stoke, but damnably close enough. "I'm not," he said, bracing himself against a wave of arousal that had nothing to do with the woman pressed against his side.

Well, not *nothing.* She was a tangible manifestation of

his desire. Not precisely what he wanted, but near enough to satisfy him. Maybe.

What the hell was he considering?

Banishing Miss Stoke from his mind. It seemed a wise—and increasingly necessary—thing to do. He thought of her far too much.

Graham pivoted slightly, and the woman looked up at him, her lips parting to reveal a rather crooked row of teeth. She wasn't Miss Stoke, and he didn't want her. That wasn't why he'd come tonight.

Before he could extricate himself from her, Ripley's butler, whom Graham had met upon his arrival before the party had started, approached. "Your Grace?"

"Yes?" The single word was a mix of relief and enthusiasm.

"If you'll come with me."

Graham cast an apologetic glance toward the woman as she took a step back. Her lips formed a slight pout as Graham practically ran after the butler.

Tibbord must have arrived! Or Osborne. Either one. Graham didn't care. Elation swept through him as he followed the butler up two flights of stairs.

As the butler led him to a door, Graham wondered what was going on. Had Ripley been able to get Tibbord —or Osborne—into a room away from the party? Was he expecting Graham?

Apprehension overtook his excitement as the butler opened the door. "Just in there," he said, gesturing for Graham to enter.

Graham moved inside, and the door closed behind him with alacrity. It was a small bedchamber, and there was no sign of a gentleman at all.

There was, however, a masked woman standing near the bed.

What the bloody hell was going on?

She moved toward him, and he was horrified to see her hair was the exact shade of Miss Stoke's. He couldn't see her eyes, not through the slits of the mask she wore that covered nearly her entire face.

As she neared, the scent of sweet pea once again washed over him, but there was no rose or any other smell to dilute it. There was no mistaking who this was.

"Arabella."

Her Christian name fell from his lips unbidden as his pulse leapt.

She reached up and untied the mask, revealing her familiar face. "I didn't want to take it off until you got here. Just in case."

He found he didn't want her to take if off at all. There was something sensual about the notion of her wearing it and nothing else. *Hell,* he was growing hard, and here they were in a bloody bedroom.

"What on earth are you doing here?" He gave in to anger—it was a far safer emotion at this point. "You aren't supposed to be here." He gritted out the last.

"I know, but I have important information." Her face scrunched up in concern. "You haven't seen Tibbord yet, have you?"

"No. What information?"

"My father thought he'd told me something the other day, but he didn't. So when he brought it up today, I was very confused." She shook her head. "Never mind all that."

She spoke quickly and avoided his gaze. Was she nervous? Of course she was; she was in the middle of a bloody Cyprian party at the Marquess of Ripley's house. She ought to be nervous. She ought to be *terrified.*

He took a step toward her so that only a foot or so separated them. "What information?"

She blinked up at him. "Are you going to take off your mask too?"

He'd forgotten he was wearing it. He was too focused on her, on what her proximity was doing to him. "Tell me why you're here. You shouldn't be."

"I can see you're angry, but it was necessary. If you accuse Tibbord of theft, he may expose your financial status. According to my father, he used that information to extort people."

His anger faded. "You came here to protect me?"

She looked at him as if it were a silly question. "I had to."

He would have done the exact same for her. In fact, much of what he was doing was for her. For him too, but he had to admit he was driven by the need to save her from ruin. He could survive it, but would she? Yes, she would. But watching her parents suffer would devastate her.

"Arabella, do you know what kind of party this is?"

"A masked one?"

"There are two things of interest here: gaming tables and Cyprians. Do you know what those are?"

She turned a fetching shade of pink. "Yes."

"I believe Ripley's butler thought you came here for an assignation with me."

"Oh. Dear. *Well.*" She averted her eyes, but the color remained in her cheeks. "I wouldn't have come if I'd known." Her head shot up, and she looked him in the face. "Yes, I would. I don't regret coming here. I was careful—I altered my gown beyond recognition, I made a mask, I walked quickly, and—"

He moved to stand directly in front of her so they barely touched. Now he swept off his mask in irritation. "You *walked?*" She nodded. "By *yourself?*"

Her eyes lit with fire. "Should I have brought one of my overworked retainers and sworn them to secrecy? Perhaps if you'd told me what sort of party this was—"

"It wouldn't have mattered. You just said you would have come anyway." He towered over her, his body teeming with unsatisfied lust. For her and no one else.

"And why didn't you tell me?" Her tone was hot and

accusatory, fanning the flames of his frustration. "Do you attend these sorts of parties often?"

She sounded… "Are you jealous?" He'd meant to provoke her the way she was provoking him, but the question came out wrong. It came out like he wanted her to say—

"Yes." Her gaze didn't waver from his. "I've no right to be. You don't belong to me."

No, he didn't. But he wanted to. If only for a short time.

There was just the two of them. He wanted her. Desperately. He was growing more and more certain she wanted him too. And there was a bed right behind her.

Oh, this was not right or honorable or acceptable. Nevertheless, he said, "I do right now."

The air around them crackled with electricity, as if a hundred lighting strikes had touched down in the room. There was searing heat and a constant thrum of energy, of desire.

He surrendered to all of it and took her in his arms, his lips descending madly on hers. She clasped her hands around his neck and stood on her toes to meet him. Her mouth met his eagerly, and the ensuing kiss became the very best moment of his life.

He'd expected to give some sort of tutorial, but she seemed to know precisely what she was doing. Her tongue swept along his lip, and he opened, joining with her in a relentless assault of mutual passion.

This might not be acceptable or honorable, but it was absolutely divine. Her fingers caressed his nape as her body came up against his, her breasts pressing into his chest.

Graham groaned and rotated his head, kissing her from another angle in order to learn every part of her. He'd wanted her for some time, but he hadn't realized how consuming his hunger had become, how desperately he needed this. How he needed *her*.

He thrust his fingers into her hair, heedless of any damage he might cause. He just wanted to feel her, to touch her, to claim her. His other hand swept down her spine and splayed against her lower back, bringing her pelvis flush against his. She felt magnificent against him, despite the layers of clothing between them.

Tearing his mouth from hers, he kissed along her jaw, murmuring, "You are so beautiful. You taste so good. You feel like heaven."

She moaned softly as he licked along her neck and snagged his teeth on her earlobe. She tugged at his hair and ran her other hand along his shoulder. Then her hand came around and moved beneath his coat. Her palm was warm and seductive. He wanted more.

"Take this off." Her command was soft but throaty and dark with longing. He felt the echo of her desire deep within himself.

She pushed at his coat, moving it off his shoulders and then tugging the sleeves down his arms. He shrugged, helping her with its removal. Then it fell to the floor and instead of kissing her again—which he wanted to do more than anything—he froze.

This *wasn't* right. Or honorable. Or acceptable.

"Arabella." No, that wasn't right either. "Miss Stoke."

"Don't you dare call me that. Not now." Her eyes narrowed as she looked up at him. "Why did you stop?"

"Because we shouldn't be doing this. I'm a complete and utter scoundrel for even remaining in this room with you, let alone kissing you."

Her chin notched up, and her gaze was devastatingly sultry. "Do you deny that you want me?"

Oh God, she was going to kill him. "Where on earth did you learn to talk like that?" Probably the same place she'd learned to kiss. Now it was his turn to be jealous. "Never mind."

She lowered her eyes to stare at his chest. "I'm not a

virgin. You may think me fast, and I suppose I am." Her cheek twitched.

He heard the self-recrimination in her voice and wanted to strike it away. "Are you sure you aren't a member of the Spitfire Society?" he asked with humor.

Her head tilted back, and she blinked up at him in surprise. "I'm sure."

"I don't think you're fast." He was surprised she wasn't a virgin, and he did want to know why, but was it really his business? Most men would say yes, especially if they had marriage on the mind. Which he did. But not with her.

Oh, this was so very wrong.

"Should we stop?" she asked, a faint tremor of doubt at last clouding her voice.

The lightning was still around them. He'd never felt such an acute longing. He just knew he'd regret it if they left without seeing this through. He dared to hope... "Do you want to?"

Her gaze was dark and steady. "No."

His body hummed with joy and hunger. "Neither do I."

"Then what do we do?" She glanced ever so briefly toward the bed. That look, along with her admission, was more than enough.

"This."

He swept her into his arms and kissed her again as the last barrier between them crumbled into dust.

~

*A*rabella gasped into his mouth as he lifted her and carried her to the bed. At least, she assumed it was the bed. She couldn't see where they were going, nor did she care. He could carry her into the fires of hell, and she would gladly go.

Yes, it was the bed, as he lowered her to the mattress.

He followed her, covering her body with his. He was a delicious weight, and she opened her legs to welcome him between them.

But there were too many clothes. She pulled at his cravat, loosening the silk so it hung about his neck. Moving her hand between them, she started on the buttons of his waistcoat. He lifted his chest from her, giving her space, and she soon had them all undone.

With both hands, she pushed the waistcoat off his shoulders and worked the garment down his arms. He grasped one side and managed to toss it away. Without delay, she tugged his shirt from the waistband of his breeches. He rose again, this time completely breaking their kiss as he got to his knees. After he whipped the shirt over his head, the garment joined his waistcoat, as did his cravat, which went flying.

She drank in the sight of his naked chest. A patch of dark hair sprouted in the center in a small triangle between his nipples. She reached up and splayed her palm against him, feeling his heat as she smoothed her way to his breast, then down his abdomen, where his muscles rippled beneath her touch.

"Why aren't you a virgin?" The question seemed to fall from his mouth without thought, for he looked instantly horrified. "Sorry, I shouldn't have asked."

She gave him a saucy stare. "Are *you* a virgin?"

He laughed. "A more than fair question, and no."

"You *shouldn't* have asked, but I understand why you did. I should be untouched, but alas, I fell in love."

"Did you?" He sounded utterly enthralled.

She nodded, feeling suddenly vulnerable in ways that had nothing to do with their position or location.

"What happened?"

"My parents refused his suit. He had neither title nor money. He had nothing to recommend himself, save charm and intelligence. He left England to find his fortune—he couldn't gain a title, so it was the best he could do to hope to win my hand."

"I didn't think I'd ever have a title."

"He did not have a duke in his line," she said wryly.

"Where is he now?"

She lifted a shoulder. "I don't know."

"So he never won your hand." He reached down and covered her hand, which had stilled against his belly.

"No."

"His loss." He lowered his head, but she halted him with her own query.

"What about the woman who claimed your virginity?"

He laughed. "She was a washerwoman at Oxford. Ten years my senior and quite, er, skilled."

Arabella narrowed her eyes at him as jealousy threatened to attack her once more. "Did you carry on with her for some time?"

"Not terribly long, no." He tipped his head to the side, his eyes glimmering with heat. "Are you jealous again?"

Warmth flushed her cheeks. "I admit it grates on me to think of you with other women. Doesn't it bother you to think of me with Miles?"

"Miles? The cad has a name? Yes, when I think of him doing things to you that I plan to do, I feel somewhat… beastly. However, he, like the washerwoman, are in the past. You are my present, and I am yours."

She smiled softly, her heart skipping as he tried again to lower his head. This time, she said nothing before he kissed her, his lips soft against hers at first and then more demanding as he claimed her mouth with his tongue.

She completely surrendered to sensation, immersing herself in his touch, scent, and taste. But she needed more. She took her hand from his abdomen and tugged at her skirt, pulling it up her legs.

He lifted his head slightly. "Do you want to take it off?"

She shook her head. "Too complicated. And I'm too impatient."

He chuckled low in his throat. "I can appreciate that." He helped her with the skirt, exposing her thighs. The dress bunched at her waist, and she realized that was going to be annoying.

"Turn over." He helped flip her to her stomach.

She felt him pluck at the laces of her gown. With each tug, her body hummed with need. Her breasts were heavy against the bed, aching to be touched. Yes, maybe she should get undressed.

He seemed to read her mind as he pulled up the back of the skirt. Cool air rushed over the backs of her knees and thighs and then her backside. He caressed her there, his hand smoothing over her curves in a tantalizing manner and then moving between her legs.

She gasped as he found her sex, his finger gliding along her folds. He let out a soft groan as he slid inside her. Rapture exploded as her muscles tightened in anticipation of release. It wasn't going to take long…

"God, I could take you like this," he whispered against her ear, his teeth tugging the lobe just before he licked her neck and sucked her flesh. His finger worked in and out of her, and she lifted her backside toward him, moaning with need.

In a series of quick movements, he had her off the bed and had removed her gown and petticoat, nearly tearing them in his haste. He muttered an apology, and she responded that she didn't care. They kissed wildly as he fought the laces of her corset. Abandoning that tack, he ripped his mouth from hers and turned her around. In short order, he removed her corset, letting it fall to the floor.

She spun back to face him, where he perched on the edge of the mattress and kissed him anew, her tongue spearing into his mouth with a desperate fervor. She'd never been this aroused. If he touched her again, she would break instantly.

He whisked the chemise up and over her head as she kicked off her slippers. Then his mouth was gone from hers once more as he kissed and licked his way down to her breasts. He clasped them, softly at first, then more firmly just before his lips closed around one nipple. She cast her head back and moaned again as he squeezed the other nipple. On and on, he tortured her until she nearly came.

"Halstead. Please."

"Graham," he said huskily. "I've scarcely been Halstead."

"Graham." She loved the feel of it on her tongue. "Please. I can't wait anymore." She reached for his fall.

"My boots." He grimaced as he moved her slightly back so he could quickly pull his boots off.

"And your breeches," she said, eager to see him naked.

With a lazy smile, he slowly flicked the buttons of his fall one by one. With a frustrated grunt, she shoved his hand away and finished the job with alacrity. Sliding her hands into the waistband, she pushed the garment down his hips, her fingers gliding down his thighs.

His cock sprang free, and her throat went dry. He disposed of his breeches and stockings, then swept her back onto the bed. She clasped his shoulders and pulled him, spreading her legs so he could nestle himself between them.

He hesitated, looking down at her. "You're certain?"

"Never more. Now, Graham. *Please.*"

He gave her a wolfish grin as he stroked her sex, his thumb giving special attention to her clitoris. It was more than she could stand. Her muscles clenched, and she wrapped her legs around him, urging him to slip inside her.

He guided his shaft into her sex, and the moment he thrust deep, she came apart. He didn't stop moving, and with each stroke, the ecstasy intensified. She whimpered as she held him, her fingers digging into his backside as she squeezed her legs around his hips.

He was relentless, and her pleasure ignited once more, building her toward another precipice from which she was more than happy to fall. He brushed her hair from her forehead and kissed her there. Then again on her temple and her cheek, her jaw, and finally her mouth, where their lips and tongues met in a mad, feverish dance.

She felt him tense and knew he must be close. She cupped his cheek and kissed him deeply. But then he was gone—from her mouth and from her sex.

"I had to—" He finished on a groan that ended with "*Arabella*" before he collapsed beside her.

She knew what he had to do. Miles had done the same thing to prevent getting her with child.

Graham's hand cupped her sex. "Please tell me you were done."

"I was. Again."

He opened one eye briefly and smiled. "Good." Then he rolled to his back.

They lay together, their sides touching, as they recaptured their breath. Her heart slowed, and her body felt heavy. She thought she could simply melt into the coverlet.

A loud knock jolted them both to a sitting position. Their heads swung toward the door as it began to open.

"Anyone in here?"

Graham bounded over her with an urgent whisper. "Hide on the other side of the bed."

She didn't see what he did next as she scurried off the other side of the mattress and fell to the floor in fear.

"Yes, someone is in here," Graham answered angrily.

She heard the door slam, followed by the distinct

sound of a lock. Relieved, she rested her back against the bed and briefly closed her eyes. When she opened them, Graham had come around the bed. And he was already wearing his breeches, which was a shame.

"I should have locked the door." He sounded rather annoyed.

"Why? Unless you *planned* to bed me."

"I certainly did not." He offered his hand and helped her to her feet, his gaze lingering on her breasts. "I expected to meet Tibbord."

She walked around the bed to fetch her clothing and began to dress. "Well, that's better than expecting to meet a courtesan."

"And why should I have done that?"

"Because that seems the point of this soirée." She turned her back to him. "Would you mind lacing my corset?"

"It's the least I can do."

She smiled. "Thank you."

They finished dressing in silence, and she poked around the room for a looking glass in which to tidy her hair. Unfortunately there wasn't one.

"What are you looking for?" he asked.

"I wanted to see my hair. It feels a mess, and I should repair it before venturing from the room."

"It's not terrible. In any case, you're going directly home, so you needn't worry."

She stopped and looked at him as he pulled on his boots. "Why? Now that I'm here—and masked—I can stay and help you interview Tibbord."

"If he shows up. It may be Osborne. It may be neither." He scowled.

"I suppose we'll have to wait and see," she said, choosing to remain optimistic. She had to. "What shall we say to them? We can't accuse them of stealing your money. Perhaps you should pretend to be someone else, someone interested in investing."

He rose from the chair after finishing with his boots and then plucked his coat from the floor. "I was going to tell you that 'we' aren't doing anything, but your plan is sound." He pulled his coat on and straightened the garment. "No, on second thought, you do have to leave. I can pretend to be someone else without you."

She frowned at him. "But I'm here. In disguise. When will I ever have another opportunity?" She crossed her arms over her chest. "Besides, you aren't my father. Or my husband."

"No, I'm not," he said softly and with a tinge of regret. "Arabella, if things were different—"

She walked toward him. "Don't say it. Things aren't different. We both have to do what we must." She tidied his cravat, tucking the ends into his waistcoat. "Tonight, it was imperative that I be with you. Maybe it's what I needed to endure the future."

He clasped her waist. "Don't say *that*. You deserve a future full of happiness and love."

She lifted her gaze to his. "So do you. Let me help you tonight. Please?"

He stared at her a long moment before finally exhaling. "It's against my better judgment. But that seems to be tonight's theme." He pulled her against him and kissed her.

She sighed and leaned into him, content to be in his embrace. After several long moments, they parted.

"Shall we go downstairs?" she asked.

"You aren't to leave my side, is that clear?" She nodded, and he smoothed her hair, tucking strands here and there. "Better."

Then he retrieved their masks and tied hers around her head. She returned the favor as he squatted in front of her. She giggled. "Here you are in this position again."

"So I am."

She heard the smile in his voice and decided that no matter what happened, she would always be grateful for their time together. It was how she felt about Miles. No regrets, just happy memories and a twinge of sadness of what could never be.

She prayed this time would only be a twinge too. However, her heart was beginning to suggest it might be a bit more than that.

CHAPTER 10

While it wasn't wise or proper for Arabella to be at this party, Graham didn't at all mind the opportunity to touch her with abandon. They walked down the stairs, her arm curled through his, their sides touching. At a Society event, they would have caused a stir, moving so closely together. Here, they fit in with everyone else. He inclined his head toward another couple on their way up who were similarly entwined.

"We'll go back to the saloon," Graham said, passing the first floor. "That seems the best place to encounter Tibbord or Osborne."

"We have to assume he—whoever it is—will be wearing a mask. And if it's Tibbord, we'll have no idea who he is."

"True. Thanks to you and your father, we should be able to recognize Osborne, even with a mask." He wanted to be optimistic.

She sent him an encouraging smile. "I hope so."

Graham escorted her into the saloon, where close to two dozen gentlemen were gambling. A handful of others stood about, most with women on their arms or draped against their sides. The women, Graham realized, were not masked. He hadn't noticed that before. He glanced toward Arabella, thinking her mask set her apart from the other women. No matter. It wasn't as if she could take it off. He just hoped she didn't attract attention.

But how could she not? She was stunning even with most of her face covered. And it was more than just her form, which was spectacular—it was her carriage and demeanor. She possessed confidence and grace, exuding an aura of strength and femininity that he found utterly alluring.

"Halstead." The Marquess of Ripley came forward and greeted him. He didn't wear a mask. As he'd told Graham earlier, what would be the point? It was his party after all. Ripley raked his gaze over Arabella, and Graham had to fight the urge to knock him down. "Have we met?" he asked her.

"This is Mrs. Devon," Graham said, pulling a name out of the air.

She dipped a curtsey. "Pleased to meet you, my lord."

Ripley inclined his head, then shot a questioning look toward Graham, which Graham chose to ignore. Instead, he subtly gestured for them to move to the corner.

"Has either Tibbord or Osborne arrived?" Graham asked.

"No." Ripley frowned. "I did my best to ensure they knew of the party and that there would be substantial gaming."

Fighting a wave of disappointment, Graham looked over the room in search of Osborne. He should be easy to find with his sharp chin, unusual height, and the likely presence of a raven-headed walking stick. He turned toward Ripley. "No walking stick?"

Ripley shook his head as Arabella said, "There." She nodded toward the back of the room near an exterior door. A man sat in a chair observing the gaming, his face almost entirely covered with a mask. Save his mouth and a very sharp chin.

"You know what he looks like?" Ripley asked in surprise.

"His Grace described the gentleman to me," she said smoothly.

Graham gazed at her with great admiration. "I thought it would be helpful to have another set of eyes."

Ripley's eyes narrowed the slightest amount and only very briefly. He looked to Graham. "What would you like to do?"

"I need to convince him to allow me to invest."

Ripley's brow creased with confusion. "I thought you were going to confront him."

"I was, but I think it will be much better if I tell him I want to invest. I don't want him—I want Tibbord."

"Good point," Ripley said. "Perhaps we should walk over there and talk about all the money you've recently lost and how you need a drastic turn of fortune."

"Perfect." Graham started toward the man they suspected to be Osborne. When they were near, Graham said, "If I don't recover at least a portion of my funds, I shall be in dire straits indeed."

"Why not play piquet?" Ripley asked benignly.

"I can't afford to lose." Graham kept his tone grave and pitched his brows low. "I need a guaranteed return."

Ripley scoffed. "Nothing is guaranteed."

The bait worked exactly as they intended. Osborne, if it was him, stood from the chair. He had several inches on both Graham and Ripley. Graham looked about for a walking stick, but didn't see one. Perhaps he hadn't brought it tonight.

"Good evening, my lord," Osborne, if it was him, said, inclining his head toward Ripley. "Thank you for the kind invitation."

Ripley smiled in response. "I'm glad you could come. Osborne, is it?"

"Yes. I must say I was surprised to be included in your soirée."

"Someone recommended I invite you." Ripley rubbed a hand along his jaw, his face briefly contemplative. "I can't recollect who, but I suppose it doesn't matter. Will you play tonight?" He gestured toward the tables. "Or I can arrange for other entertainment?"

Osborne's gaze drifted to Graham. "Actually, I thought I might speak to your friend. I couldn't help but overhear your conversation, and I might have a solution for his troubles." Beneath his mask, Osborne cast a placid smile toward Graham, who felt a sudden urge to wipe it from the man's face. He and his employer had fleeced any number of people, carelessly ruining lives as they filled their own coffers.

"Indeed?" Graham asked, leaning slightly forward. "How can you possibly help?"

Arabella gripped his arm, and he resisted the urge to soothe her tension.

Osborne darted a guarded look toward Arabella but continued. "I facilitate investments. My employer is quite good at selecting sound investment schemes that earn a great deal of money for his clients. He's saved many a gentleman from debtor's prison." His tone was smug and wholly deceptive. The urge to commit physical violence was growing stronger.

"That sounds very intriguing," Graham said slowly, infusing his voice with a mix of curiosity and skepticism. "What sort of investments?"

"A wide range. Building schemes. Shipping ventures. This is probably not the right place to discuss it further." Again, Osborne sent a circumspect glance at Arabella, but then gave Ripley an apologetic look. "Forgive me. This is a night for entertainments, not business."

Graham wasn't letting him get away, not without securing a future meeting. He detached himself from Arabella and stepped closer to Osborne. "Perhaps we can arrange a time to pursue our conversation."

"That would be amenable. How about Monday evening at Hosenby's in Leicester Square, nine o'clock?"

Anticipation curled through Graham. "I'll be there."

Osborne let out a light chuckle. "I do beg your pardon, but how shall we recognize each other without masks?"

"Perhaps we should just wear them," Graham said with a laugh.

"That will garner us a few stares."

Graham looked up at him. "I daresay I will recognize you just fine. You are rather tall."

"Very well. I'll see you then."

"Does this appointment include me?" Ripley asked, surprising Graham.

Osborne seemed to look down his nose at Ripley. "I wasn't given to believe that you were in need, my lord. My employer is rather...discerning." He nodded toward Graham. "Good evening." He turned and left.

Ripley stared after him. "I do feel as if I've been given the cut direct by a scoundrel. Even for me, this is a new low."

Graham couldn't help but smile at Ripley's self-deprecating humor. "And Osborne doesn't even know who I am."

"How do you know he doesn't?" Ripley asked with a sly smile.

Graham moved back to Arabella, and she didn't hesitate to curl her hand around his arm. "I suppose I don't, but I've never met the man, and I'm not exactly known around town yet, especially with a mask on."

"Will you tell him who you are, or wait for him to puzzle it out?" Ripley asked.

"I think I have to tell him." Graham's mind churned as he contemplated what his plan should be. "I'll need to ponder this."

"Do let me know if you require assistance." Ripley's gaze strayed once more to Arabella.

"I will," Graham said, pulling her against him. "I've been considering how to proceed, provided I obtain an interview with Tibbord. Absent extortion, it seems I must strike him where he lives—the gaming hells."

Ripley narrowed his eyes. "What do you have in mind?"

"If he can't go to the hells, he doesn't have a hunting ground. What good is my title if I can't get a swindler banished from a gaming hell or five?"

"What good indeed." Ripley flashed a brief smile. "Bravo, you're learning."

"I have to ensure he no longer takes advantage of the gullible. Not that he has to know that." Graham let out a soft chuckle. "Now, it is time for us to depart. Thank you for a very helpful evening. I am in your debt." He winced inwardly at his poor choice of words.

"Careful, Halstead, I do like to collect." Ripley flashed a grin.

Graham offered Arabella his arm and guided her toward the door they'd entered earlier. Just before they left, he shot a look toward Ripley. He was watching them with interest, one of his brows elevated. Graham suspected he was wondering who Arabella really was. Surely he was aware of who he'd invited to his own bloody party, and Mrs. Devon hadn't been on his list.

Shrugging away the bead of unease working its way down his spine, Graham escorted Arabella from the house. Once they were outside on the pavement, he stopped short.

"You really walked here?" he asked.

"It's not that far."

No, it wasn't, but thinking of her walking alone made him distinctly uncomfortable. "I realize I am not your father—or your husband—but would you promise not to do that again?"

"I won't promise anything except to be careful."

They started walking through the square toward Oxford Street. "You really should be a member of the Spitfire Society."

"I would if I could." She didn't have the luxury of choice, however.

Neither did he. Not if he wanted to keep Brixton Park. And he did, more than anything. But if they'd been able to choose… "Would you truly prefer spinsterhood to marriage?"

"The word spinster is tossed about as if it were a degradation. However, there are many things to recommend that state."

"And what are those?" He was genuinely interested.

"Independence to not only do what you want but to control your own funds."

"I imagine that in particular would be attractive to you." He knew it was for him. He wanted to throttle the former duke for behaving so carelessly.

"Yes."

"You wouldn't miss the companionship of a husband?" he asked.

"It's difficult to miss what you haven't had. And if you're referring to what we just did, clearly marriage isn't a requirement." She cast him a sidelong glance cloaked in heat.

Had she just suggested a liaison? No, he was simply looking for a reason to repeat their encounter. Time to change the subject. "I suppose we don't need to meet in the morning," he said, feeling a trifle disappointed about that. "I was looking forward to our next fencing lesson."

"We could meet Tuesday. I'll be most anxious to hear how things go with Osborne. Unless I can come." She gave him a hopeful smile.

"Absolutely not. You can't show your face at a gaming hell in Leicester Square."

Surprisingly, she didn't argue. "Speaking of showing your face, when you tell Osborne who you are, won't he realize you don't have money to invest?"

"He would obviously know how much money he stole from the prior duke, but was he also aware the duke had mortgaged Brixton Park and was essentially bankrupt? Even if he was, he can't know *my* financial situation. I was not destitute when I inherited the dukedom."

She slowed. "So you have money to invest?" She sounded surprised.

"I would have had six months ago; however I've had to spend most of my savings just to keep Brixton Park and Halstead Manor running."

"It's strange to think you are financially insolvent when you own two grand houses."

He didn't disagree with her. "Well, if I can't lay my hands on a good sum of money, I will no longer own Brixton Park. I am, however, stuck with Halstead Manor and its excess of problems."

She peered up at him as they waited to cross Oxford Street, which was still busy even at this late hour. "What's wrong with it?"

There was an opening in the traffic, and he ushered her quickly across the street. "Too many things to list. It seems the previous dukes paid little attention to it after Brixton Park was built. In fact, I wonder why they didn't entail Brixton Park. That's yet another question I shall never have answered. It's a shame because they could have sent my great-great-grandfather there to take care of it." Graham's father had often railed about that. Instead of exiling his brother from the family entirely, the third duke should have sent him to Halstead Manor to manage the estate.

"Who was your great-great-grandfather?" she asked.

"Richard Kinsley—he was the younger brother of Robert, the third Duke of Halstead. He ought to have been the duke, for he was far smarter than his elder brother. Richard designed Brixton Park and oversaw its construction—the house and the gardens. When it was finished, Robert rewarded him by sending him away and disinheriting him completely."

Her sharp intake of breath was gratifying. "Why would he do that?"

"Because his wife told him to. Richard discovered she was having an affair and planned to tell Robert. However, the duchess beat him to it—only she told Robert that his brother Richard had assaulted her. She wanted Robert to kill him, but he couldn't murder his brother, so he sent him away instead. All of it was a lie by the duchess to protect herself. And it ensured my Kinsley branch was utterly cut off from the family."

She stopped. "My house is there."

So it was. He'd become so wrapped up in his story that he'd lost track of where they were. "How will you get inside without being detected? I'm assuming you slipped out earlier?"

She nodded, turning toward him and taking his hands in hers. "I'm so sorry your family was wronged. I can see why Brixton Park is so important to you."

"It symbolizes what we lost. My father was overjoyed that it was coming back to us—or that we were going back to it—that we were going to be the future of the Kinsley family. I'm just glad he knew that would happen before he died—and I'm glad he didn't know how badly the prior duke had botched things."

"If anyone can make it right, it's you," she said softly. "You will find a way to keep Brixton Park." Her forehead creased. "You mentioned extortion. Would you really re-sort to that?"

"Normally, I'd rather not, but in this case, I will do what I must—for me and for you. I *will* find a way to save your family." He tipped his head down and squeezed her hands. "I promise you that."

She smiled, but there was an edge of sadness to it. "My marriage prospects are good, I think. No one terribly wealthy, but hopefully situated well enough to keep my parents from debtor's prison."

His chest twisted, because he knew she didn't want to

wed and yet she would do whatever she must to protect her parents. "That isn't really a threat, is it?"

She shrugged. "My parents say it is, but I don't know if that's true. My future husband will have to promise to care for them as best he can. I suppose that will need to be negotiated before the marriage." Uncertainty crept into her voice. Her prospects might be good, but there was every chance a potential groom might balk upon hearing the truth of their financial state.

It was more important than ever that he get their money back from Tibbord. Graham was absolutely committed, whatever the cost.

He lifted his hand and caressed her jawline. He'd cared for her for some time, but after tonight, it was more than that. She couldn't be his, but she had been, if only for a short time. And he would cherish the memory for all his days.

"I should go inside," she whispered.

"Yes."

But they didn't move. Time stretched between them, as if neither wanted the night to end. He knew he didn't. But it must.

She realized it too, standing on her toes to briefly press her lips to his. The kiss was gentle and lovely, but so bittersweet.

Stepping back from him, she said, "I'll see you Tuesday."

He let her go. "Same time and place?"

She nodded, then turned and crept down to the servants' entrance of her house.

As he watched her go, the frustrating sensation of being trapped crept over him. It was strange to think that now he was a duke, with all the prestige and power that title carried, he was far more encumbered than he'd ever been as a secretary.

What good was being a duke if he couldn't use that

power? And how could he use it to help Arabella? He wasn't sure, but he was determined to work it out.

~

*J*t began to rain as Arabella walked through the gate to Phoebe's garden late Monday morning. She dashed toward the garden room, where Phoebe was seated at the table.

Phoebe jumped up to open the door. "Come in!"

Arabella hurried inside before she was too wet. "Thank you. I hope I'm not disturbing you." She brushed at the dampness on her skirt.

"Never," Phoebe said, retaking her chair. "Join me. I was just having tea and cakes. No butter biscuits, I'm afraid."

Arabella sat down at the round table. "That's quite all right. Since Mrs. Woodcock began making them, I've had more than enough. And that's with my father devouring most of them."

"He's feeling better, I hope?" Phoebe asked.

"He is." He'd actually come downstairs for breakfast the day before. He seemed to be generally improved since she'd talked to him about Tibbord. He'd asked her yesterday for an update. She'd told him she hadn't heard anything.

In truth, she had a difficult time focusing on the Tibbord matter when her mind was so very occupied by Graham. More accurately, what had happened with Graham the other night. She'd surrendered to temptation again. Really, one would think she'd regret it by now, but she just couldn't. Too much was beyond her control, and she would cherish the things that were hers and hers alone.

"How goes the husband hunt?" Phoebe asked before sipping her tea.

Arabella poured herself a cup. "Fine. I think Sir Ethelbert may be coming around."

Phoebe pursed her lips. "Doesn't he have an over-bearing mother?"

Overbearing was perhaps a strong description. "His mother is usually with him, if that's what you mean."

"Yes, that. Does she like you? I think she will need to like you if you're to have a chance with him."

Arabella had spoken to her on a few occasions, but hadn't noticed if the woman cared for her or not. "I think so?"

"How could anyone *not* like you?" Phoebe asked. "Is there anyone else besides Sir Ethelbert? The Duke of Halstead, perhaps?"

Having just taken a sip of tea, Arabella had to fight not to choke on it. She swallowed, then coughed delicately as she set her cup down. "Why would you mention His Grace?"

"Jane and I found it interesting that he went to help you the other day. He's also attractive, charming, and, may be in search of marriage. He's been a tad wily about it."

"We would not suit," Arabella forced herself to say. Because they wouldn't. They both needed something the other could not provide.

"You've already determined that?" Phoebe asked.

"Yes. We've spent some time together. He did call on me one day."

"Did he? Well, I'm surprised you wouldn't suit. It seems as if two people whose company I enjoy ought to enjoy each other's company." Phoebe exhaled. "Alas, en-joying someone's company doesn't mean you wish to *wed* them. It's good you are being selective." She peered closely at Arabella. "Or are you perhaps not entirely en-thused about marriage? I truly hope you aren't hunting for a husband because you think you must."

Arabella felt a rush of bitterness as she picked up a cake. "I do not have the freedoms you enjoy. I am hunting for a husband to secure my future." She stuffed the cake in her mouth and chewed with irritated enthusiasm.

Phoebe lifted her hand to her cheek. "Oh dear, I have quite forgotten myself. I'm so sorry, Arabella. My goodness, it hasn't taken me overly long to forget about the requirements and expectations placed upon young ladies by their families and society." She gave Arabella an apologetic smile. "I support whatever you want or need to do."

Arabella let go of the tension in her muscles. She was on edge and had been since Saturday night. One would think the activity she'd shared with Graham would have put her at considerable ease. And it had for a while. But it had been a fleeting occasion, a wonderful moment that would never be repeated.

Curiosity drove her to ask, "Will you be sad not to marry?"

"Heavens, no." Phoebe's shoulders twitched. "Why should I be?"

"There are certain…advantages to marriage."

"And what would those be?" Phoebe asked with a hint of humor.

Arabella had had sexual intercourse with two men—inwardly, she winced—and enjoyed it immensely. She couldn't imagine going a lifetime without it. She picked up her teacup and peered at them over the rim. "Sex."

Phoebe set her cup down with a loud clack. "Some would argue that isn't an advantage but a chore."

Arabella supposed that would be possible if the gentleman wasn't very good at it. Apparently, she'd been fortunate. Twice. She thought of the courtesans and gentlemen she'd seen together at Ripley's party. They all seemed quite enthralled, and she doubted sex was a hardship for any of them. "Some say it's quite pleasurable."

"It isn't for everyone," Phoebe said quietly.

Arabella noted that she'd gone pale and worried she'd upset her. "Are you all right?"

Phoebe took a shallow breath. "Most people think I

refused to wed my betrothed because of his philandering ways, and while that is accurate, that is not the entire story." She paused briefly. "Sainsbury tried to force himself on me. If the footman hadn't interrupted or if Sainsbury hadn't been so inebriated, I shudder to think what might have happened. And I knew it's what would happen on my wedding night. I never wanted him to touch me again. I'm not sure I ever want any man to touch me again."

Anger and sadness twisted through Arabella. "Oh, Phoebe, that's horrible."

She summoned a smile. "I managed to humiliate him on his wedding day. Though that hadn't been my intent, it was a small comfort." She cocked her head to the side. "It seems your opinion on the matter of sex differs from mine."

Arabella wanted Phoebe to know that it wasn't all bad, that not all men were repellent. "It does."

"You're speaking from experience?" Phoebe asked.

"I am," Arabella said.

Phoebe arched a brow. "Your former love?"

Arabella nodded. "He, ah, led me to believe that sexual activities are quite nice." She shook her head. "No, not nice. *Splendid.*" That word didn't do it justice either, especially when she thought of Graham. Devastating. Beautiful. *Divine.*

Phoebe's eyes widened. "Perchance, did you do more than just kiss him?"

Arabella's cheeks heated, and she glanced down at her teacup. "Yes." She hoped Phoebe wouldn't think less of her.

"Well, this is a day for revelations," Phoebe said. "*Secret* revelations. Nothing said here will be repeated."

Lifting her head, Arabella regarded her with gratitude. "I hope someday you're able to experience what I have. You would change your mind about the advantages of marriage."

"Or maybe I'd just find a new activity to entertain me," Phoebe said with the ghost of a smile. "Who says you need to be married to have sex?"

Arabella grinned, recalling how she'd said pretty much the same thing to Graham. "Men certainly don't."

"Hear, hear," Phoebe said, lifting her teacup. "The Spitfire Society makes its own rules. To freedom!"

"To independence!" Arabella picked up her cup in response, and they tapped them together before drinking.

Arabella wished she could be a member and then recalled that Phoebe had said she was. She would tell Graham that next time she saw him since he kept saying she should be.

Tomorrow. She would see him tomorrow. Alone in the park. It wasn't a bedroom, but...

No! There would be no kissing or anything else. He might very well tell her that he'd concluded his business with Tibbord, and then their association would be over.

She'd known their relationship was temporary. Not that she'd considered that the other night. She hadn't considered anything beyond how much she'd wanted him and how wonderful being with him felt.

The sooner she accepted that he would be nothing but a lovely memory—like Miles—the better off she would be.

CHAPTER 11

*A*fter arriving early at Hosenby's on Monday evening, Graham nursed a tankard of ale as he awaited Osborne's appearance. He sat at a table against the wall with a clear view of the door, which he watched like a bird of prey. Therefore, the arrival of Ripley and Colton was impossible for him to miss.

The marquess and viscount scanned the room and quickly found Graham. What the bloody hell were they doing here?

They made their way to Graham's table and didn't wait to be invited to sit down. "'Evening, Halstead," Colton said.

"Good evening. What a surprise to see you here," Graham said without diluting the irony.

Colton inclined his head toward a serving maid. "We thought you might want moral support."

Graham didn't, but he refrained from saying so. He didn't want to scare Osborne off, and the man had made it clear he wasn't interested in working with Ripley.

The serving maid brought two more tankards of ale for Graham's unwanted guests. As was usual, her gaze lingered on Ripley. But then she also looked toward Colton. Graham supposed she'd given him the same manner of interest, but he hadn't returned it. Ripley and Colton, however, smiled at her. She bounced away with a sly grin.

"Do you ever go out without looking for women?" Graham asked, lifting his ale for a drink.

"I never do anything without looking for women," Ripley said. "Life would be tragically boring without them. I wondered if you were remotely interested in them until I saw you with—what was her name, Mrs. Devon?" He sipped his ale. "She's a comely piece. Did you bring her? I don't recall meeting her, and I did my best to meet all the Cyprians who came to my house the other night."

"No, I didn't bring her. You must have just missed her." Graham prayed he would drop this line of conversation. Or that Osborne would arrive. The latter would be ideal.

"But you left with her," Ripley said.

Colton leaned forward across the table toward Graham, his red-rimmed eyes alight with interest. "Did you?"

"We departed at the same time. I didn't leave *with* her." Hopefully, no one saw them walking away together. Even if they did, Graham would say they were mistaken.

Ripley turned toward Graham and draped his arm over the back of his chair. "I assumed you had some sort of association with her since you recruited her assistance with locating Osborne and allowed her presence when you spoke with him."

"Only because it seemed prudent to have help." Thankfully, Osborne entered at that moment. Even without the mask, the man was completely recognizable thanks to his height and the walking stick. Graham quickly stood. "If you'll excuse me. While I appreciate the support, it's best if I speak with Osborne alone."

"I agree," Ripley said, making Graham relax slightly. He removed his hand from the chair and looked up at Graham with a measured expression that conveyed seriousness instead of his usual dry wit. "As Colton said, we only wanted to provide moral support—or any other kind of support should you need it."

"Thank you." Graham hurried to meet Osborne just inside the door. "Good evening, Mr. Osborne."

Osborne's gaze flicked over him. "Good evening. Yes, you are the man I met the other night."

Graham extended his hand. "Halstead."

Surprise flashed in Osborne's dark eyes, and he blinked, perhaps in an effort to mask the emotion. "Your Grace, it's an honor to meet you."

"Come, let us find a quiet place to sit. If there is such a thing at a gaming hell." He smiled blandly and led Osborne to a table in the corner on the opposite side of the common room from Ripley and Colton.

They sat, and Osborne said, "Yes, they can be rather loud, but usually not terribly so, especially if you stay out of the gaming rooms."

"I'm surprised this is where you'd choose to conduct business," Graham said. "Haven't you an office?"

"That's an expense my employer doesn't wish to incur. It's hardly necessary as he only works with a small group of select clientele."

Graham wondered how he'd managed to become "select" but supposed it was entirely based on the conversation Osborne had overheard Saturday night. "Your employer… When do I get to meet him?"

"That is not how we work, I'm afraid. You meet with me. My employer is focused on investing your money to its best advantage."

What utter horseshit. Graham had to practically bite his tongue.

A different serving maid deposited two tankards of ale on the table before hurrying on her way.

"Then I'm afraid I won't be able to invest," Graham said. It was a huge risk, but he had to meet Tibbord face-to-face. He picked up his tankard and took a drink, hoping to appear careless.

Osborne frowned but didn't say anything. Graham pressed his advantage—if he had one. "I can't be the first client to request a meeting with your employer."

"No." Osborne's lips stretched into a tight, humorless smile. "However, that is a privilege reserved for very few."

"One might argue I'm the epitome of privilege." For the first time, Graham wielded his title like a hammer. "If your employer won't meet with a duke, I have to wonder if his investments are sound at all."

Osborne narrowed his eyes. "Do you actually have money to invest?"

Graham wondered if this would come up. He tensed, feeling as if he were in the midst of a fencing match. "I do."

"I have to ask, of course." The pompous smile returned. "The prior duke, who also demanded to meet my employer, was not all that solvent, and from your conversation the other night, it seemed you might be in a similar situation."

Graham hid his shock at the mention of the prior duke. He hadn't expected Osborne to mention him, but how could Osborne know if Graham possessed knowledge of Tibbord and his schemes or not? "The prior duke invested with your employer?" he asked in mock surprise. "I was not aware of it."

"What a coincidence," Osborne said smoothly, reaching for his tankard. "The duke liked to exert his privilege. I'm afraid he didn't have much else when he died." He said this with a mix of pity and disdain.

Graham almost felt sorry for the duke. "I have my own money. When can I meet with your employer? He is welcome to come to Brixton Park. Presumably, he knows where that is if he worked with my predecessor."

"He does. I will confer with him and send you a notice of the meeting. You must keep this confidential, of course. This is not a service we extend to many."

"Of course," Graham agreed, though he intended to tell Arabella in the morning. He could hardly wait. Victory was within their grasp.

Osborne took another drink of ale, then stood. "You'll hear from me soon." Picking up his walking stick, which he'd leaned against the table, he departed the hell.

Graham swept up his tankard then went back to his previous table. His backside had barely hit the chair before Ripley said, "Well?"

"Tibbord will meet me at Brixton Park—the date is yet to be determined."

Ripley grinned. "Excellent."

Colton lifted his mug. "To... What are we drinking to?"

"To restitution." Graham tapped his tankard to the other's and took a long drink.

Ripley set his ale down. "Have you decided what to do if he refuses to return the investment?"

"I can do what I mentioned the other night—seek to have him banished from his usual gaming hells. And any new ones." Graham didn't doubt he could make this happen. The owners of the hells wouldn't want it spread around that they allowed a known swindler among their clientele.

"You could also threaten legal action," Colton suggested.

Graham acknowledged that anything he did would likely ensure Tibbord publicized the state of the prior duke's financial affairs. Given what Osborne had said tonight, Tibbord was clearly aware of how desperate the duke had been.

However, Graham refused to be extorted. And if he had to choose between recovering the money or keeping everything secret, he would choose the former. If he got the investment back, he would no longer be destitute, and there would be nothing to expose.

"Or just tell him you're the Duke of Halstead and you have the means to make his life completely miserable," Colton said with a snort. "Which you do. You have powerful friends and connections."

Graham didn't either, but he supposed he could. He thought of the Duke of Kendal and Satterfield's invitation to join them at the club. He would do that. Perhaps when he was finished here.

"That seems a rather vague threat," Graham said.

Colton shrugged. "It might be to some, but if this man is skirting the law, and propriety, then it seems like you might be able to frighten him with ducal bluster. I know it works for the Duke of Holborn. Everyone's intimidated by him."

"I'm not." Ripley smirked as he picked up his tankard.

Colton laughed. "You don't count."

Ripley smacked his empty mug on the table. "Where are we off to next, lads?"

"I'm for White's," Graham said, intending to establish a connection with Satterfield's stepson, the Duke of Kendal.

"Forget the stodgy old club," Colton said. "Come with us."

Graham could well imagine where they were going, and he wasn't interested. "Thank you, but I have a prior engagement."

"I suspect Halstead has a mistress." Ripley gave him a knowing look.

Not wishing to encourage the man, Graham said nothing and busied himself with drinking his ale.

"The woman he left your house with the other night?" Colton asked. "Sorry I missed meeting her, but I was otherwise engaged." A gratified smile spread his lips.

Ripley chuckled. "Halstead's being rather coy. And we'll leave him to it."

Graham breathed a sigh of relief. He didn't want to discuss Arabella. She already occupied too much of his mind.

He parted ways with Ripley and Colton, then caught a hack to White's. So far, tonight had gone quite well, and he could only hope it would continue in that vein. He was grateful not to have to return to Brixton Park, but wished David was here.

Graham regretted keeping his financial problems from his best friend. It would be nice to have someone to talk to. Except he did—Arabella.

Maybe he wanted someone to talk to about her. Graham laughed aloud in the empty hack. That he was perhaps falling in love with the woman his best friend had been supposed to marry was incredibly ironic.

Falling in love.

Was that what was happening to him? No, that wasn't possible. It couldn't be. Not when he knew they had no future. If she was free of her duty, she'd choose not to wed. She'd choose to be a member of the Spitfire Society, and he couldn't blame her for that.

Soon, they would go their separate ways, and he would simply be glad for having known her, if only for a short time.

~

*A*nticipation thrummed through Graham as he lunged and parried. The morning was warm, and a faint sheen of sweet dappled his forehead and the back of his neck. He'd removed his coat, but now paused to shed his waistcoat as well. He leaned his sword against a tree and was just stripping the garment away when he heard Biscuit's familiar bark.

"Good morning," he greeted as Arabella came into

the small private clearing. He liked practicing here because the trees and shrubbery obscured him from the surrounding area. It was also the perfect place to meet Arabella without drawing notice.

Particularly when she was dressed as a maid, with her floppy cap and oversized work gown. She looked incredibly nondescript.

But not to him. To him, she was beautiful, her moss-green eyes smartly assessing everyone around her with curiosity and empathy, while her smile lit up the world.

She seemed to falter, stopping short as she saw him, her gaze arresting on his midsection. She was taking in his state of undress. And now he was thinking about *her* in a state of undress. Perhaps he should at least have left his waistcoat on.

"Good morning," she said, coming farther into the clearing.

Graham went to take the leash from her hand, then bent to pet Biscuit quite thoroughly. The dog knew him now, not that she'd ever shied away from his attention, and set out licking his wrist and nuzzling his hand. "That's a good girl," he cooed, rubbing her belly and chin as she flopped onto her back. Her lids came down halfway, and her tongue lolled to the side.

"She adores you," Arabella said.

Graham looked up to see her staring down at them. "She's a smart dog." He returned his attention to Biscuit, scratching her head. "Aren't you, Biscuit? Aren't you the smartest dog?"

She barked in response, then leapt to her feet.

After securing her to the same tree as last time, he went to his coat, where he withdrew a bone wrapped in paper from David's kitchen. "I brought you a treat."

Arabella laughed. "Oh, she's going to be insufferable now."

Graham shrugged but didn't apologize. "I think I told you I loved dogs."

"You didn't have to tell me. I can see it. Why didn't you get another after Zeus?"

It had been too painful to contemplate at first. He'd poured all his energy into Uther instead. But now, after spending time with Biscuit, he wondered if it was time. He was going to miss her when he no longer saw Arabella. He ignored the pang of anguish that sucked at his chest.

"I just didn't. Perhaps I will—after everything is settled." He had a hard time imagining when that would be. Aside from dealing with the financial disaster, he was still trying to navigate being a duke. It felt overwhelming when he truly stopped to think about it. The tenants at Halstead Manor, his role in the government, the weight of the past and future generations depending on him.

"How did it go last night?"

He was grateful for the question so he could shift his mind. "Very well. I demanded to meet Osborne's employer before I would commit to making an investment."

Her eyes widened. "And he agreed?"

"It took some persuasion, but yes." She grinned, and he couldn't stop himself from joining her. It felt so good to share this with her. "I invoked my privilege as a duke."

She giggled. "How *noble* of you."

He snorted. "Yes, that's what we dukes do. He said the previous duke did the same thing."

She blinked in surprise. "You discussed him?"

"Osborne brought him up. I think he was trying to ascertain what I knew. I pretended as though I was unaware of any investment between him and Tibbord. Osborne also wanted to be sure I actually had money to invest."

"Which you don't."

"Correct, but I said I did."

"And he believed you because, well, you're a duke." She smirked.

He grinned again. "Just so."

"When will you meet with Tibbord?"

"He hasn't said—he's going to send a note informing me of the time. I suppose I will have to rearrange my schedule since Osborne didn't indicate I would have a say in setting the appointment. He'll come to Brixton Park." He realized he wanted her to see Brixton Park, the place his ancestor had built and which gave him a sense of pride and connection. Connection to his father and the Kinsleys, who'd come before them, a line of people who'd been forsaken, and Graham would make sure it wasn't for naught. He would make them all proud.

"I hope you'll let me know when," she said.

"Of course. In the meantime, I think you should visit Brixton Park. Your mother wanted to see it, didn't she?" He didn't particularly want her mother to come, but he couldn't very well invite Arabella for a private tour, much as he wanted to.

"She would love that." She grimaced. "But, she would also take that as a sign that you're interested in courtship, and she'll be horribly disappointed when we decide we don't suit. She's already been pestering me as to whether you'll call again. She's noticed you haven't been at any of the events we've attended."

No, he'd been busy with hunting Tibbord. "Should I call again? I want to do whatever makes things easier for you."

Her features softened. "Thank you. I do appreciate your concern. What if you host a small picnic? We can include Phoebe and Jane."

"*We.*" It almost sounded as if they were hosting it to-gether. A vision of her as his duchess flashed in his mind. He shoved the image away. "An excellent idea." He tried to think of friends he could invite, but decided Ripley, and to a lesser extent Colton, would not be acceptable with the ladies in attendance. "Is tomorrow too soon?"

The bridge of her nose wrinkled. "What if Tibbord wants to visit tomorrow?"

"Then I shall come down with an inconvenient injury or illness that will require me to postpone our picnic." He retrieved his sword and sliced it through the air. "Ready for your fencing lesson?"

"If you think I must."

He lowered his arm, frowning. "I thought you enjoyed it."

She shook her head gently, a small smile teasing her lips. "I did. I'm sorry. It's just... Never mind." She squared her shoulders and assumed the position he'd taught her, then held out her hand. "My sword, if you please."

He wished he could give her a sword—one that belonged to her. With a jeweled handle and her name inscribed at the base of the blade. He shook himself from the reverie and offered her the weapon with a great flourish, bowing.

She took it from him, and he straightened. "You remember how to lunge?" he asked.

She responded by leading with her foot and sword. Her form was excellent.

He nodded approvingly. "Wonderful. Now, to parry. This is a defensive act, and you will not move your feet. It's important that you stand your ground and use the sword as your defense. Keep your arm as straight as possible."

Perhaps he should have brought another sword, but he hadn't thought of that and would have had to plan to bring one from Brixton Park. Assuming he could find one there. Surely there was a sword there somewhere. He glanced around the clearing and saw a small branch on the ground.

He went to pick it up, and Biscuit immediately started yapping and running about.

Arabella laughed. "She thinks you're going to throw it."

Of course she did. Zeus had loved to chase sticks.

"And I shall. After you perfect your parry. Given your natural ability, this shouldn't take long." He moved to stand opposite her and positioned himself to lunge.

"I'm to defend myself against your stick?" she asked skeptically.

"You think you can't? It's a stick. You have a sword."

"Therein lies my concern. I will cut your stick in two, and you will be defenseless."

He laughed. "You can try. Ready?" She nodded, and he lunged.

She parried, but wasn't fast enough to strike his stick. He could have scored a hit.

"You didn't move your feet," he said appreciatively.

"You told me not to."

"I did, but most people, when they are learning, step back without thinking. It's the natural thing to do when you are being attacked." Unsurprisingly, she showed bravery and fortitude along with grace and wit.

"Again," she said.

He lunged again, and this time, she struck the stick in defense. "Well done!" he cried.

"I want to lunge, and you parry," she said.

"All right." He admired her vigor. "Ready?" She nodded just before she lunged. He parried, then riposted.

She stumbled back. "What the bloody hell was that?" She scowled before lunging toward him again, her form perfect.

She really was magnificent. He parried, and she riposted without him even showing her what to do. He hadn't meant to do it, but it was second nature to him. "I'm sorry," he said. "I didn't mean to counterattack."

She lunged again, and he was forced to move back as he parried. She came at him with a riposte, which he quickly parried, then followed with his own lunge. She wasn't as fast as him, but she was keeping up better than he could have expected. They continued for a few minutes until he noticed she was breathing heavily, and her sword arm was beginning to sag. Also, Biscuit was in a near frenzy because of the stick.

He stopped and pointed his branch at the ground. "Enough." He tossed the branch where Biscuit could easily get it. She promptly sat down and began to gnaw on the bark.

"I hope she doesn't think it's another bone," Arabella said.

Graham laughed softly as he moved toward her. Working to recover her breath, she handed him the sword. Listening to her, watching her chest rise and fall, he was reminded of the other night as they lay tangled in bed. His cock hardened, and he was all too aware of how alone they were in this secluded place.

"I see why you removed your clothing," she said. "It's quite easy to become overheated."

"It is."

"I might remove my clothing, if I could." She lifted her skirt to her calves and shook them, likely creating a breeze that cooled her legs.

He tried not to look at them, the elegant turn of her ankle and the slope of her calf. He imagined her knee and then her thigh. He wanted to bury himself between them. Before he could think of what he was about, he was standing before her.

"What are you going to do with your sword?" she asked, her voice dark and husky.

For a moment, he thought she meant his cock, but realized he was still carrying his sword. "Sheath it." He turned abruptly and found the scabbard.

"I wish you would." She was right behind him, and this time, there was no mistaking her meaning.

He pivoted, still gripping the now-sheathed sword. "You are sorely tempting me."

She moved toward him and curled her arms around his waist. "Am I? Good."

He let the sword fall to the ground and grabbed her.

Sweeping her to his chest, he kissed her with wild abandon, unable to stop the torrent of lust pouring through
him.

She clutched at his waist and backside, greedily returning his kisses and pulling him taut against her. She
rotated her hips, and he groaned, his desire cresting to a
desperate height. This was madness. Delicious insanity,
and he wanted every moment of it.

He reached down, their arms switching positions as
she clasped his shoulders and neck while he grasped her
skirt and pulled it higher than she had. He lifted it higher
still, until he could slide his hand along her thigh. The
skirt fell over his hand and forearm as he stroked toward
her sex.

She moaned as he found her slick folds. She was
ready and eager for him, her pelvis pressing into his
touch. He gave her what she sought, sliding his fingers
along her clitoris and then into her sheath. Her muscles
clamped around him, and he was desperate to feel her
around his cock.

He moved his mouth from hers, dragging kisses along
her jaw and neck. "Arabella, let me…"

"Yes. *Please.*"

He rotated them both and guided her to a tree—not
the one with the dog. He lifted her against it, then
paused, looking into her face. She opened her eyes with
alarm. "Why did you stop?"

"This can't be comfortable."

"What isn't comfortable is you leaving me wanting."
She narrowed her eyes at him. "Please don't."

"So demanding," he whispered, lifting her skirts once
more so they bunched between them.

"Is that a problem?"

"Not even a little bit." He loved it. "Wrap your legs
around my waist." As she did what he demanded, he
opened his fall and withdrew his cock.

She moaned, holding him tight as she ground against

him. He slid his shaft along her crease, glorying in the sweet anticipation. Then he guided himself inside, and desperation took hold. She dug her feet into his backside, and he thrust deep.

"Go fast, please," she said. "I need you."

God, she aroused him like no other woman could. He gave her what she asked for, driving relentlessly into her. Her muscles clenched hard around him, and he knew she was close. With just a few more strokes, she came apart around him, squeezing him until he thought he would die from the pleasure of it.

Damn, he was going to come. And he couldn't. Not inside her. But he couldn't…get…out…

He withdrew just before he spilled himself. He dropped his forehead against the tree trunk beside her head, heedless of the coarse bark.

She held him, her hands caressing his nape and upper back, her lips grazing his ear, temple, and cheek. It was just a moment before he eased her to her feet, holding her until she was steady. "All right?" he asked softly.

She nodded, smoothing her skirts down her legs as he stepped back.

"That was probably ill-advised," he said.

"Probably. As with the other night, however, I won't regret it." She was absolutely incomparable.

What had he ever done to deserve the time he had with this woman? Most men would go a lifetime without experiencing this depth of desire and satisfaction, this utter bliss.

He managed to find his voice. "Neither will I."

"Still, we should probably stop doing this," she said, readjusting her cap, which had gone quite askew during their…exercise. "I suppose we'll have to when it comes time."

Did that mean she was content to continue their… liaison? For that was what this had become. Or so it seemed she was saying. "Are we having an affair?" he asked.

She tipped her head to the side, her tongue darting out to lick her lip, and damn if he didn't want her again right now. Maybe this time, he'd bend her over that rock…

"Yes, I think we are. How very Spitfire Society of me."

He barked out a laugh. "Is *that* what they do?"

"Goodness, no. They do nothing of the sort. I just thought it seemed like something a spitfire *might* do. And I am an honorary member."

"Are you?" He smiled. "Well, that makes sense."

Biscuit barked, having grown bored with her stick. Graham went and loosened her from the tree. "You should let her chase the stick for a while."

"I think I will," Arabella replied. "I don't think I can go home yet. I imagine I'm rather flushed."

"You are. Beautifully so." Her cheeks were pink, her lips red and slightly swollen, her eyes glowing with satisfaction.

"Thank you. I'll see you tomorrow for the picnic, then?"

"Yes, I'll send a formal invitation to you and to the Misses Lennox and Pemberton."

"You'll need to include Jane's mother." He nodded, and she smiled. "I look forward to it."

"No more than I." He noted the glint in her eye.

"We should be on our best behavior." She sounded somewhat disappointed. "My mother will be there, after all."

He lifted his hand in a pledge. "I promise to keep my hands to myself."

"I will try to do the same." She gave him a saucy smile before taking Biscuit's leash and leaving the clearing.

Graham had to wait some time before he was cool

enough to don his outer garments once more. What on earth was he doing carrying on an affair with an unmarried woman who was in search of a husband? He was a cad, a scoundrel, an absolute jackanapes.

And he was also, quite probably, in love.

CHAPTER 12

The sun glowed warm overhead as Arabella arrived at Brixton Park with her mother the following afternoon. Graham stood outside the portico. Behind him, tall pillars stretched to the towering roofline. Dozens of windows gleamed in the sunlight. It was a magnificent house, and she could already see why he loved it so much.

As they approached, Graham held his arms out wide in greeting. "Welcome to Brixton Hall. We have been blessed with a very fine day, perfect for a picnic." He bowed as Arabella and her mother curtsied.

"We have indeed," Mama said as she rose. "We are delighted to be your guests." She'd been absolutely thrilled to receive his invitation yesterday. As expected, she'd immediately concluded that it must mean something, that courtship or even a proposal was imminent.

Graham's gaze connected with Arabella's, and a flash of heat blazed through her. It was becoming rather torturous to spend time with him. Or maybe it was just because they weren't alone today. She'd become rather accustomed to having him to herself.

The sound of another vehicle drew Arabella and her mother to turn their heads back toward the long drive. It had to be Phoebe or the Pembertons. Arabella hadn't told her mother they were coming, for Mama would have asked how Arabella knew.

"There are other guests?" Mama murmured.

"Apparently, "Arabella replied, keeping her voice bright.

The coach came to a halt, and Arabella noted that it didn't belong to Phoebe or the Pembertons. It bore a crest.

Graham's groom rushed to open the door, and Phoebe immediately stepped down, her gaze widening as she took in the house. Jane came out after her, and a third person—presumably the owner of the coach—descended last.

It was Lady Clifton. Why hadn't Graham mentioned inviting her?

"Good afternoon, ladies," Graham said. "Welcome to Brixton Hall." He bowed again, and all three ladies curtsied.

Phoebe came forward and gave Arabella and her mother a warm smile. "I'm so pleased to see you here."

Lady Clifton glided toward them, a willowy figure who moved with elegant grace.

"Lady Clifton," Phoebe said. "Allow me to present my dear friend Miss Arabella Stoke, and her charming mother, Mrs. Stoke."

Arabella and her mother performed another curtsey. "It's lovely to make your acquaintance," Arabella said.

"Indeed it is," Lady Clifton agreed before moving past them to address Graham. "Thank you so much for including me in your kind invitation for the picnic today."

"It was my pleasure." Graham's voice was smooth and warm, and Arabella wondered how this invitation had come about. Since Lady Clifton had thanked him for including her, perhaps Phoebe was behind it. But why? If she'd been looking for ladies to bring along, why not bring Arabella? Phoebe didn't know she was already coming.

Why would they? You made it clear to them that there was nothing between you and Graham, that you did not suit.

"Yes, thank you, Your Grace," Jane said. "My mother wasn't able to come, and Lady Clifton is a welcome chaperone. I appreciate you including her."

He inclined his head, then gestured toward the house. "Shall we go inside for a brief tour before we repair to the garden for the picnic?"

"Yes, let's," Lady Clifton said, and since she was closest, Graham offered her his arm. Or perhaps it was because she outranked the rest of them.

Arabella linked arms with her mother as they walked toward the entry.

"I didn't realize there would be other people here," Mama whispered with grave disappointment.

"It's quite all right," Arabella said. "I did tell you not to get your hopes up about the duke."

"It's hard not to when he invites us to his house." Mama pursed her lips as they moved inside.

The entry hall was large, with a pale marble floor and green wall coverings. A single portrait hung over a small accent table. It was of a woman with dark hair and secretive eyes.

"That is a past duchess," Graham said, prompting Arabella to wonder if it was the duplicitous duchess who'd had his family banished. "The most recent duke's mother." Not her, then. *Good,* Arabella hoped he'd sold any portraits of her.

It seemed he'd sold plenty given the dearth of artwork on the walls. She hoped she was the only one to notice that.

"You'll find my decorating taste is plainer than what you might see at other ducal houses," Graham said. "I'm afraid it's hard to leave behind my humbler background.

Living in a house of this size and splendor is an adjustment, and I've striven to make it feel like my home instead of a museum."

That was a most excellent explanation for the lack of art. Arabella wanted to applaud his ingenuity. Plus, she wondered if it was true. She knew he loved the estate and would do anything to keep it, but was he finding it difficult to adjust to opulence and splendor when it came to his living quarters?

"Allow me to show you the saloon and the ballroom. This way." He took them through the hall, past a wide, gorgeous staircase with intricately designed polished wood banisters. There were flowers and leaves entwined along the stair rail and newel posts.

"The detail on the staircase is stunning," Arabella said, wanting to run her fingers over the wood.

"My ancestor carved that himself, or at least part of it. He loved the gardens—he planned those as well—and sought to bring them inside whenever possible. You'll see the flowered cornice in the ballroom."

Graham took them to the saloon, which was painted in the colors of a garden. Indeed, a garden mural adorned one wall.

"This is so charming," Lady Clifton enthused. "It reminds me of your garden room, Miss Lennox."

"It does indeed," Phoebe agreed.

Arabella noted that it seemed quite large, likely because there were only two seating areas, and it really could—and should—have supported much more. Again, she hoped no one else was paying attention to such details. Although, if her mother determined he didn't have enough wealth, perhaps she'd surrender her hope that he and Arabella would suit.

Next they moved into the ballroom, and just as he'd said, the ceiling was trimmed with carved flowers around the edges. It was gorgeous, and Arabella feared she would get a crick in her neck from staring up at it for so long.

"Shall we go outside?" Graham gestured toward the wide doors that led out to the gardens. Laid out in a grid with paths between them were sectioned areas, and off to the left, a maze.

A footman held the door as they went out, and Graham led them toward the maze. Just past the last square lay a sprawling, beautiful green lawn. Two blankets were situated with six place settings so they would sit in a circle.

"On our way," Graham said, "let me show you the keystone laid by my great-great-grandfather in 1715." He took them to the corner of the house and pointed to a stone about four feet up from the ground. It read: R. Kinsley 1715.

Arabella knew the R meant Richard, Graham's great-great-grandfather, not Robert, the duke. This was Richard's creation, his passion. And it had been stripped from him. She looked at Graham, who stood staring at the stone with such pride that she felt it in her chest.

"I will do my best to ensure you sit next to him," Mama whispered, breaking the moment.

She didn't have to, as it turned out, because Graham guided Lady Clifton to a place, then stood next to her. He looked toward Arabella in silent communication. His message was clear—at least to Arabella—she was to sit on his other side.

"Oh good," Mama murmured as they took their seats.

A footman served a delicious meal of cold pheasant, cheese, bread, and an assortment of fruit and nuts. There was also lemonade.

"Your great-great-grandfather designed this house?" Lady Clifton asked. "And the gardens?"

"Yes. It took him nearly ten years. It was a great deal of work. We have his diaries."

Lady Clifton smiled, her attention completely focused on Graham. "How wonderful. I should love to read them. Have you considered having them published?"

"I have not."

Perhaps he should. It could be a source of income. Arabella inwardly winced, hating that she saw everything in terms of bettering one's financial state. However, she knew he needed it as much as she did. She suddenly wondered if Lady Clifton was wealthy. Arabella's stomach sank.

"Did your great-great-grandfather design anything else? He seems so talented that he ought to have been known, and yet I've never heard of him." Lady Clifton dipped her chin. "Granted, I am not an architectural expert."

"He designed the gardens at Huntwell in Huntingdonshire. He went there to become the secretary."

"And your family has served as secretary there ever since," Phoebe said. "Until recently. I wonder what your ancestor would say to see you here now as the duke in the garden he designed and the house he built."

Arabella felt the rise of pride and passion in Graham beside her as much as she saw his chest inflate and his shoulders square.

"He would be quite pleased, I think."

"Did he design the maze too?" Jane asked, looking toward the large, intertwined rows and alleys of hedges.

"That was his favorite aspect," Graham said, smiling. "He created it for his children. It is specifically designed for a challenging game of hide-and-seek. There are all sorts of nooks and crannies that are perfect for hiding oneself."

"How splendid!" Lady Clifton exclaimed.

"I don't know," Phoebe said skeptically. "Wouldn't it be easy to become lost?"

Graham cocked his head to the side. "Yes, but if you put your hand—right or left, it doesn't matter—on the shrubbery and keep it there as you walk, you will eventually find your way out."

"We should play," Lady Clifton said.

Jane nodded in agreement. "Oh yes, I think we should."

Graham lifted a shoulder, then looked from Phoebe to Arabella's mother to Arabella, his gaze settling warmly on her. "What say you?"

If there was any way Arabella could get lost in a maze with Graham for even a few minutes, she would take it. "Yes, please," she said, looking him square in the eye as a tremor of anticipation tripped through her.

"All right, I'll give it a go," Phoebe said with a hint of reluctance. "Since you explained how I can find my way out. However, if I can't get out, I will scream at the top of my lungs, and you will be forced to rescue me."

He chuckled. "I would be happy to." He looked back at Arabella's mother. "Mrs. Stoke?"

She shook her head. "I will leave this to you younger people." She gave Arabella an encouraging smile. Clearly, she hoped Arabella would turn this to her advantage somehow. Oh, if she only knew how wrong this all was, and how there was absolutely no hope for her and Graham.

They all stood, save Arabella's mother, and made their way to the opening of the maze, which was not visible from where they'd picnicked.

"Wait, who's doing the searching?" Jane asked.

"His Grace, obviously," Phoebe said. "Not only because he'll have to play rescuer if need be, but he's the only man."

"Yes, it must be him," Lady Clifton agreed. "How much time do we have to hide?"

"I'll give you five minutes, and then I'll call out." He pulled his pocket watch out and glanced down at the face.

Everyone stood there for a moment before Jane said,

"Let's go!" She led the way into the maze, with Lady Clifton behind her and Phoebe trailing. Arabella purposely went last.

She looked back to Graham, who mouthed, *Go to the left.*

Anticipation curled through her again as she entered the maze. She passed a right turn and another right turn and another one. Was there a left?

He'd said there were nooks and crannies. Perhaps she'd missed something. She backtracked, this time looking to the right, and finally saw it, a narrow opening. Graham called out that he was coming to find them.

Sliding between the hedges, she slipped into a small space, glad to find it empty. After situating herself to wait, she heard the gentle crunch of pebbles followed by the press of leaves as Graham inserted himself into the nook. It was just large enough for them to stand and barely touch.

"Oh good, you found it," he whispered.

She put her hand on his chest and felt his heart beating sure and strong beneath her palm. "You've clearly spent time in this maze."

"I've been rather obsessed with it since moving here. I would have loved this as a child."

She heard regret in his voice. "You're angry this was denied you."

"I didn't have to live here, but to be welcomed and embraced by family is all my father ever wanted."

"Family is so important." It was why she would do anything to save her parents, including forfeit her own happiness. She didn't want to think about that right now. Not when happiness—however fleeting—was standing right in front of her.

"We don't have much time," he said.

"Then you better kiss me." She'd intended to ask him about Lady Clifton, but she didn't want to waste their time together. Maybe the widow was his future, but Arabella was his present, and he was hers.

His mouth came down over hers as she curled her arms around his neck. He swept her up against him, bringing their bodies flush. She longed to wrap her legs about his waist as she'd done in the park. Instead, she stood on her toes and pushed her pelvis against his, feeling the delicious length of his shaft even through their layers of clothes.

He caressed her breast through her gown as his tongue explored her mouth. He put his other hand on her backside, encouraging her movements against him. Desire roiled through her, arousing her to a fevered state.

This was not conducive to coupling, but there were other things they could do… If not for the time.

He kissed along her cheek and down her neck, suckling lightly at her flesh. "I would take you here if I could."

She dug her fingers into the hair at his nape and gloried in this moment, in his touch, in their mutual longing. Oh, how she wished things were different!

They parted, their breath coming fast as he clasped her waist and she put her hands high on his chest.

He leaned his forehead against hers. "I think the time is up."

Yes, their time was up. Graham would either recover their money, or they'd be forced to marry—and not each other. As if that had ever been anything more than a dream. For a brief moment, she wondered what would happen if he managed to get the money from Tibbord. And in that moment, she realized she never really expected that to come to pass.

He seemed to read her thoughts, for he said, "I'm going to get your father's money. You're going to be free to be a true member of the Spitfire Society."

She smiled up at him. "I know you'll do your best."

She leaned up and kissed him quickly. "Go. I'm going to sit with my mother."

He nodded, then kissed her once more before turning and slipping out of the nook. The air turned cold, and Arabella wrapped her arms around herself. They couldn't continue like this. He needed to marry Lady Clifton or someone else. She needed to marry Sir Ethelbert or someone else.

Arabella left the maze and returned to her mother, who frowned slightly upon seeing her. "I was hoping you would be the last one out."

"Why?" Arabella sat beside her on the blanket.

"So that you could spend some time with His Grace, of course."

Arabella was glad her mother couldn't tell how fast her heart was still beating or detect the glow she felt lingering about her after being in his arms. "Mama, you mustn't get your hopes up about a match with the duke."

"I'll get my hopes up however I like," she said primly. But then her gaze darkened. "Though I must say, I was disappointed to see Lady Clifton arrive. Surely he'd rather choose a young lady who has never been married and who doesn't already have children."

"Then why shouldn't he look toward Phoebe or Jane?"

"They don't signify, dear. They've quite consigned themselves to the shelf with their Spitfire Society."

Before Arabella could defend their choice—and their independence—Jane came from the maze laughing.

"Oh my," she said, catching her breath as she joined them. "I startled His Grace quite marvelously."

Phoebe came out a moment later, but it was several minutes before Graham emerged with Lady Clifton on his arm. She nestled against his side quite closely and laughed gaily as they made their way to the blanket. Arabella shoved away the sharp stab of jealousy that she had no right to feel.

A short while later, the ladies took their leave, each of them thanking Graham for the lovely afternoon. None, however, was more effusive than Arabella's mother.

"Your Grace, we are simply *thrilled* you took us up on our suggestion to visit—when you recently called on Arabella." She said all this so that everyone, especially Lady Clifton, could hear.

"I'm so pleased you could come," Graham said evenly. He gave her a charming bow before turning to Arabella. His gaze brushed over her like a flame, and Arabella would have given anything to return to the maze with him.

Then his attention moved to Lady Clifton, who smiled prettily. She dipped a curtsey. "Thank you, Duke, for including me in this brilliant excursion. I especially enjoyed the maze." She tipped her head coyly, prompting Arabella to wonder *why* she'd enjoyed it *especially*. Had Graham kissed her too?

Of course not!

Her head told her he would never be so callous. However, her head also knew that Graham had to find an heiress, and if Lady Clifton possessed a fortune, she was precisely what he needed. Her heart, on the other hand, told her she should stake her claim on Graham and never let him go.

But she couldn't. She had to accept that she—and Graham—needed to move on.

How was she supposed to do that when she was falling in love with him?

～

*G*raham paced the library at Brixton Hall as he awaited Tibbord's arrival. The man had sent word late yesterday asking to meet this afternoon. The end was nigh—he'd solve his money woes *and* Arabella's and then—

And then what?

Then she would embrace her future as a member of the Spitfire Society, and Graham would set to work refurbishing Halstead Manor and focusing on his new role as duke. A small voice at the back of his mind wondered if their affair could possibly continue. Or maybe even lead to something else. Would she want that? She certainly hadn't given him the impression she did. History—her history—said that intimacy between them did not need to result in marriage.

Hedge's voice carried into the library just before he came to the door. "His Grace is just in here." Exactly as they'd planned—Hedge would show Tibbord directly to the library and speak loudly enough that Graham could hear them approach.

Graham inhaled deeply and straightened his coat as Tibbord moved past the butler into the library. He was short and stocky with a thick neck. He handed his hat to Hedge, revealing a head of thick, dark hair. His eyes were light—gray perhaps—and quickly scanned the room before settling on Graham. It was an odd perusal, as if he were searching for exits.

"Welcome to Brixton Park," Graham said.

Tibbord bowed. "Thank you, Your Grace." He moved forward, and Graham extended his hand in greeting. Tibbord shook it and offered a bland smile. "I'm pleased to have been invited to return. You've a new butler, I see." He flicked a glance toward Hedge.

"Yes. Several of Brixton Park's retainers left after the prior duke died. How kind of you to recall them. Did you visit here often?"

"A few times," Tibbord said smoothly as he sauntered to the window looking out toward the maze. "I never had a chance to visit the gardens, however. The maze always intrigued me."

"It's rather amusing." Graham longed to lure Tibbord into the center and leave him there overnight. Hopefully, he wouldn't know how to escape. Graham looked toward Hedge and inclined his head. The butler took himself off with Tibbord's hat.

Tibbord's clothing was exceptionally well cut and crafted from fine materials. He seemed to be doing well, but then why shouldn't he be?

"Shall we discuss business?" Graham asked.

Turning from the window, Tibbord exhaled. "I suppose. That is why I'm here." His lips pulled back in a self-important grin.

Graham moved toward a seating arrangement near the windows and gestured Tibbord toward the settee, while he sat in a chair.

Tibbord perched on the settee with a flick of his coat-tails. "Osborne says you have money to invest. That is excellent to hear, since it seems the prior duke overextended himself."

"You must have known the Duke rather well to be privy to such information."

"He shared many details about his financial situation. I know he had to pay annuities to countless relatives, and it was an endless drain on his coffers. Brixton Park has also long been mortgaged, and he was forced to increase the debt to support his dependents. I was more than happy to help him try to reverse his fortune."

"Except you didn't." Graham kept his tone somewhat light. He didn't want to scare the man off—not yet. Not until he understood precisely what would be required of him. "You took his money and failed to provide a return. Some people would call that theft."

Tibbord frowned, his brow forming deep grooves. "I dearly hope you aren't accusing me of something criminal. There was a return—not as large as I'd hoped—but His Grace insisted I invest it in a risky scheme. I did not recommend it, but he was adamant. Unfortunately, he lost the entire investment."

"Is that also what happened with the Stokes and your other clients?" Graham asked with deceptive calm.

Tibbord showed no sign of concern. Instead, he smiled condescendingly. "I shouldn't speak of other clients.

"Then allow me," Graham said. "All these people simply made poor choices that you facilitated? That seems an unlikely coincidence."

At last, Tibbord's eyes hardened, and his muscles seemed to tense. "I assure you it is. Why are you bringing this up? I begin to wonder if you are truly interested in investing with me."

"I am not, actually." Graham leaned back in his chair and assumed a nonchalant posture while inside, his blood was roiling. "I invited you here to demand the return of the duke's investment. I believe you stole it, and if you don't return it, I'll sue you for fraud and theft."

Tibbord's nostrils flared, but that was the only reaction he betrayed. "That sounds rather expensive."

"I'll also ensure you aren't welcome in any gaming hell in London. Since that's where you hunt the desperate, how will you find your marks then?"

As Tibbord hesitated, Graham wondered if he'd finally broken through the man's bravado. "Let me save you the trouble. I can't return the investment because I don't have it. As I said, it was a risky scheme, and the money was lost."

Graham stared at Tibbord with unconcealed malice. "Show me the proof of the investment and how it was lost."

Tibbord leaned forward, bracing his elbows on his knees. "What is your goal here?"

"To have my money—and that of the Stokes —returned."

Tibbord held up his hands briefly before scooting back onto the settee. "Well, that simply won't happen. The money is gone. Furthermore, His Grace didn't care.

He suspected there would be no return, but as he was not long for this world, he said it would be your problem and he didn't give a fig if you were bankrupted or not."

Graham felt as though he'd been punched in the gut. "He told you that?"

"Yes." Tibbord looked at him with pity. "You can't prove the duke ever invested with me. I am very careful. Though not careful enough, apparently, for I should never have met with you today. What a tedious waste." He stood abruptly.

Fury coursed through Graham, driving him to his feet. "I'm so sorry to bore you. You're discussing people's lives. This isn't about me and whether I can have a new horse or buy another country house. People at Halstead Manor count on me, and that estate needs attention."

"Don't forget all those pesky relatives and their annuities. It sounds as if you'll need to sell Brixton Park. As it happens, I know of a buyer. I'd be happy to facilitate the sale."

Graham glared at him. "I wouldn't let you facilitate a use of the privy. Forget about me." How it grated to say that! "You must return the Stokes' money. You preyed on them and have made Mr. Stoke quite ill, leaving his wife and daughter vulnerable."

Tibbord snorted. "Stoke is an idiot who doesn't know when to quit. He wagered himself into a corner, racking up losses he couldn't hope to regain. He deserves whatever he gets."

Graham fought not to hit the man. How could he be so heartless? "And so do his wife and daughter?"

Tibbord shrugged. "They are not my problem, and neither are you. You've wasted both of our times today."

Graham advanced on the man, baring his teeth. "I am a bloody *duke*. You can't steal from me and walk away."

A shadow of fear crept into Tibbord's gaze. "Are you threatening me?"

"I should call you out. In fact, I will if you mention any of this to anyone—no one is to know about the Stokes' financial state. Or mine."

Tibbord narrowed his eyes. "You don't have any money to invest at all, do you?"

Graham clenched his jaw but didn't say a word. "I ought to squeeze you until you bleed the money you stole."

A bit of color leached from Tibbord's face. "You could try, but there would be nothing."

"Where did it go?" Graham gritted the question out through his teeth.

Tibbord shrugged again. "I like to spend."

Unable to control his anger a moment longer, Graham lunged for him, grabbing Tibbord by his lapel. "You're a blackguard. I'm getting the money you owe us."

"You can't because there is none." Tibbord's eyes bulged, and he worked to suck in a breath. "My cousin will tell you."

"Who the hell is your cousin?" Graham demanded, pulling on the man's coat with both hands until the fabric went completely taut.

"The Marquess of Ripley."

Graham let Tibbord go, shoving the scoundrel in the process.

Tibbord managed to keep his balance as he stumbled backward, then smoothed his hand over his ruffled coat. "Ripley will confirm that I have nothing to my name. Or very little, anyway. I owed money to…some people."

Graham shook his head. "And you have the gall to speak ill of Stoke. You disgust me. Get out."

Tibbord inhaled deeply and lifted his chin. Then he spun on his heel and left.

Graham stared at the doorway long after the man had departed. There was no money. If Tibbord was to be believed.

It seemed Graham would need to ask Ripley. But

how was he entangled in all this? He'd known all along that his cousin had stolen from Graham? And he'd helped Graham? Now Graham had to wonder…

He shook his head, trying to clear his brain of the anger and disappointment and confusion. If there was no money, he had to sell Brixton Park. He was nearly out of time anyway. There was less than a fortnight to repay the bank, and the sum was simply exorbitant. Plus, quarterly payments were due to all his bloody relatives. Who despised his line of the family. The irony was so deep, it hurt.

But none of that compared to what this would do to the Stokes. They were barely keeping their household together. Arabella would need to marry, and as far as he knew, she didn't want to. He couldn't see her trapped in a loveless marriage. He'd do anything to stop it.

Including sell Brixton Park.

He turned and went to the window and looked out at the maze. His chest tightened as he thought of the cornerstone with his great-great-grandfather's name outside this very wall.

He should have sold it months ago when he'd learned of his financial woes. Then he wouldn't have wasted most of his savings, and he could already have started improving Halstead Manor. He'd allowed pride and love for his father to overshadow everything else.

Including his love for Arabella.

The ache in his chest intensified. Not because he realized he was in love, but because he was almost entirely certain the emotion wasn't reciprocated. She wanted to be an independent woman, able to make her own choices. She was already that woman, as evidenced by the decisions she made for herself, and he would ensure she was able to remain that woman.

He'd tell her and her parents that he was able to recover their money from Tibbord. The sale of Brixton Park would allow him to do that, plus have a little left over to invest in Halstead Manor. He supposed he could spend the rest of the Season ensconced at David's town house. David wouldn't mind.

Knowing David, he would try to give Graham money, or at least lend it, in order to help him keep Brixton Park. However, Graham was past that. He couldn't sacrifice another moment clinging to this place. It was never meant to be his.

Turning from the window, he decided to write to David at once. He would ask for a short-term loan so that he could pay the Stokes immediately. Then when the sale of Brixton Park went through, he would pay him back.

Graham paused in walking to the door. David would wait to be repaid, but what of the bank? They expected payment of the mortgage by the end of the month. That didn't give Graham much time to sell the estate. Could he even do it that quickly? Or would the bank be patient if he at least had a committed buyer.

His mind turned, aggravatingly, to Tibbord. He'd said he had a buyer. Was that true? The man couldn't be trusted. And yet, Graham didn't even know where to begin to find one.

Trudging from the library, Graham hadn't felt this despondent since his father had died. Maybe because he was letting him down by selling Brixton Park. No, he refused to think of it like that. Selling Brixton Park was the right thing to do—for his tenants, for himself, and definitely for Arabella. She was not his responsibility, but he would care for her for the rest of his days. And if he had the means to ensure she could live the life she wanted, he was going to do it.

Love was worth the price.

CHAPTER 13

"*Y*our Grace?"

Graham blinked but couldn't see through the fog. He heard the man's voice, but had no idea who he was talking to. Graham didn't know any dukes, and those were the only people addressed as Your Grace.

"Your Grace. I do beg your pardon."

The brush of a hand on Graham's shoulder made him flinch. Who was touching him?

"*Your Grace.* You have guests, and they are most insistent. I did try to tell them you were indisposed."

Your Grace.

Graham was the duke. He'd become a duke over six months ago, yet it still felt foreign. Would it ever be comfortable? He was a secretary, not a duke.

And now more than ever, he had no business with a title.

He pried one eye open to see the pillow beneath his face. Closing it again, he summoned the energy to roll over. Murky sunlight greeted the backs of his eyes, which he squinted open.

Beside the bed stood his valet, whom he'd promoted from footman. He was younger than Graham by several years and probably had no business being a valet. However, he was far cheaper than a trained valet would be. Plus, it suited Graham to have a manservant who was as inexperienced as he, even if that wasn't perhaps the best strategy. He'd reasoned they would work it out together.

Graham squeezed his eyes closed. "I realize you are still relatively new to this position, Boone, however, I think it's likely frowned upon to wake your employer up, particularly after a late night of drinking too much port."

The former duke's dwindling wine collection had been impossible to ignore last night following Graham's appointment with Tibbord. Just the thought of the man's name nearly sent Graham into a fit of anger.

"My apologies, sir," Boone said. "However, the Marquess of Ripley and the Viscount Colton are here, and they demand to see you. Hedge did try to say you were indisposed, but they said they would just come up."

"Bloody hell," Graham muttered as he tried to work himself up into a sitting position. The room tilted sideways, and his stomach did a little flip.

"Water, sir?" Boone asked.

"Yes, please." Graham swayed as he managed to keep himself upright. He closed his eyes, and that seemed to improve matters.

A moment later, Boone returned. "I have your water."

Graham opened one eye and held out his hand for the glass. Taking a tentative sip, he pried his other eye open again. After another sip and upon realizing his stomach was not going to empty its contents, Graham handed the glass back to Boone. "I'd also appreciate it if you didn't open the curtains after a night like that."

"I would never, Your Grace. It's just that I was trying to see if you might rouse… The marquess—"

Graham held up his hand. "Yes, yes, the marquess. As it happens, I am quite eager to speak with him. If not, I would have you send them on their way. As it is, we will make them wait a bit. I think I need a bath."

It was close to an hour before Graham finally made

his way down to the drawing room. His queasiness was
gone, but his head still ached like the very devil. He supposed he deserved that for trying to bury his sorrow in
drink.

"At last, the Duke has arrived!" Colton didn't bother
rising from the settee where he was sprawled, a glass of
something dangling from his fingertips.

Ripley looked less carefree than normal. His gaze was
hooded, his forehead pinched in the center. "Are you all
right?" he asked somewhat cautiously. Unlike Colton, he
stood from his chair.

"Fine, thank you." Graham wouldn't beleaguer them
with his problems. He would write to David shortly, and
that would steal enough of his pride.

"Good to hear," Colton said. "Shame to let this place
go, but can't imagine it means much to you, and it's always better to restock the coffers if you need to."

Graham froze, then slowly pivoted toward Colton on
the settee. "I beg your pardon?"

"We heard you're selling the place." Colton sipped
whatever he was drinking.

"Also that you're dead broke," Ripley said quietly.
"That's why we came—thought you might like some
support."

Anger mixed with shock, and Graham's head began to
pound. He made his way to a chair and dropped into it
as his emotions gave way to a blissful sense of numbness.

"I suspected this would upset you," Ripley said, grimacing. "Not something we typically like others to know.
It does make sense now, given your interest in pursuing
that Tibbord fellow. I assume he swindled you?"

The numbness evaporated in an instant, and Graham
vaulted out of the chair toward Ripley. "'That Tibbord
fellow'? You mean your bloody cousin?"

The indentation in Ripley's forehead deepened. "I
don't have a cousin named Tibbord."

Had the blackguard lied about that too? Why would

he do that? Why the fuck had he done anything? "He said he was your cousin and that you could confirm his penniless state. He said he likes to spend."

Ripley swore under his breath. "Shorter chap?" Ripley held a hand up at his shoulder height. "Devious grin?"

"That's him."

"His name isn't Tibbord." Ripley shook his head, his lips pressed into an angry line. "His name is Archibald Drobbit. And yes, he is my mother's sister's idiot son. *He's* the one behind these fraudulent investments?"

"Yes, and he can't return any of them—including the one he took from the former duke, which was the cause of my financial state—or so he says. Is that true?" Graham had to ask even as he was nearly certain there was no money.

"Yes. Unfortunately. He spends money he doesn't have—I often wondered where he got it all, but he keeps dubious company. I never would have imagined he could pull something like that off. He's a fucking imbecile."

"Apparently not, since he's been fleecing people for some time, and you weren't even aware of it."

"I hardly pay attention to him. Indeed, I try to pretend he doesn't exist. He used to try to trade on my name, but I put a stop to that several years ago. Ran up a bunch of debts. I bailed him out once and told him never again. I've no idea what he's been up to the past few years."

"Swindling people," Colton offered.

Graham squeezed his hands into fists. "I'm going to call him out."

Ripley's eyes widened briefly. "You can't do that."

"Why, because he's your family?" Graham sneered.

"Halstead *should* call him out," Colton said. "Sounds like the ass deserves it."

"He does deserve it, but you'll kill him. Beyond being stupid, he's hopeless with a pistol."

"It'll be swords," Graham said, determined to find satisfaction.

Ripley snorted. "Even worse. You'll cut him down in no time. Where's the satisfaction in that?"

Graham glowered at Ripley. "This isn't just about me. He stole from countless people, and I've every reason to expect he'll do it again. What's more, I warned him not to reveal my problems and he went and did precisely that. He knew the consequences, and still he chose to expose me."

Colton clenched his jaw. "Sounds like he absolutely deserves it. I'll be your second if you'd like. Ripley will probably have to stand for his cousin."

"The hell I will." Ripley took a step toward Graham. "You don't have to do this. It won't help. I will personally promise you that he won't continue this behavior. He won't expose anyone else, and he won't engage in any more fraudulent practices."

Graham heard the man's earnestness, but Tibbord—Drobbit—was a criminal, and he wasn't to be trusted. "How can you guarantee that?"

"You're going to have to trust me," Ripley said. "On my honor, and I do have some despite what anyone says. I give you my word, and if I don't live up to it, you can call *me* out. I'm fairly shit at swordplay."

"But not at pistols," Colton said. "Word of warning."

Honor was important to Graham. His father had raised him with a strong sense of loyalty, family, and pride. Though he hadn't known Ripley long, he wouldn't discount the man's pledge.

He nodded at Ripley. The numbness was creeping back. All of this was so out of his control, but then that was what he'd been dealing with since inheriting this god-forsaken title in the first place. "I do realize becoming a duke would be a dream come true for most, but I find it incredibly demanding. My life was so much simpler when I was a secretary." He looked about the room sadly.

"Did you know my great-great-grandfather built this house? He designed it and the gardens, and his brother, the duke, threw him off the estate because of a lie by his duplicitous wife. My father thought it was divine intervention that Brixton Park had come back to us."

"Do you have to sell it?" Ripley asked.

"I do. The mortgage is due, and the dukedom has too many debts and bills. I inherited a nightmare."

Both Ripley and Colton winced, their eyes dark with pity. Colton tipped the rest of his drink down his gullet, then set the glass on a table near the settee. He stood. "There's a bright side, if you're interested. There are several wagers as to which heiresses will attempt to buy their way into becoming your duchess. You could peruse the betting book and see if any of the names strike your fancy." Colton shrugged.

Graham couldn't think of anything that might have depressed him further. He didn't want an heiress. He wanted Arabella. His throat dried up, and he went to the sideboard and poured himself a glass of port.

"How can I help?" Ripley asked from somewhere close behind Graham, indicating he'd followed him at least partway to the sideboard.

Graham turned as he sipped the port, welcoming the sweet, wet elixir. He hadn't sent the letter to David yet. He'd tried to write one but had been too angry, so he'd gotten drunk instead.

"I need a short-term loan," Graham said before he could lose his nerve.

Ripley's eyes glowed with ferocity. "Done."

"I didn't even tell you how much."

"Doesn't matter," Colton said. "He's rich as Croesus. He could probably fund the government."

"I'll have it deposited to your account this afternoon," Ripley said.

Graham went to a small desk in the corner and scratched out the amount he needed, then handed the paper to Ripley. "Thank you. I'll pay it back as soon as Brixton Park is sold."

Ripley didn't even glance at the amount before tucking the parchment into his coat. "I'm sorry it's come to that." He sounded genuinely remorseful. "It sounds as though this property is an important part of your heritage."

"It's just a pile of stone. And I've another pile of stone in Essex that's more important. I have tenants there. As well as several cousins who depend on my financial support."

"You *did* inherit a nightmare," Colton said. "My deepest condolences."

Graham laughed, but with little humor. Still, it felt good to let something out. And it felt good to have a pair of friends at his side in this moment.

Ripley smiled. "I'll take my leave. Colton, you should stay and keep him company. I think our friend needs a little more of the hair of the dog that bit him last night."

"Is it that obvious?" Graham asked.

"When you take an hour to come downstairs and your eyes are red-rimmed and your face is pale, it doesn't take a scholar. Add in what you revealed to us, and I would have been surprised if you *hadn't* gotten drunk."

"Just make sure Colton paces himself. He gets carried away sometimes." He gave Colton a dark stare, to which Colton replied by shrugging and lifting his hands. Ripley offered his hand to Graham. "I am truly sorry about Drobbit. And I will make this right—as right as I can. I'll send word when I've transferred the money to you."

"Thank you, Ripley. I appreciate your kindness."

"It's what friends do." Ripley inclined his head, then left.

"I think I need to see your maze," Colton said. "I've heard it's spectacular, but the former duke never entertained. Shame you have to sell this place before having one big raucous house party. Perhaps Ripley and I can talk you into having one first." Colton winked.

Graham could well imagine an event like that if it included Ripley and Colton. However, such a party didn't interest him. He would be far happier with another intimate picnic. This time with just him and Arabella.

But that wouldn't happen. He would sell this place, and with it enable her to live the life she deserved. If it was the one good thing that could come of all this, then he would count himself lucky.

∿

*A*fter so many years on the Marriage Mart, balls had begun to grow tedious, but this Season in particular, Arabella found them positively banal. Or maybe that was just since she'd stopped seeing Graham at them.

Not that she'd seen him many times, and they'd danced only once. Still, knowing he was somewhere else and not here was disappointing.

Mama turned toward her with a slight frown. "I find it odd no one has asked you to dance. You've never been in want of partners."

That was true, and it *was* odd. Arabella also didn't mind. Though dancing would take her mind off Graham, and perhaps she could stop brooding over him.

"It's early yet," Arabella said, glancing about the room. She saw Sir Ethelbert over near the refreshment table. And he saw her. Instead of smiling or acknowledging her in some way, he turned his back.

Had he just cut her? It wasn't quite the cut direct, but it had the same chilling effect.

Perhaps he hadn't really seen her. Yes, that made far more sense. Arabella shook off the discomforting sensation.

"It's your gown," Mama said. "I told you it was time to retire it. The style is far too old."

"I highly doubt my gown would preclude a gentleman from asking me to dance." Arabella spotted Lady Satterfield and her stepdaughter-in-law, the Duchess of Kendal. They stood with a few other ladies in close conversation. Arabella noted several other groups of ladies clustered together. One of the ladies in one gathering looked toward Arabella and her mother, her gaze lingering just the slightest moment.

A bead of apprehension worked its way down Arabella's spine. Something was wrong. The usual people who might have stopped and exchanged pleasantries with them had not. A second person seemed to look their way, but Arabella couldn't be quite sure.

The next set finished, and still no gentleman approached. Arabella was now almost certain something was amiss. And she'd be willing to wager it wasn't her gown.

The Duchess of Kendal and Lady Satterfield came toward them, and Arabella relaxed. It was apparently all in her mind. She was quite relieved to be wrong.

Lady Satterfield greeted them. "Good evening, Mrs. Stoke, Miss Stoke."

"Good evening," Mama said, curtseying. Arabella did the same.

"Would you mind if we stepped to the side?" Lady Satterfield asked softly.

Arabella's apprehension slithered back. Her pulse tripped as they moved toward the wall. "Is everything all right?" She hadn't meant to ask, but alarm was growing inside her.

"I'm afraid there's a distressing rumor going about," Lady Satterfield said. "About your financial situation."

The duchess gazed at them with sympathy. "We thought it best to come and speak with you, to lend our support. We do not care one whit about your finances."

Mama had gone quite pale. Arabella gently clasped her elbow to keep her steady. "It will be all right, Mama," she whispered, even as she knew it wouldn't be. If everyone knew—

"What are they saying?" Mama asked, her voice sounding strained.

"That Mr. Stoke gambled all your money away, and that Miss Stoke is desperate to marry as soon as possible."

"Desperate?" Mama croaked.

Arabella truly worried she might swoon. "We should go."

"Let us escort you," the duchess offered.

Tears filled Mama's eyes. "That isn't necessary."

"Yes, thank you," Arabella said firmly. She needed to get her mother out of the ballroom before she fainted or began to cry.

They left the ballroom, Lady Satterfield guiding Arabella's mother, while Arabella walked closely behind with the duchess at her side. "I hope you won't credit anything you hear," the duchess said with great encouragement. "People can be cruel. Some take joy in other's misfortune because it makes them feel better about their own tragedies and disappointments."

"I appreciate you and Lady Satterfield coming to our aid. You are most kind."

"I know a thing or two about being the center of unwanted attention—far worse than this, mind you." She lowered her voice to barely a whisper. "*A scandal.* I spent nine years in exile until I came to work as Lady Satterfield's companion."

"Then you married her stepson."

"I did." She smiled, her brown eyes lighting with mirth. "Sometimes even scandal has a happy ever after."

When they reached the foyer, the footman sent for their gig. Arabella's mother, still pale, turned to Lady Satterfield. "What will we do?"

"The rumor will die down."

"It isn't a rumor," Mama breathed. "Arabella must marry. If she doesn't—" Her voice trailed off with a croak, and she bowed her head.

Lady Satterfield patted her shoulder. "You poor dear." She looked to Arabella. "Should we accompany you home?"

They couldn't, even if Arabella wanted them to, since the gig wouldn't support all of them. She summoned an appreciative smile. "No, thank you. We'll be fine. I'll take good care of her."

The footman indicated their vehicle would be waiting in just a moment.

Arabella took her mother's arm. "Thank you, Your Grace, my lady. We are deeply grateful for your kindness and concern." She escorted her mother outside and to their waiting gig.

Their groom handed Arabella the reins, and, once he and her mother were situated, she drove them into the street.

Mama leaned her head back and closed her eyes. "You can't tell your father."

"No." He'd been doing so much better since Arabella had lied about the investigation. He was eating again and was getting dressed every day. The exposure of their financial devastation would likely send him right back into the pit of despair and illness.

What were they going to do? She had to pray Graham would be able to recover their money from Tibbord. She'd never thought it would truly happen, but she now realized she'd hoped it would—with everything she had.

"How on earth did someone find out?" Mama cried. "We've been so careful."

They had, but all it took was one shopkeeper to whom Papa owed a debt to mention something to someone who enjoyed spreading gossip. "It's possible someone simply puzzled it out," Arabella said. "It's not hard to see we are struggling. We have only this gig. None of my gowns are from this Season. We live in a smaller house every year." It hardly seemed likely that anyone would pay attention to their house, but what did Arabella know? Mama used to invite friends over, and now she didn't. Perhaps that had been noted.

"It hardly matters how they know. Now we have nothing. No money, no prospects, no support," her mother said flatly. "I had hoped the Duke of Halstead might come up to snuff, but I daresay not even he will want you."

If she only knew… Arabella's gut twisted. She hated the lack of emotion in her mother's voice more than anything else. "Mama—"

"We'll have to sell off whatever we have left. And leave London. We'll find a village somewhere we can afford to live—if such a thing exists. I really have no idea how much debt your father owes. We'll look for a village with a nice vicar in need of a wife. That would see you settled, and then I needn't worry."

"Mama," Arabella said more forcefully. "There may be another way. Don't ask me to explain, but please have faith for a little longer."

"Don't ask you to explain? Your father keeps things from me, and now you will too?" Her emotion was back —anger, sadness, frustration.

Arabella wished she wasn't driving the gig so she could look at her mother, so she could take her hand and try to infuse her with strength and calm. With strength, at least—that, Arabella had. Calmness was something else entirely. It was one thing to convince her mother to trust that things would work out and another to believe it. Which made her nothing more than a fraud.

Perhaps her mother was right. Perhaps it was time they took matters into their own hands instead of letting men try to sort it out for them. "My apologies, Mama. I know of someone who is trying to get Papa's investment back, but I don't know if it will work. I trust that this person is doing his best, but you're right—we should determine the truth of our finances and plan accordingly. I'm sure we can find a vicar in want of a wife." Arabella was proud of herself for not choking on the words.

She didn't want a vicar. If she was going to take a husband, she wanted Graham. But would he want her? She had no way of knowing. Maybe it was time she found out.

CHAPTER 14

*B*y Monday morning, Arabella was exhausted. They'd tried to keep the news of their situation from Papa, but a pair of creditors had called on Saturday and demanded to be paid. After that, Papa had finally laid out the amount of their debt. It was, unfortunately, far more distressing than either Arabella or her mother had realized.

This had sent Papa into a downward spiral of agony in his gut, and he'd taken to his bed, where he'd remained since. Arabella had done most of the nursing—she'd sensed her mother needed time to organize her emotions as well as their finances.

Arabella walked into the small breakfast room to see her mother seated at the table, her blonde hair swept into a simple but elegant style. Her face was pale, but her eyes were no longer red from crying, and she held herself quite regally, if truth be told. Arabella smiled, grateful to see her mother in such a state.

"You look well this morning, Mama." Arabella pressed a kiss to her cheek before sitting across the small table from her.

Mama spread butter on a roll. "Thank you, dear. I have appointments today, with the property agent and with two more of your father's creditors. I am hopeful we will be able to settle the accounts with something we have here, or with the funds from selling the rest of our things." She gave Arabella a determined look, and it was truly as if a new woman had been born from the ashes of their financial destruction.

Arabella plucked a roll from the basket in the middle of the table. "You've been very busy."

"I have, and I do appreciate you tending to your father."

Arabella noted she didn't ask how he was faring. "I think he slept better last night. Mrs. Woodcock's new tonic seems to be helping."

"That's good to hear," Mama said somewhat absent-mindedly as she perused a newspaper next to her plate. "I'm looking for villages in need of a vicar. Sometimes such information is published in the paper, and we can use it to find a village where a new vicar takes up a living and is thus in need of a wife."

That seemed a difficult situation to find, but Arabella wouldn't try to stop her mother from trying, especially if it made her feel better. She was on a dedicated mission to save them, and Arabella only wished she'd been able to do so.

She hadn't heard from Graham and tried not to dwell on her disappointment. Perhaps he hadn't yet met with Tibbord.

"Is there room for me?" Papa asked from the doorway.

Both Arabella and her mother swung their heads toward him in shock.

"Of course," Arabella said, standing to go help him.

He was actually *dressed*, or mostly anyway, with a banyan over his shirt and cravat. He also wore breeches, stockings, and slippers. Arabella had assumed all the progress he'd recently made would disappear.

Papa held up his hand before she could offer to guide

him to the table. He gave her a nod, then looked toward her mother. "Is it all right with you, Mariah?"

Mama hesitated the slightest moment, dropping her gaze to her plate, then looked toward them once more. "Yes."

Arabella stood back as her father made his way to the table, then retook her seat. Papa angled himself toward Mama, and Arabella briefly wondered if she should leave.

"I owe you a sincere apology." He turned to look at Arabella, his lips stretching briefly into a sad smile. "And you. I did so many things wrong, not the least of which was trying to shield you from my mistakes. If I'd shared the depth of my misdeeds with you long ago, perhaps we could have come up with a plan to fix it all—together."

"Yes, that would have been nice." Icicles clung to Mama's voice.

"Mama," Arabella murmured.

Mama relaxed her shoulders and looked at her husband with a fierce stare. "It is going to take some time for me to forgive you."

He nodded. "I understand."

"I was foolish too," Mama said, briefly pursing her lips. "I should have known how bad things were. We should have abandoned London and our extravagant style of living long ago." She shifted her gaze to Arabella. "I only wanted you to have the ability to make a good match—you deserve that."

Since everyone was baring themselves, Arabella decided to do the same. "Making a good marriage was your dream, Mama, not mine."

"I know," she said, grimacing as she reached over and squeezed Arabella's hand. "I was a fool about that too."

Their butler, Baxter, entered. "Sorry to disturb you, but you've a visitor."

"We are still eating breakfast," Mama said, letting go of Arabella and picking up her buttered roll.

"I can see that, Mrs. Stoke. However, His Grace, the

Duke of Halstead is here, and he says the matter is urgent."

Arabella's heart began to thud. The pounding in her chest felt as if everyone in the room would hear the sound.

Mama snapped her gaze to Arabella. "His Grace is here for an urgent matter. Can it be he heard of your situation and wishes to rescue you?"

Oh, it was a fairy-tale ending to be sure. However, Arabella didn't think fairy tales were true—at least not for her. Still, she couldn't deny the excitement racing through her.

"Let us find out," Papa said, rising from the table. "Give us a moment, Baxter, and then show His Grace to the sitting room."

Arabella got to her feet but held her hands out toward them. "Wait! He may not be here for that purpose. Please do not raise your hopes."

They both gave her a single nod but didn't appear convinced. Arabella quickly preceded them from the room.

She strove to calm her nerves on the way to the sitting room. Once there, she took a position in front of the settee.

Mama and Papa entered, and went to stand before their favorite chairs. Seeing her father here looking better than he had in months gave Arabella courage for whatever came next. To think that in a few moments they might be saved was nearly overwhelming. Her hands began to shake. She clasped them tightly before her just as Baxter showed Graham in.

Arabella realized this was the most number of days she'd gone without seeing him since they'd met. Her heart squeezed as she took in his dark hair, neatly styled, his crisp, handsome appearance, and the intensity of his dark eyes. She tried to read the emotion buried within—

was there happiness? Sorrow? Remorse? She couldn't decipher anything.

She and her mother curtsied, while her father bowed.

"Good morning," Graham said, extending a leg. He acknowledged Arabella's mother briefly and then Arabella —but his eyes didn't linger on hers, which Arabella took as a bad sign—before settling his gaze on Papa. "It's a pleasure to make your acquaintance, Mr. Stoke."

"It is my honor and privilege," Papa said. "I am sorry I wasn't able to receive you before."

"I understood you were unwell. May I say how wonderful it is to see you looking so hale?"

"Thank you, Your Grace." Papa gestured toward the settee. "Please, sit and tell us the purpose of this welcome call."

Arabella waited until he came to the settee before she sat. She tried to silently ask for reassurance, but he didn't even look at her. When they sat, he arranged himself as far to the edge away from her as possible.

This was worse than a bad sign. Arabella's stomach dropped straight into the basement, and she took a deep breath to keep herself from feeling light-headed.

"I come bearing excellent news," Graham said, surprising Arabella. Now he glanced toward her and smiled, though it was somewhat brief. "I've been working to collect money that was stolen by a Mr. Piers Tibbord." He looked toward Arabella's father. "I believe you know him?"

Papa sucked in a sharp breath and coughed. "He's an utter blackguard. How are you involved in all this?" He shot a look of surprise at Arabella. "This is the party who was investigating him?"

"What party? What investigation?" Mama asked, sounding both confused and annoyed. She shifted her gaze to Arabella too. "Is this what you were hinting at the other night?"

"Allow me to explain," Graham said easily. Arabella

was grateful for his interjection. "Yes, I investigated Mr. Tibbord. He's been fleecing people for some time. His name is not Piers Tibbord, but Drobbit. He is a cousin to the Marquess of Ripley."

Arabella thought her parents gasped in shock, but wasn't sure she heard them accurately over her own sharp intake of breath.

"Not only is he a thief, but he hides behind a false identity?" Papa asked derisively.

"He is a horrid person altogether." Graham's voice held a dark quality that Arabella wasn't sure she'd ever heard. "But the good news I bring is that I was able to secure your investment from him and am happy to return it." He withdrew a bank note from his coat and stood so he could hand it to her father.

Mama's hand went instantly to her mouth, while her eyes widened to a rather extreme degree. Papa stared at the note, a muscle in his jaw twitching. Then he dashed a finger over his eye. "This is…a miracle."

It was indeed. Arabella could scarcely believe Graham had been successful. She'd never expected Tibbord—or Drobbit—to return the money. However, since Drobbit's cousin was the marquess, perhaps he'd helped make this happen. Arabella longed to ask for the details but didn't want her parents to see how involved she'd been—with the investigation, but more importantly, with Graham. She longed to throw her arms around him and thank him. Instead, she clasped her hands together and squeezed until her knuckles turned white.

"A miracle, I say!" her father shouted, grinning. He looked at Arabella's mother, who now had tears streaming from her eyes—happy tears, unlike the ones she'd shed following the ball.

Papa turned his attention to Arabella, his eyes bright. "Now you can marry however you like—or no one at all! I'm so sorry for the burden I placed on you, my dear. I will support whatever you choose. Whomever you choose. Or not."

Mama sniffed. "I will too. If you truly wish to remain unwed, that is your decision. I want you to be happy above all else."

A month ago, Arabella would have celebrated in their joy and basked in the chance to choose her own future. But everything had changed once she'd met Graham. She looked over at him. He was watching her parents with pleasant satisfaction.

Arabella leaned toward him slightly. "Did you—"

Graham turned his head and smiled at her. "I told you everything would work out, and it has. I hope you're as pleased as I am."

Pleased.

She nodded mutely, unable to find the words to say how pleased wasn't at all what she felt. He, however, looked quite content. That was it, then. He'd done what he'd set out to do. He'd recovered their money, and now they would go their separate ways. Why should she have expected anything else? They hadn't discussed a future. Never mind the intimacy they'd shared. It hadn't been based on declarations or promises. They shared lovely moments together, moments she would cherish her entire life. Moments that were now in the past.

Arabella feared if he didn't leave soon, she was going to humiliate herself by dissolving into a puddle of tears. No, she wasn't going to do that. She was strong. She'd weathered Miles leaving and the nightmare of the past several months of uncertainty. She would survive this too.

"Thank you, Your Grace," she said with a serenity she didn't feel. "We are indebted to you."

"Indeed we are," Papa said with grave solemnity. "If there is anything I can ever do for you... Though how I could ever help a duke..." He laughed somewhat awkwardly.

Graham stood, and everyone else followed suit. Papa

came toward him and shook his hand with more vigor than Arabella would have thought he had. "I can't thank you enough."

"There's no need," Graham said. "I am happy to have brought about a positive outcome for you." He let go of Papa's hand, then turned to Mama and inclined his head. "Mrs. Stoke."

"Your Grace," she murmured, curtseying.

Then Graham turned to Arabella. "It has been my pleasure to make your acquaintance, Miss Stoke. I wish you every happiness in the future—wherever it takes you." His gaze held hers, and she feared her heart was going to split in two. Then he turned and left.

Her heart didn't break in half. Instead, it fractured into dozens and hundreds and thousands of tiny pieces that couldn't ever mend themselves back together again.

She fought to take a deep breath while her parents began to dance around the room. They laughed and hugged, and Arabella slipped quietly into the garden.

Outside, she barely noted the gray sky or the cool breeze. Tears stung her eyes, but she blinked them away. Pain tore through her, and she wondered if she'd ever find joy again.

I wish you every happiness…

But there was only one she wanted.

Without thinking, she went through the gate into Phoebe's garden. She walked toward the garden room, the door to which stood slightly ajar. Phoebe and Jane sat at the table, and the former jumped up to welcome Arabella inside.

"Come in, Arabella! You can celebrate with us."

"Yes, do," Jane said, grinning.

Arabella had hoped they would take her mind off the devastation that had just occurred, and now she felt quite fortunate that she'd stumbled onto a celebration. "Perfect, I'm in the mood for good news. What are we celebrating?"

"Jane's matchmaking skills," Phoebe said, looking toward Jane. "I do think you may need to take this up as an occupation."

"I might. I must admit, I feel rather accomplished." She preened for a moment, then they all laughed.

Oh, this was precisely what Arabella needed.

"Pour Arabella some ratafia," Jane said.

Phoebe complied, then handed Arabella the glass. "Shall we drink a toast to the couple Jane has matched in matrimony?"

"Yes, who are we celebrating?" Arabella asked eagerly, hoping it was someone she knew.

Jane lifted her glass. "To Lady Clifton and the Duke of Halstead."

"Huzzah!" Phoebe said.

Arabella nearly dropped her glass. She managed to set it on the table, but did so a bit too hard, and ratafia splashed over her hand.

Phoebe and Jane sipped their drinks while Arabella could only stare.

"What's the matter?" Phoebe asked Arabella. "I thought you liked ratafia."

"When did they become betrothed?" Arabella managed to get the question out even as the world around her seemed to be turning gray.

"Today," Jane said. "Or they will, anyway. Lady Clifton will be on her way to Brixton Park shortly." Jane frowned at her glass, then looked over at Phoebe. "I'm not sure I deserve credit for this match. If not for His Grace's situation—"

"Nonsense," Phoebe said. "If not for you, Lady Clifton wouldn't have met him at all, and it's not as if she's proposing just because he's broke. They clearly suit, and she doesn't give a fig about his finances."

Arabella's breath snagged in her lungs. "How do you know he's broke?"

"It's all over town," Phoebe said. "He put Brixton

Park up for sale the other day. That was the deciding factor for Constance—Lady Clifton—I think. She saw how important it was to him when we went for the picnic."

Jane nodded, her brow creasing with sympathy. "Oh yes, it's just awful to think he would have had to part with it."

"But not now." Phoebe smiled brightly. "Now he has Lady Clifton's fortune to save the day."

Arabella hadn't thought her day could get any worse. She'd presumed Graham had recovered the duke's investment in addition to theirs. However, now she had to wonder, especially since both of their secrets had been exposed. It was too much of a coincidence.

"You're certain he's destitute?" Arabella asked, trying to make sense of everything.

Phoebe looked at her in question. "Why do you doubt it?"

"I just…" Arabella tried to summon a reason that wouldn't require her to explain the truth. The truth. What was that? She thought she'd known, but sitting here listening to them talk about Graham and Lady Clifton as if theirs was a divine match made her question everything. "You said they 'clearly suit'?" she asked Phoebe.

"That's what Lady Clifton said. She found him quite engaging—so genuine and unassuming. Absolutely unlike almost every other gentleman in Society, especially of a lofty rank."

Jane nodded. "That's true. If I wasn't a committed spinster, he might have turned my head."

The world had turned completely upside down. Arabella's family was no longer destitute. She no longer had to marry, and indeed had her parents' support to become a full member of the Spitfire Society. Graham was still insolvent, *and* he was selling the thing he loved most:

Brixton Park. But Lady Clifton was about to swoop in and save the day.

The pieces of Arabella's heart further splintered. She should be the one to save him. But she couldn't. She had nothing to give him, save her love.

She thought of Miles. Her parents had refused his suit, he'd begged Arabella to run away with him, and she'd tearfully let him go.

She wasn't going to make the same mistake twice. She hadn't fought for Miles, but she was going to fight for Graham. It might be a losing battle, but at least she wouldn't regret doing nothing.

Picking up the glass of ratafia, Arabella took a long drink. Then she looked at Phoebe and Jane with determination. "I'm sure Lady Clifton is lovely, and if Graham wants to marry her, I will not interfere. However, I am in love with him, and if I don't tell him, I will always wonder what might have been."

Their jaws dropped in precise unison.

Phoebe was the first to find her voice. "You said you didn't suit."

"I lied."

Jane gave her hand an empathetic pat. "You didn't have to."

"I did. My family was destitute. Graham was destitute. We were trying to help each other *not* be destitute. Then…things…happened."

"That's twice you've called him Graham," Jane noted.

"I, ah, know him quite well." She tried to keep the heat from rising up her neck and flooding her cheeks and was fairly certain she'd failed miserably.

"Apparently," Phoebe murmured. She gave Arabella a pained look. "We had no idea how you felt about him. Does he feel the same?"

"I don't know. But we had…something." Arabella stood. "I have to find out."

Jane stood too. "Of course you do. How can we help?"

Phoebe rose. "Yes, let us help. If we can."

"I need to get to Brixton Park." She felt a wave of despair as she said the name—how could she compete with Lady Clifton when the countess could save his beloved heritage? Her shoulders drooped in defeat. "It's pointless. If he chooses me, he'll lose Brixton Park. I don't want him to have to make that choice." And yet he'd already made a choice by returning her father's investment when he could have kept it to perhaps save Brixton Park.

"So you'll let him marry Lady Clifton without him knowing you love him?" Jane frowned deeply, her brow pinching. "What if he loves you in return?"

Phoebe blew out a breath. "Wouldn't he have told her that?"

Arabella shook her head. "I'm afraid not. He thinks I want to remain unwed and be a spitfire more than anything." Her father's speech in front of him earlier had certainly supported that belief—she couldn't blame Graham for thinking it. That was what she'd wanted.

"That isn't what you want?" Phoebe asked softly.

"No. I want to marry him. If he'll have me."

"Then go tell him. You'll determine what to do about Brixton Park—together."

Yes, *together*. Assuming he wanted her too.

She could assume nothing beyond the fact that she was running out of time. "Phoebe, may I borrow one of your vehicles."

"Of course. Take the curricle. It's fastest." Phoebe clenched her jaw. "Damn, I knew I should have bought a phaeton."

"I wouldn't know how to drive it," Arabella said, smiling. "But a curricle I can manage." Even if driving alone to Brixton Park would probably ruin her reputation —she had nothing to lose. "I need to write a note to my parents to tell them where I've gone—will you deliver it?"

"Certainly," Phoebe said.

Jane started toward the door. "I'll fetch writing utensils."

Phoebe gave Arabella an encouraging smile. "Have faith. Everything will all work out as it should."

People kept saying that, but so far, Arabella wasn't convinced.

CHAPTER 15

*G*raham took his time tending Uther when he returned to Brixton Park. The ride back had been melancholy as he contemplated the future. The loss of Brixton Park was painful, but it was nothing compared to losing Arabella.

How could he lose someone he'd never had?

An angry voice in his head asked, *And whose fault was that?*

Uther whinnied softly, as if he too could hear the voice berating Graham. "I deserve it," he told the horse. "I should have told her how I feel, even if it meant she chose the Spitfire Society. Now I'll never know."

Unless he went and told her now. He'd just left! And after listening to her parents support her wish to choose her own future, he'd felt certain he was doing the right thing. If she'd wanted that future to include him, she would have said so.

Just like you told her how you feel?

Oh, he was an ass. An ass who was going to lose his family's legacy and the only romantic love he'd ever known.

He'd already unsaddled his horse and completely groomed him, but what did it matter? "Come on, Uther, we have to go back."

The horse tossed his head in response—and in, Graham felt certain, agreement.

Dyster, the head groom, appeared in the doorway of the stable. "Your Grace, a coach has arrived. I've sent Lowell to assist."

Graham frowned. He didn't have time for interruption. "What sort of coach?"

"I'm not certain."

Exhaling, Graham rubbed Uther's neck. "Give me a moment," he whispered. Then to Dyster, he said, "Please resaddle Uther in a few minutes—he needs a short respite." This delay forced Graham to do that, which was probably best for Uther. "I have to return to town. I'll be back shortly."

Graham strode toward the drive, where Lowell was helping the coachman tend to the vehicle. The crest on the door designated the owner—Lady Clifton. What the devil was she doing here?

He peered into the coach, but it was empty.

"She's gone inside," Lowell said.

With a nod, Graham turned and went toward the door. A footman greeted him. "Where's Hedge?" Graham asked.

"He's showing Lady Clifton to the drawing room."

Graham quickly made his way to the drawing room, passing the butler just outside.

"There you are, Your Grace. I took the liberty of taking Lady Clifton to the drawing room. I understood you were just in the stables."

"I was. I came when I heard she arrived. Thank you, Hedge."

"I'll be right back with refreshment."

Graham blinked. "Why?"

"Because it's a five-mile journey from town, and it's polite?" Hedge turned a faint pink. "I do beg your pardon, sir, but you have asked me to be as honest and helpful as possible as you adjust to your new role."

"Yes, of course it's polite. You're quite right. I'm just… Never mind." Graham swallowed his impatience. He could spare Lady Clifton a short interview.

"Might I also suggest you would benefit from a visit with Boone?" He dipped his gaze over Graham, who looked down and noted his dust-laden clothing.

"Yes, I suppose I would." Graham suppressed a frown. He didn't have time for such nonsense, particularly when he was just going to ride right back to town. Still, he dashed upstairs, suffered Boone's ministrations for as long as he could manage, then hurried to the drawing room.

Lady Clifton stood near the windows, turning as he entered, likely hearing the sound of his boots upon the floor.

"Good afternoon, Lady Clifton." Graham bowed. "To what do I owe this distinct pleasure?"

She smiled prettily and dipped a brief curtsey. "I hope you won't think me too forward for visiting."

"Not at all." Graham moved farther into the room.

She pivoted halfway back toward the windows. "I was just looking at your maze. I had such a lovely time at our picnic. Didn't you?"

The sensation of Arabella pressed against him, her taste and scent enveloping him in heat and rapture, washed over him. "Yes, it was lovely."

To think that may have been the last time he'd kiss her… His impatience turned to desperation. He couldn't lose her.

Lady Clifton came toward him, a pair of lines marring her perfect brow beneath the brim of her hat. "I heard you put Brixton Park up for sale."

The world seemed to stop for just a moment. She was here…about Brixton Park? "You want to buy it?"

Surprise flickered in her gaze, and the lines in her forehead eased. "I suppose I could."

Hedge arrived with a tray of refreshments, placing it

on a small round table near the window with a pair of chairs. It was for playing chess or other games, but was the closest surface, and Graham supposed it would do.

There was lemonade, cakes, and a small plate of butter biscuits—the recipe Arabella's mother had given him. Graham's heart clenched as he eyed the confection. Forever in his mind, they would remind him of Arabella.

Lady Clifton removed her hat and gloves and handed them to Hedge with a smile. "Thank you."

Hedge inclined his head, then looked to Graham in question. Graham longed to ask the butler how long "polite" would take but didn't. He gave a slight nod in response and murmured, "Thank you, Hedge."

Lady Clifton took one of the chairs at the table, and Graham sat opposite her. He then poured lemonade into the two glasses. She reached for a butter biscuit, and Graham stared out the window. He tried to set thoughts of Arabella aside and focus on the point of Lady Clifton's visit.

He returned his attention to her. "You came to offer to buy Brixton Park?"

"I didn't, actually. And truly, there's no need, unless you really want to sell it. I had the impression you were quite attached to the property. But then I heard you were...ah, that you..."

"That I'm insolvent?" he supplied, realizing what had prompted her to come here.

Pink rushed up her cheeks. "Yes. I do apologize for having to discuss such an indelicate topic; however, it is wise for us to do so."

"It is?" Graham picked up his lemonade and took a long drink. The perfect blend of tart and sweet greeted his tongue, and he was again reminded of Arabella. Would *everything* bring her to his mind?

Yes, idiot, because you're in love with her.

"It is," Lady Clifton said, dragging him back to the conversation he was fast losing interest in. Which was bad—she was here to save him from financial ruin. "I think it wise for husbands and wives to speak frankly about all things, including financial matters."

Graham had been about to reach for a cake, but his hand arrested halfway, hovering above the table. "I beg your pardon?"

The blush returned to her face, but more intensely this time. "I didn't come to offer to buy Brixton Park, though I could. I came to propose marriage so that you may keep it. By aligning ourselves, you can keep the estate."

Dear God, this was not what he expected and yet it was precisely what he needed, what he'd hoped for. It was not, however, what he wanted. The floor seemed to yawn and gape beneath him. He clutched the side of the table to keep from falling through it. Graham fought for logic, for the brain he'd relied upon for twenty-eight years and which had served him well. "And what do you get from the bargain?"

"A happy marriage, I hope. And yes, I'll become a duchess, which is an improvement over countess, of course, but that isn't important to me. I do think we can be happy, and what's more, I think you would be an excellent role model for my son, which he desperately needs. You clearly served the Earl of St. Ives with great success." She flashed him a small smile. "I've done some research since learning about your financial situation."

She was bloody investigating him. He couldn't help but feel impressed. "As you should."

"It seems you inherited this disaster."

"I did." Nevertheless, he hated that he wasn't able to right things. But there simply weren't enough resources to work with—not between the mortgage, the other debts, and the relatives with their vampiric annuities.

She leaned over the table, her blue eyes glimmering in the sunlight spilling through the windows. "Then let me help you fix it. With my money, you can keep Brixton Park."

He could also tend to Halstead Manor. Everything he needed was right here before him. But, again, it wasn't what he wanted. Without Arabella, none of it mattered. Brixton Park was a pile of stones. She was flesh and blood and the reason his heart was beating.

He worked to summon the words he needed to say. He reached for a cake again just as she reached for his hand. He startled, and the cake he'd just picked up went flying onto the floor.

They locked gazes for a moment, then began to laugh. It was ridiculous, but it felt quite good to let go of some emotion through laughter.

Graham knelt on the floor and found the cake beneath the table.

A sharp gasp from the doorway drew him and Lady Clifton to swivel their heads in unison toward the sound.

Like a dream become real, Arabella stood there gaping at them as the color completely drained from her face.

CHAPTER 16

$\mathcal{S}$he was too late. Arabella watched as they laughed together, looking so intimate at the small table overlooking the garden with the maze beyond. The next thing she knew, he was kneeling before Lady Clifton. Arabella had thought *she* was the one proposing. But maybe he'd known all along. Maybe that was why he'd given Arabella's father the money. He didn't need it. He knew salvation was his in the form of Lady Clifton.

"I'm interrupting," Arabella said softly.

Graham jumped to his feet, knocking the table in his haste. Lemonade sloshed, and Lady Clifton grabbed two plates in an effort to keep them from tottering from the table. Wait, were those *butter biscuits* on one of the plates? He was eating those with Lady Clifton?

Arabella wanted to disappear into the floor. Or throw a plate of butter biscuits at his head. Both sounded equally pleasing.

"You aren't," Graham said. He glanced about, opening his mouth, then snapping it shut again. He seemed to realize she'd come, scandalously, alone. But then so had Lady Clifton, it seemed. However, she was allowed. Widows had much different rules.

Arabella looked toward Lady Clifton, who was sipping her lemonade. "It really looks as though I am. I understand you are to be congratulated. That's why I came, actually." It was, she hoped, a believable excuse.

She feared it wasn't.

Particularly given the way his eyes narrowed in that skeptical fashion. "You came here to congratulate us?" Now his eyes widened. "You knew?"

She nodded, somewhat enjoying the look of shock on his duplicitous face. "Phoebe and Jane told me. I wanted to rush right over and offer my congratulations." She looked from him to Lady Clifton. "Congratulations!"

The countess lifted her glass. "Thank you."

As Arabella started to turn, Graham raced forward and clasped her arm. "Wait. There's nothing to congratulate." She peered at him in surprise. "Just…wait." He gave her a firm stare, then turned and strode back to Lady Clifton.

He knelt again in front of her, and Arabella thought she might be sick, especially when he took the countess's hand. "I deeply appreciate your generosity, and in another situation, we might have found happiness. However, I find myself in love with another, and I cannot accept your kind proposal."

Lady Clifton flicked a glance toward Arabella before staring into Graham's face with concern. "Miss Stoke? But she's as penniless as you. You'll lose Brixton Park."

"It means nothing to me when compared with her. I would give a thousand Brixton Parks if it meant she would be my wife. I only hope it isn't too late." Graham looked toward Arabella, his beloved gaze warm and steady.

Arabella's legs shook. She had to grasp the frame of the doorway to keep from swaying.

Graham let go of Lady Clifton's hand and rose, turning to Arabella. His gaze told her everything he'd just said and more. They'd both been ridiculous fools.

Arabella walked toward him. "It's not too late."

"Thank God." He rushed forward and took her in his

arms, holding her tight against him.

Her lips found his, and she poured every drop of love she had into their kiss.

The sound of Lady Clifton coughing forced them apart—but Arabella didn't let go of him, and he didn't let go of her. He slid his arm around Arabella's shoulders and held her snug to his side.

"My apologies, Lady Clifton," Graham said. "I believe I am already betrothed."

Arabella tightened her hold on his waist. "Yes, he is."

Lady Clifton stood, her lips pursing. "This is disappointing." She looked to Graham. "Jane and Phoebe insisted we would suit—and I agreed. They also led me to believe you were looking to wed, but apparently, you were only interested in my fortune."

Graham flinched. "I am not proud of that," he said quietly. "You deserve someone who will love you."

"Yes, I do. Having had that already, I realize now I could never settle for less. A love match is worth, as you said, a thousand estates. I know that from experience," she added softly, with a tinge of sadness.

"I won't forget your kindness," Graham said. "If I can ever be of service—to you or your son—I hope you'll let me know."

"That is most generous of you. However, I believe our association is concluded." Lady Clifton sounded perhaps more than disappointed; she sounded annoyed. "I wish you the best."

"We wish you the same," Arabella said, hating that the countess felt used. Yet, she also felt relieved that she'd reached Graham before he and the countess had made a mistake that would have led to misery for all of them.

Lady Clifton inclined her head, then took her leave. She was scarcely gone from the room before Arabella turned toward Graham and he turned toward her. They both spoke at once.

"I am such a fool," she said.

"I am a giant ass," he said.

They startled, their gazes locking. Then they both smiled with relief and happiness.

Graham pulled her to his chest and brushed his lips against her forehead. "Oh, my dearest love, to think we almost walked headlong into disaster."

She looked up at him in question. "I assumed you'd recovered your money as well as my father's. Why didn't you?"

He grimaced. "There was, in fact, no money. The sale of Brixton Park will provide what we both needed—the return of your father's investment and a path for me to rebuild the ducal coffers."

"You're selling Brixton Park for us?" The question ended on a squeak. She couldn't quite believe his selflessness. Only she could. That was absolutely the man she'd fallen in love with.

He nodded. "I meant what I said. I'd forfeit a thousand of them, more, if necessary, if it meant we could be together. Or, in this case, if it meant I could save you and your family. I didn't think you wanted me."

"You thought I wanted to be a spitfire."

"Didn't you?"

"Not as badly as I want to be your wife." She stood on her toes and pressed her lips briefly to his. "Can I still be a spitfire?"

"My love, I wouldn't have you any other way." He clasped her back, his hands on her spine and the upper curve of her backside, and kissed her.

After a long moment, she eased her lips from his. "I love you, Graham."

"I love you, Arabella."

"I regret that Lady Clifton felt badly."

"The blame is mine," Graham said. "I should have been direct with her—and with Miss Lennox and Miss Pemberton—from the beginning."

"And how would that have appeared?" Arabella asked.

"You couldn't have gone around telling people you were searching for an heiress."

"Colton seemed to think I could. He said that plenty of women—or their fathers—would be interested in purchasing my title."

It was true, of course. Arabella shook her head.

"I hate that you're losing Brixton Park. I wish there was a way to save it." A thought occurred to her. "How did you pay my father? You can't have sold it yet."

He shook his head. "I have a loan from the Marquess of Ripley."

"Can he be trusted? What of his cousin?"

"No one was more surprised than Ripley that Tibbord was actually his cousin Drobbit. He's quite offended. I daresay Tibbord, Drobbit, whatever, won't be harming anyone else with his schemes or by spreading gossip about people's fortunes."

She sucked in a breath. "He's the one who told everyone we were destitute?" She clenched her jaw in anger. "From now on, I propose we call him the Swindler. He doesn't deserve the right to have a name, let alone two."

He gazed down at her in admiration and love. "My spitfire… You are quite correct." He dropped another quick kiss on her mouth. "Now, must you return home immediately, or can I persuade you to take a tour of the upstairs?"

She gave him a sultry smile. "What part of the upstairs?"

"My bedchamber, of course."

"You're a naughty gentleman, Your Grace."

Graham swept her into his arms. "I have it on good authority you like me that way."

"I do indeed." She curled her arms around his neck and kissed his jaw. "In fact, I *love* you that way."

Then he took her upstairs and showed her just how naughty he could be.

EPILOGUE

HUNTWELL, HUNTINGDONSHIRE

ONE MONTH LATER

"*H*e is so precious," Arabella gazed down at David and Fanny's son, and Graham hoped to see that same look on his wife's face soon —when they welcomed their own child into the world. They weren't expecting an arrival yet, but it wasn't for lack of them trying...

"We wanted to ask if you would do us the honor of being Graham's godparents," David said from beside his wife, who was spending her first day away from her bedchamber.

Arabella looked over at them, but it was Graham who spoke. "You do *us* the honor," he said softly. "Truly, I am overcome. You already named him after me."

"I can think of no one finer," David said. "With my father's name in the middle," he added.

"Are you sure you want me to be his godmother?" Arabella asked. She looked to Fanny. "I know you have a sister and close friends."

Fanny gave her a warm smile. "We discussed it at length. Given the close relationship between your father and David's, we really thought this was the perfect way to unify our families."

Arabella gently swayed with the baby in her arms. "My father will be delighted."

Mr. Stoke had been thrilled to welcome Graham into their family. And as a member of their family, Graham now knew how upset he'd been when David had failed to marry his daughter. Mr. Stoke had even admitted his disappointment was part of what led to some of his poor decisions. He was desperate to show that they didn't need the *Earl* of St. Ives.

"Are you done with Brixton Park, then?" David asked.

Graham nodded. There was only a slight sense of loss, but he was too eager for what was yet to come to brood on the past. "We said goodbye before we came here to welcome young Graham."

"I hope Ripley paid you enough," David said.

Graham exchanged a look with Arabella. He'd paid *too* much, but they hadn't been able to stop him. Plus, he'd invited Arabella and Graham to use it whenever and however they chose. "He was quite generous."

"Good, you deserve that, especially given his cousin's involvement."

Graham had told David everything, and David had chastised him profusely for not asking for help, even as he understood the pesky issues of pride and self-reliance.

"Ghastly news about him," Fanny said with a shudder.

"About who?" Arabella asked.

"You didn't read the paper this morning?" David glanced toward a table where a newspaper lay.

"We may have overslept." Or something. Graham traded another look with his wife, this one full of heat.

"Apparently, Drobbit was found dead a few days ago," David said grimly. "Bullet straight through his heart."

A cold sense of dread tripped up Graham's spine. Again, he and Arabella looked toward each other. He gave his head an infinitesimal shake. They'd discuss it later.

Graham looked at David, his heart pounding. "He was murdered?"

"Seems so, though they don't know the culprit. I imagine it will be the talk of London upon your return."

They were due to go back in a few days, but Graham wondered if they should return sooner. Why? What could they possibly do? In fact, it might be wiser to increase their distance from Ripley. His reputation was bad enough, but now…

Fanny changed the course of the conversation to her friend, Lady Lavinia. She and her husband had welcomed a son a fortnight before. "And our other friend, Sarah, Lady Ware, will deliver soon—in the next few weeks to be sure."

Sarah was Anthony Colton's sister, of course, and mention of her brought Colton to Graham's mind. Colton should probably move away from Ripley for a while. Their close friendship had become a focal point of the Season, along with Colton's decline from eligible bachelor to unseemly rake. More often than not, he was seen gambling or suffering from excessive drink. He'd had a notorious assignation with a married woman a few weeks ago—they'd been caught in the act of fornication at a ball. It troubled Graham to see him fall so far, but he was utterly impervious to counsel. Still, Graham would try again, particularly where Ripley was concerned.

After a short time, young Graham began to fuss, and Fanny declared it was time for him to be changed and fed before her sister, the Duchess of Clare, arrived, which was due to happen shortly. Graham looked forward to meeting the Duke and Duchess, whom David had said were lovely people. He'd also noted that the Duke was a welcome ally for people like them—gentlemen who weren't yet at ease in their positions. While David had expected his, he hadn't been quite ready to embrace it when his father had died suddenly.

As soon as they were alone—David had escorted his wife and son upstairs—Arabella turned to Graham. "You don't think Ripley—"

Graham didn't want her to say it out loud. "I don't know, but many will probably say he did."

Her brow creased with concern. "If only they hadn't fought in the park."

Ripley and Drobbit had come to blows one day in Rotten Row. A number of gentlemen had heard Ripley tell his cousin that he should be lucky he wasn't dead, and that if it were up to him, he would be. Add that to the countless comments Graham and Arabella had heard him make about regretting his cousin's behavior and all the damage he'd caused, and it seemed at least possible he could be the one to have shot him.

It was also likely that any of the other men Drobbit had fleeced could have committed the crime. A few had come forward when an actual investigator had begun to look into Drobbit's affairs—at Graham's request and Ripley's expense.

No, Graham didn't want to think Ripley would have killed Drobbit. The marquess was a rake and more than a bit of a scoundrel, but he was, at his core, a decent person. Or so it seemed to Graham. Why else would he have supported the investigation of his cousin and purchased Brixton Park at such an exorbitant price?

Graham stood. "Come, let's walk in the garden and put this from our minds for a while." He held out his hand.

She put her fingers in his, and he still felt a jolt of excitement when they touched. He hoped it would always be that way and had to imagine it would. Every day, his love for her increased and his passion for their future grew.

Arabella curled her arm through his, and they made their way outside into the lovely spring day. Trees were filled with green, and flowers blossomed along the path. "I look forward to when we go to Halstead Manor. My mother's letter was so descriptive of the gardens and all we could do to improve them."

Her parents had traveled to Halstead Manor, where they planned to live in the dower house—as soon as it was made hospitable. Graham's first order of business after selling Brixton Park had been to hire a steward for the estate. He had sent Graham his preliminary report, and it was all Graham could do not to rush to Essex and bury himself in repairing the damage the last several dukes had done.

However, he still had duties in London, and they would stay in David's town house for the remainder of the Season. "You sound excited to get there." Graham looked askance at her with a smile.

"I am, because we're getting a dog. Or two."

Graham laughed. They'd discussed the need for canine companionship. It was just a question of how many. "I am amazed that the secret of a happy life is love, butter biscuits, and a dog."

"Or *two*," she repeated. "I'm excited to be wherever you are. And to rebuild Halstead Manor together."

He was excited for that too. "There is no one I'd rather have at my side."

They were a good distance from the house and from prying eyes, in the shade of a large maple tree. She pivoted into his embrace, wrapping her arms around his neck. "Good, because you're stuck with me."

"Forever," he whispered against her lips.

"And ever," she murmured just before he kissed her.

Want to find out if the Marquess of Ripley killed his
cousin? And if Phoebe can heal the hole in his heart?
Don't miss the next book in The Spitfire Society series, A
DUKE IS NEVER ENOUGH, coming in early 2020.

THANK YOU!

Thank you so much for reading *Never Have I Ever with a Duke*. I hope you enjoyed it!

Would you like to know when my next book is available and to hear about sales and deals? Sign up for my VIP newsletter at http://www.darcyburke.com/readergroup, follow me on social media:

Facebook: http://facebook.com/DarcyBurkeFans
Twitter at @darcyburke
Instagram at darcyburkeauthor
Pinterest at darcyburkewrite

And follow me on Bookbub to receive updates on pre-orders, new releases, and deals!

Want to read about some of the characters in this book such as Lavinia, the Marchioness of Northam, David and Fanny, the Earl and Countess of St. Ives, and Sarah, the Countess of Ware? Grab *The Duke of Seduction*, *The Duke of Kisses*, and *The Duke of Distraction*!

Never Have I Ever With a Duke is the first book in The Spitfire Society series. Catch up with my other historical series: The Untouchables, Wicked Dukes Club, Secrets and Scandals, and Legendary Rogues. If you like contemporary romance, I hope you'll check out my Ribbon Ridge series available from Avon Impulse, and the continuation of Ribbon Ridge in So Hot.

I hope you'll consider leaving a review at your favorite online vendor or networking site!

I appreciate my readers so much. Thank you, thank you, *thank you*.

One Night of Passion
One Night of Scandal
One Night to Remember
One Night of Temptation

Secrets and Scandals

Her Wicked Ways
His Wicked Heart
To Seduce a Scoundrel
To Love a Thief (a novella)
Never Love a Scoundrel
Scoundrel Ever After

Legendary Rogues

Lady of Desire
Romancing the Earl
Lord of Fortune
Captivating the Scoundrel

Contemporary Romance

Ribbon Ridge

Where the Heart Is (a prequel novella)
Only in My Dreams
Yours to Hold
When Love Happens
The Idea of You
When We Kiss
You're Still the One

Ribbon Ridge: So Hot

So Good
So Right
So Wrong

The Untouchables Series

THE FORBIDDEN DUKE

"I LOVED this story!!" 5 Stars

-Historical Romance Lover

"This is a wonderful read and I can't wait to see what comes next in this amazing series..." 5 Stars

-Teatime and Books

THE DUKE of DARING

"You will not be able to put it down once you start. Such a good read."

-Books Need TLC

"An unconventional beauty set on life as a spinster meets the one man who might change her mind, only to find his painful past makes it impossible to love. A wonderfully emotional journey from attraction, to friendship, to a love that conquers all."

-Bronwen Evans, *USA Today* Bestselling Author

THE DUKE of DECEPTION

"...an enjoyable, well-paced story ... Ned and Aquilla are an engaging, well-matched couple – strong, caring and compassionate; and ...it's easy to believe that they will continue to be happy together long after the book is ended."

"This is my favorite so far in the series! They had chemistry from the moment they met...their passion leaps off the pages."

THE DUKE of DESIRE

"Masterfully written with great characterization...with a flourish toward characters, secrets, and romance... Must read addition to "The Untouchables" series!"

"If you are looking for a truly endearing story about two people who take the path least travelled to find the other, with a side of 'YAH THAT'S HOT!' then this book is absolutely for you!"

THE DUKE of DEFIANCE

"This story was so beautifully written, and it hooked me from page one. I couldn't put the book down and just had to read it in one sitting even though it meant reading into the wee hours of the morning."

"I loved the Duke of Defiance! This is the kind of book

you hate when it is over and I had to make myself stop reading just so I wouldn't have to leave the fun of Knighton's (aka Bran) and Joanna's story!"

-Behind Closed Doors Book Review

THE DUKE of DANGER

"The sparks fly between them right from the start... the HEA is certainly very hard-won, and well-deserved."

-All About Romance

"Another book hangover by Darcy! Every time I pick a favorite in this series, she tops it. The ending was perfect and made me want more."

-Sassy Book Lover

THE DUKE of ICE

"Each book gets better and better, and this novel was no exception. I think this one may be my fave yet! 5 out 5 for this reader!"

-Front Porch Romance

"An incredibly emotional story...I dare anyone to stop reading once the second half gets under way because this is intense!"

-Buried Under Romance

THE DUKE of RUIN

"This is a fast paced novel that held me until the last page."

"Don't miss this magnificent read. It has some comedic fun, heartfelt relationships, heartbreaking moments, and horrifying danger."

-The Reading Café

"...my favorite story in the series. Fans of Regency romances will definitely enjoy this book."

-Two Ends of the Pen

THE DUKE of DISTRACTION

"Count on Burke to break a heart as only she can. This couple will get under the skin before they steal your heart."

-Hopeless Romantic

"Darcy Burke never disappoints. Her storytelling is just so magical and filled with passion. You will fall in love with the characters and the world she creates!"

-Teatime and Books

Secrets & Scandals Series

HER WICKED WAYS

"A bad girl heroine steals both the show and a highwayman's heart in Darcy Burke's deliciously wicked debut."

–Courtney Milan, *NYT* Bestselling Author

"...fast paced, very sexy, with engaging characters."

–Smexybooks

HIS WICKED HEART

"Intense and intriguing. Cinderella meets *Fight Club* in a historical romance packed with passion, action and secrets."

—Anna Campbell, *Seven Nights in a Rogue's Bed*

"A romance...to make you smile and sigh...a wonderful read!"

—*Rogues Under the Covers*

TO SEDUCE A SCOUNDREL

"Darcy Burke pulls no punches with this sexy, romantic page-turner. Sevrin and Philippa's story grabs you from the first scene and doesn't let go. *To Seduce a Scoundrel* is simply delicious!"

—Tessa Dare, *NYT* Bestselling Author

"I was captivated on the first page and didn't let go until this glorious book was finished!"

—*Romancing the Book*

TO LOVE A THIEF

"With refreshing circumstances surrounding both the hero and the heroine, a nice little mystery, and a touch of heat, this novella was a perfect way to pass the day."

—*The Romanceaholic*

"A refreshing read with a dash of danger and a little heat.

For fans of honorable heroes and fun heroines who know what they want and take it."

NEVER LOVE A SCOUNDREL

"I loved the story of these two misfits thumbing their noses at society and finding love." Five stars.

"A nice mix of intrigue and passion...wonderfully complex characters, with flaws and quirks that will draw you in and steal your heart."

SCOUNDREL EVER AFTER

"There is something so delicious about a bad boy, no matter what era he is from, and Ethan was definitely delicious."

"I loved the chemistry between the two main characters...Jagger/Ethan is not what he seems at all and neither is sweet society Miss Audrey. They are believably compatible."

Legendary Rogues Series

LADY of DESIRE

"A fast-paced mixture of adventure and romance, very much in the mould of *Romancing the Stone* or *Indiana Jones*."

"...gave me such a book hangover! ...addictive...one of the most entertaining stories I've read this year!"

ROMANCING the EARL

"Once again Darcy Burke takes an interesting story and...turns it into magic. An exceptionally well-written book."

"...A fast paced story that was exciting and interesting. This is a definite must add to your book lists!"

LORD of FORTUNE

"I don't think I know enough superlatives to describe this book! It is wonderfully, magically delicious. It sucked me in from the very first sentence and didn't turn me loose— not even at the end ..."

"If you love a deep, passionate romance with a bit of mystery, then this is the book for you!"
-Teatime and Books

CAPTIVATING the SCOUNDREL

"I am in absolute awe of this story. Gideon and Daphne stole all of my heart and then some. This book was such a delight to read."

-Beneath the Covers Blog

"Darcy knows how to end a series with a bang! Daphne and Gideon are a mix of enemies and allies turned lovers that will have you on the edge of your seat at every turn."

-Sassy Booklover

Contemporary Romance

Ribbon Ridge Series

A contemporary family saga featuring the Archer family of sextuplets who return to their small Oregon wine country town to confront tragedy and find love...

The "multilayered plot keeps readers invested in the story line, and the explicit sensuality adds to the excitement that will have readers craving the next Ribbon Ridge offering."

-Library Journal Starred Review on YOURS TO HOLD

"Darcy Burke writes a uniquely touching and heart-warming series about the love, pain, and joys of family as well as the love that feeds your soul when you meet "the one.""

-The Many Faces of Romance

I can't tell you how much I love this series. Each book gets better and better.

-Romancing the Readers

"Darcy Burke's Ribbon Ridge series is one of my all-time favorites. Fall in love with the Archer family, I know I did."

-Forever Book Lover

Ribbon Ridge: So Hot

SO GOOD

" ...worth the read with its well-written words, beautiful descriptions, and likeable characters...they are flirty, sexy and a match made in wine heaven."

-Harlequin Junkie Top Pick

"I absolutely love the characters in this book and the families. I honestly could not put it down and finished it in a day."

-Chin Up Mom

SO RIGHT

"This is another great story by Darcy Burke. Painting pictures with her words that make you want to sit and stare at them for hours. I love the banter between the characters and the general sense of fun and friendliness."

-The Ardent Reader

SO WRONG

ABOUT THE AUTHOR

Darcy Burke is the USA Today Bestselling Author of sexy, emotional historical and contemporary romance. Darcy wrote her first book at age 11, a happily ever after about a swan addicted to magic and the female swan who loved him, with exceedingly poor illustrations. Join her Reader Club at http://www.darcyburke.com/readerclub.

A native Oregonian, Darcy lives on the edge of wine country with her guitar-strumming husband, their two hilarious kids who seem to have inherited the writing gene. They're a crazy cat family with two Bengal cats, a small, fame-seeking cat named after a fruit, and an older rescue Maine Coon who is the master of chill and five a.m. serenading. In her "spare" time Darcy is a serial volunteer enrolled in a 12-step program where one learns to say "no," but she keeps having to start over. Her happy places are Disneyland and Labor Day weekend at the Gorge. Visit Darcy online at http://www.darcyburke.com and follow her social media: Facebook at http://www.facebook.com/darcyburkefans, Twitter @darcyburke at http://www.twitter.com/darcyburke, Instagram at http://www.instagram/darcyburkeauthor, and Pinterest at http://www.pinterest.com/darcyburkewrite.

CPSIA information can be obtained
at www.ICGtesting.com
Printed in the USA
LVHW111000150919
631110LV00003B/587/P